THE
SEVEN
MADMEN

A NOVEL BY **Roberto Arlt**

TRANSLATED BY **Naomi Lindstrom**

DAVID R. GODINE · PUBLISHER
BOSTON

THE
SEVEN
MADMEN

First English language edition published in 1984 by
David R. Godine, Publisher, Inc.
306 Dartmouth Street
Boston, Massachusetts 02116

Library of Congress Cataloging in Publication Data

Arlt, Roberto, 1900–1942.
  The seven madmen.

  Translation of: Los siete locos.
  I. Title.
PQ7797.A66S513 1984   863   83-20508
ISBN 0-87923-492-X

First edition

Printed in the United States of America

INTRODUCTION

Recent critical reappraisal has brought Roberto Arlt and *The Seven Madmen* out of literary obscurity and has accorded both author and novel an important place in the history of Latin-American fiction. Although when first published in 1929, Arlt seemed no more than an unpolished, realistic writer, in the sixties and seventies he attracted the notice of critics searching for the roots of the wildly inventive fiction coming out of contemporary Latin America. Arlt is now recognized as a long-lost ancestor of the so-called "boom" of imaginative fiction which the American reader associates with such names as Julio Cortázar, Jorge Luis Borges, and Gabriel García Márquez.

Arlt was a newspaperman with a style that was often rough, blunt, and defiantly agrammatical. His unpolished mode of expression and the swarm of low-life characters with whom he populated his novel gave his fiction a naturalistic tone. Many of Arlt's contemporaries saw no more in *The Seven Madmen* than a harsh, rough-hewn "proletarian" novel, full of scabrous scenes, crude words, sleazy characters, and unforgivable grammar. Arlt caricatures this type of reader aptly when he imagines how a critic will greet his work after *The Seven Madmen*: "Mr. Roberto Arlt keeps on in the same old rut: realism in the worst possible taste." Arlt himself did much to enhance his image as a "proletarian" author. Disheveled, impulsive, and denunciatory, he looked and acted the part of the angry young man. In his column, he praised a number of socialist realist writers, both Soviet and Argentine. He scorned spelling and proper grammar as elitist, fetishistic concerns, and gave no thought to standardizing his erratic Spanish.

Thoughtful readers, however, found Arlt singularly imaginative, willing to violate the tenets of realism in favor of bold invention. As Adolfo Prieto puts it, "along with his undeniable realistic intentions, Arlt nurtured a predilection for creating forms in which fantasy and real-life experience played a hallucinatory counterpoint." His fusion of the fancifully distorted and the realistically faithful set Arlt's work apart from that of the social realists of his time. But many who were unsure how to evaluate Arlt's blend of the real and the unreal and his rough, deviant mode of expression simply concluded "that Arlt didn't know how to write." Even readers who appreciated Arlt's originality were hard-pressed to understand it. Thus Arlt, who died in 1942, remained a minor, enigmatic, almost freakish figure in Argentine literary history.

Then, in the wake of the explosion of Latin-American literature in the fifties and sixties, a new generation of readers rediscovered Arlt and his eccentric fictional experiments. These new Arlt readers had grown up on Borges, Cortázar, García Márquez, and other practitioners of "magical realism," a mythic representation of serious human realities. To such readers, the coexistence of the fantastic and the serious was not a shock. What was surprising was to find such a mélange in a novel written so long before the official boom, which brought worldwide fame to the authors of Latin America, exploded. Thus, people immediately began pointing to Arlt as a misunderstood innovator whose work was inspirational to the latter-day magical realists.

In recent years, a number of creative writers and literary critics have proclaimed Arlt's seminal influence. Julio Cortázar cited Arlt as one of the two great influences on his literary development, along with Borges. Jorge Lafforgue, the influential critic, wrote: "to avoid any possible misunderstanding let me say here and now: Roberto Arlt and Juan Carlos Onetti represent the beginnings of current Argentine–Uruguayan fiction and I could count on the fingers of one hand figures comparable to them in this part of the world." Juan Carlos Onetti, known in this country for *The Shipyard* (1958) and *A Brief Life* (1976), prefaced the Italian translation of *The Seven Madmen* with this tribute: "if any inhabitant of our humble shores managed to achieve literary genius, his name was Roberto Arlt."

Ordinary readers, too, had begun to appreciate Arlt. From 1968 on, Latin-American publishing houses began to reprint not only *The Seven Madmen* but also Arlt's other novels, short stories, newspaper writings, and the dramatic works which occupied his last years. Odd musings and sketches of city life which had only appeared in journalistic form were dug out and published in book form—a sure sign of a writer's canonization. The times had finally caught up with Arlt's dizzying, disconcerting style.

Readers of contemporary Latin-American authors will immediately recognize the realm of uncertainty and ambiguity that is Arlt's fictional world. *The Seven Madmen* is the story of a revolutionary conspiracy, and it is the story of human beings in the greatest anguish. Yet neither the reader nor the hero, Remo Erdosain, knows the exact nature of either the conspiracy or the suffering. The conspiracy appears protean: its cryptic leader, the Astrologer, is capable of waxing enthusiastic over Mussolini and the Ku Klux Klan one minute and advancing Bolshevik or anarchist ideas the next. When questioned too closely about the goals and feasibility of his plot, the Astrologer retreats behind a smoke-screen of enigmatic language.

It is equally hard to grasp what exactly ails Arlt's characters. They are tremendously unhappy, but no diagnosis or possible remedy for their sorrow is ever specified. Existential anguish seems at fault when Erdosain broods on his relations with God, his fellows, and destiny, or speaks of crime as a confirmation of selfhood, but shortly afterward, he can be found railing at the capitalist system, bourgeois values, and his alienation as a clerk on a corporate treadmill. Erdosain also exhibits severe psychological disturbances, and the reader is left unsure whether he has entered the realm of existentialism, political protest, or abnormal psychology.

The reader seeking some central reality to hang on to will get no help from the narrator of *The Seven Madmen*. To the increasingly unreal tangle of events which form the plot, he adds a few gnarls of his own. He enjoys adding footnotes to the text which contradict statements he himself has asserted as facts. He withholds the information which the reader needs to make sense of the plot, bombards him with pointless details about the characters' past lives, and claims to possess vast reserves of additional information which he may or may not disclose at a future time. The narrator never reveals his identity or credentials (one may even suspect him of being the Astrologer).

The reader embarking on the treacherous first reading of *The Seven Madmen* will do well to remember what he has learned in reading the fiction of the more recent Latin–American authors. Arlt's readers must give up the expectation that, if they read carefully, they will find out what "really" happened among these madmen. They must not belabor separating what the characters fear, hope, or imagine from what the characters actually do. In *The Seven Madmen,* as in other recent Latin–American fiction, apparent chaos generates meaning and comments on real-world conditions. But the novel requires the cooperation of readers willing to examine man and society through a distorted lens.

— Naomi Lindstrom

THE
SEVEN
MADMEN

1

THE SURPRISE

The moment he opened the door to the manager's office, with its milk-glass panels, Erdosain tried to back out; he could see he was done for, but it was too late.

They were waiting for him: the manager, a man with a pig's head, a true snout and implacability oozing out of his small fish gray pupils; Gualdi, the accountant, small, slight, bland as honey, with eyes that missed nothing; and the assistant manager, the son of the pig-headed man, thirty, good-looking, his hair gone completely white, an air of great cynicism about him, an edge to his voice and the harsh eyes of his progenitor. These three characters, the boss, bending over the payroll, the assistant manager, lolling in an easy chair with one leg dangling over the back, and Mr. Gualdi standing respectfully by the desk, did not return Erdosain's greeting. Only the assistant manager went so far as to raise his head:

"We hear that you're an embezzler, that you've taken six hundred pesos from us."

"And seven cents," added Mr. Gualdi, applying his blotter to the signature on the payroll that his boss had checked off. The latter then looked up from the paper with an abrupt movement of his bull neck. Hands clasped against the front of his jacket, the boss was evidently calculating behind his half-closed lids as he coolly examined Erdosain's gaunt, impassive face.

"Why are you so badly dressed?"

"Because I don't make much as a bill collector."

"What about the money you stole from us?"

"I didn't steal anything. That's a lie."

"All right then, can you square up your accounts?"

"By today at noon, if you want."

That answer saved him for the moment. The three men exchanged glances, and finally, the assistant manager, with the tacit consent of his father, said:

"No . . . you have until three tomorrow. Bring the payroll with you and all the receipts . . . You can go now."

This turn of events came as such a surprise that Erdosain just kept standing there, forlorn, looking at the three of them. Yes, just looking at them. Mr. Gualdi, who despite his professed socialism had humiliated him so deeply; the assistant manager, who had stared with such rude persistence at his frayed tie; the manager, whose stiff, close-cropped, pig head was aimed right at him, with obscene cynicism seeping through the gray slit in his half-closed lids.

And still, Erdosain did not leave . . . He wanted to find words that would make them grasp the immense sorrow that weighed upon his life; and so he kept on standing there like that, sadly, the great black mass of the iron cash register looming up in front of him, feeling himself grow more hunched with each passing minute while he nervously fingered the brim of his black hat and his eyes took on the sad look of a hunted man. Then, suddenly, he asked:

"So, can I go now?"

"Yes . . ."

"No . . . Give Suárez the receipts and be here tomorrow at three sharp and have the whole amount with you then."

"Yes . . . the whole amount . . ." and, turning, he left without saying good-bye.

He walked down Chile Street to the Paseo Colón. He felt some invisible force fencing him in. The setting sun lit up the most revolting inner recesses of the sloping street. Conflicting thoughts seethed inside him, such a crazy mix that they would have taken hours to sort out.

Later he realized that he had never even thought to ask who had blown the whistle on him.

STATES OF CONSCIOUSNESS

He knew he was a thief. But the name they gave him didn't much affect him. Perhaps the word thief didn't strike a chord with his inner state. What he did feel was a round silence that bored through his skull like a steel cylinder, anesthetizing him to anything unrelated to his unhappiness.

This circle of silence and darkness cut into the flow of his ideas, so Erdosain could not associate, with his deteriorating reason, his home, now known as a house, with some institution called a jail.

He thought telegraphically, skipping prepositions, which is enervating. He had known empty hours when he might have committed any crime without feeling the least responsibility. Of course a judge would never understand that sort of thing. But now he was drained empty, he was the shell of a man kept in motion by force of habit.

If he stayed on at the Sugar Company, it would not be to keep stealing more money but because he was waiting for something extraordinary to happen—immensely extraordinary—that would give his life an unexpected charge and save him from the catastrophe looming in his future.

Erdosain had a name for the atmosphere compounded of dreaming and restlessness that kept him wandering in circles like a sleepwalker through the days of his life: "the anguish zone."

Erdosain pictured this zone as lying two meters above the city streets, and he could see it quite graphically, shaped like those great salt flats or deserts that are shown on maps as ovals full of dots, thick as herring roe.

This anguish zone came out of all the suffering of mankind. And like a cloud of poison gas it moved heavily from one place to another, penetrating solid walls and slicing through buildings without losing its flat, horizontal form; two-dimensional anguish that slashed through throats like a guillotine, leaving an aftertaste of bitter sobbing.

That was the explanation Erdosain came up with when he felt the first waves of nauseous grief.

"What am I doing with my life?" he would then ask himself, perhaps hoping to clarify with this question the source of an anxiety that made him long for a life where each tomorrow would not simply be more of today, but something novel and always unexpected, like the sudden turns of plot in an American movie, where yesterday's beggar is today's underground chieftain and the gold-digging secretary is a multimillionairess incognito.

His thirst for marvels, which could never possibly be slaked—since he was a frustrated inventor and a crook about to land in jail—and the rationalizations and doubts it always entailed left him churning with acidity and gritting his teeth as if he had bit into a lemon.

At such times, he could fall back on a stock of absurd notions. He imagined that the wealthy, tired of hearing the snivelings of the oppressed, built great horse-drawn cages. Hangmen, picked for their inhuman strength, pursued the wretches with choke collars, until he envisaged a whole scene: a mother, tall and disheveled, ran behind the cage where, from behind bars, her cross-eyed child cried out to her, until a "dogcatcher," tired of hearing her screams, knocked her out by clobbering her over the head with the butt end of his whip.

After this nightmare vision dissolved, Erdosain wondered, in self-revulsion:

"What kind of soul do I have?" And as his imagination was still racing from the last nightmare scene, he went on to another. "I must have been born to be a lackey. One of those vile perfumed lackeys rich prostitutes keep around to do up their bras, while the lover lounges on the sofa with a cigar."

And his thoughts again slithered down to the kitchen in the basement of a luxurious mansion. Maids flitted around the table, and there was a chauffeur and an Arab vending garters and perfume. In this setting he would wear a black jacket that came just to his rear and a little white tie. Suddenly the "master" would call him: a man exactly like him physically, except with a mustache and glasses. He did not know what his boss wanted him for, but he would never forget the funny look the man gave him as he left the estate. And he went back to the kitchen for some locker-room talk with the chauffeur, who delighted the maids and bored the Arab pederast by telling how he had ruined the daughter of a great lady, a child of tender years.

And again he repeated to himself:

"Yes, I am a lackey. I have the soul of a true lackey," and he clenched his teeth with pleasure at the way he insulted and debased himself in his own eyes.

At other times he saw himself emerge from the bedroom of some devout old maid, unctuously bearing a heavy chamberpot, but just then he would be met by an assiduous priest, attached to the household, who, with smiling neutrality, would ask:

"Keeping up with our religious duties, Ernesto?" And

he, Ernesto, Ambrosio, or José, would live the slimy life of an obscene, hypocritical servant.

Just the thought of it sent a shiver of madness coursing through him.

He knew, ah, how well he knew, that he was bruising and soiling his soul out of sheer perversity. Deliberately wallowing in the mire, he suffered the terror of one who, in a nightmare, falls down the abyss but does not die.

Because at times he longed for humiliation, like those saints who would kiss the sores of lepers, not from compassion but to be yet more unworthy of God's love, since they would revolt Him by their repulsive deeds.

But these images faded, and all that was left in his mind was the "desire to know the meaning of life," and he would tell himself:

"No, I am no lackey . . . no, I am not . . ." and he would have liked to ask his wife to take pity on him, to feel grief and pity for his horrible, vile thoughts. But remembering how she had made so many sacrifices for him filled him with blind fury, and at such times he would have liked to kill her.

And he knew all too well that some day she would turn to another man and that was yet more fuel added to everything that went to make up his anguish.

So when he stole the first twenty pesos, he was surprised how easily he could "do it," since before he got started he had thought he would have to overcome any number of scruples which he was no longer in a condition to feel. Then he reflected:

"It's just a matter of working up one's will and doing it, simple as that."

And "it" made life a little easier, with "it" he had money that felt alien, since it was acquired through no effort of his own. And the amazing thing for Erdosain was not the thievery itself, but that his face should

show no sign of his crime. He was forced to steal because his monthly pay was so meager. Eighty, a hundred,
a hundred and twenty pesos, since it depended on how
much he collected; he was paid a commission per
hundred pesos of bills he collected.

So, some days he carried four to five thousand pesos
on his undernourished person and made do with a
stinking, fake leather billfold, inside of which happiness piled up in the form of paper money, checks, money
orders, and vouchers.

His wife nagged about the way she was always deprived of this or that; he would hear out her reproaches
in silence and later, alone, he would wonder:

"What can I do?"

When he got the idea, when that idea started to grow,
how he might steal from his bosses, he felt like an
inventor yelling eureka. Steal? But how come he had
only thought of it now?

And Erdosain was amazed by his own oversight, even
accusing himself of lacking drive, since in those days
(three months before the events of this story), he was
painfully deprived of all kinds of necessary things, although vast sums of money streamed through his hands
every day.

And what made his thievery so easy was the lax way
the Sugar Company kept its books.

TERROR IN THE STREET

His life was most certainly strange, because sometimes hope welled up inside him and drove him
out into the street.

Then he would get on a bus and ride to some ritzy
neighborhood like Palermo or Belgrano. He would wan-

der, lost in thought, down quiet avenues, saying to himself:

"Some young creature will spot me, a tall, pale, high-strung young girl, driving aimlessly around in her Rolls-Royce. Suddenly she spots me and knows I will be the one love of her life, and those eyes, that withered foolish suitors, will come to rest on me and will fill with sudden tears."

The dream pried loose from its framework of nonsense and slid slowly down into the shade of the tall facades and the green plantain trees that cast their shadows in triangular shapes on the white tiling below.

"She will be a millionairess, but I will tell her, 'Señorita, I cannot touch you. Even should you offer yourself to me, I would not take you.' She will look at me in surprise, then I will say, 'It's no use, do you understand? It's no use, I am married.' But she will pay Elsa a fortune to divorce me, and then we will marry and sail off to Brazil on her yacht."

And the bare simplicity of his dream took on rich nuances at the word "Brazil," which, hot and fervid, summoned up a pink and white coast, jutting and jettying out at points into the tender blue sea. Now his lady had lost her tragic air and was—under the white silk of her simple schoolgirl dress—a smiling creature, simultaneously timid and daring.

And Erdosain thought:

"We will never have sex. To make our love last forever, we will deny our desires, and I will never kiss her mouth, only her hand."

He pictured this happiness which would purify his life, if such an impossible dream could happen. But it would be easier to make the earth stand still than turn his crazy dream into reality.

Then he would mutter, discomfited by a vague sense of ill-being:

"So then, I'll be a pimp." And all at once a terror greater than any other undid the fabric of his thoughts. He felt his soul being bled dry out of every furrow, like a creature pressed in a vise. With his powers of reason paralyzed, he ran off in search of a brothel. Then he knew the full terror of the thief, luminous terror like a sunny day smashing against a convex salt flat.

He abandoned himself to the impulses that twist a man who finds himself facing jail for the first time, blind forces that impel some wretch to stake his life on a card or a woman. Perhaps seeking in that card or woman a sour, harsh consolation, perhaps seeking in the vilest, lowest depths a certain affirmation of purity that might once and forever save him.

And in the warmth of the siesta hour, he wandered the sidewalks, whose tiles baked in the yellow sun, seeking the filthiest of whorehouses.

He liked best the one where he saw orange peels and trickles of ash in the doorway and the windows were lined with red or green flannel and armored with chicken wire.

He would enter, plunged deep into darkest despair. In the courtyard, under the checkered blue sky, there was usually a bench painted ocher, onto which he would wilt, exhausted, enduring the icy stare of the madam while he waited for one of her girls to show up, inevitably either horrendously thin or horrendously fat.

And the prostitute yelled from the half-open bedroom door, where a man could be heard getting dressed again:

"Ready, love?" and Erdosain went into the other bedroom, his ears buzzing and smoke churning in front of his eyes.

Later he lay back on the bed, varnished a liver-like color, on top of the shoe-grimed covers which protected the mattress.

Suddenly he felt like crying, like asking that horrible pig of a woman what love was, the angelic love that celestial choruses sang at the foot of the throne of the living God, but anguish formed a plug in his larynx and his stomach was a clenched fist of disgust.

And as the prostitute let his hand wander over her clothes, Erdosain wondered:

"What have I done with my life?"

A ray of sun bounced off the cobweb-covered transom, and the prostitute, with one cheek against the pillow and one leg resting on his, slowly moved his hand for him while he thought sadly:

"What have I made of my life?"

Suddenly remorse darkened his soul, he thought of his wife who, in her poverty, had to do laundry although she was sick, and then, filled with self-loathing, he leaped out of bed, paid the girl, and without having taken her, ran off to a new hell to spend the money that was not rightfully his, to descend still farther into his ever-howling madness.

A STRANGE MAN

At ten that morning Erdosain arrived at the corner of Peru and Avenida de Mayo. He knew he was doomed to jail, for Barsut would never give him the money. All at once he got a surprise.

At a café table was the pharmacist Ergueta.

With his hat down to his ears and his hands touching thumbs across his vast expanse of belly, he sat nodding with a puffed-up, sour expression on his yellow face.

His glassy, protruding, toad eyes, his great hook nose, his flaccid cheeks, and pendulous lower lip all combined to make him look like a cretin.

His great hulking body inhabited a cinnamon-brown

suit, and from time to time he would bend over and rest his teeth on the pommel of his cane.

That disgusting habit and his churlish, bored expression made him resemble a white slaver. He suddenly caught sight of Erdosain walking toward him, and the pharmacist's face lit up with an infantile grin. He was still smiling as he stretched out his hand to Erdosain, who thought:

"How many women have loved him for just that smile."

Erdosain was unable to hold back the question:

"So did you and Hipólita get married?"

"Right, only when they found out at home all hell broke loose."

"What—they knew she was a prostitute?"

"No . . . but she told them that afterward. You know before Hipólita was a prostitute she had been a servant?"

"So?"

"Right after we got married, Mama, Hipólita, me, and my sister all went to visit a family. You know how some people remember things? Ten years later they recognized Hipólita who had been their servant. That really put us on the spot. Mama and Juana versus me and Hipólita. It destroyed the cover story I had worked up to make Hipólita seem all right to marry."

"But why did she tell them she had been a prostitute?"

"She was furious. But, wasn't she right? Hadn't she gone straight? Couldn't she live in peace with me, something they'd never managed to do?"

"So how's it going?"

"Pretty well. The pharmacy brings in seventy pesos a day. In all of Pico nobody knows the Bible like me. I challenged the priest to a debate and he wouldn't take me up on it."

Erdosain looked at his strange friend with sudden hope. Then he asked:

"You still gamble?"

"Yes, because of my innocence, Jesus has seen fit to reveal to me the secret of roulette."

"What is it?"

"You don't know—the great secret—a law of static synchronism—I used it twice in Montevideo already and won a lot of money, but tonight Hipólita and I are going to break the bank."

And all at once he launched into an involved explanation:

"Look, in theory you play X amount on the first three balls, one out of each dozen. If you don't get different dozens, then, automatically, the whole thing is off balance. So you keep track of the dozen that come out. For the three balls after that, the dozen you're keeping your eye on will stay the same. Of course the zero doesn't count and you play your dozens in series of three balls. So then you raise by one the amount you have riding on the dozen without a cross, you go down one, I mean, two units on the dozen with three crosses, and on the basis of that you figure the unit smaller than those bigger ones and play the difference on the dozen or dozens that come out of that move."

Erdosain had not understood. He suppressed a laugh as his hope grew, for there was no denying that Ergueta was mad. So he replied:

"Jesus knows how to reveal such secrets to those whose souls are full of light."

"And also to idiots," argued Ergueta, looking at him mockingly and winking with his left eye. "Since I've gotten into these mysteries, I've done some hair-raising things, for instance, marrying that dummy."

"And are you happy with her?"

". . . to believe that people are good, when everyone is out to get you, to label you as crazy . . ."

Erdosain frowned in impatience, then:

"Why shouldn't they think you're crazy? You were, as you yourself put it, a great sinner. Then suddenly you hear some divine call, you marry a prostitute because it is written in the Bible, you talk about the fourth seal and the pale horse—sure, people are going to think you're crazy because you don't know anything at all about these things. Didn't they call me crazy, too, because I said they should set up shops to dry-clean and dye dogs and metallize shirtcuffs? But I don't think you're mad. No, I don't think so. Your problem is you have too much life, love, and neighborly feeling. Now, about Jesus revealing to you the secret of roulette, that's going a bit far—"

"But both times I won five thousand pesos—"

"So what? What saves you isn't the secret of roulette, but the beautiful soul that you have. You're someone who can do good, have mercy on some poor wretch about to go to jail . . ."

"That's the truth," Ergueta interrupted. "And look, there's another pharmacist in town who's an old miser. His son stole five thousand pesos from him, and later the son came to me for advice. You know what I told him to do? To blackmail his father saying he'd send him to jail for selling cocaine if he tried to report the crime."

"See how I understand you? You want to save the old man's soul by making the son commit a sin, a sin which he'll repent his whole life long. Isn't that it?"

"Yes, in the Bible it is written: 'And the father shall rise up against the son, and the son against the father.' "

"See? I understand you. I don't know what future fate awaits you—the destiny of man is always uncertain. But I believe a magnificent road stretches before you. You know? A strange road . . ."

"I shall be King of the World. Can't you see it? I will win at every roulette wheel, all the money I could want.

I will journey to Palestine, to Jerusalem, and rebuild the great temple of Solomon—"

"And save many good people from misery. How many are there who, from dire need, steal from their bosses, take the money that is given into their keeping? You know? Wretchedness—a wretched man doesn't know what he's doing—Today he robs one peso, tomorrow five, the next day twenty, and before he knows it he owes hundreds of pesos. And so the man thinks, 'It's not much . . .' and suddenly it's five hundred that's disappeared, no, six hundred pesos and seven cents. You see? Those are the people who must be saved—the wretches." The pharmacist thought a minute. A somber expression came over his puffy face; then he agreed coolly: "You're right—the world is full of stupid wretches, but what is to be done? That's what worries me. How can we share the sacred truths with those of little faith?"

"But if what people need is money—not sacred truths."

"No, that's what happens when man will not heed the word of God. A man who bears within him the sacred truths doesn't rob his boss, defraud his company, get himself into a spot where he could go to jail overnight."

Then he scratched his nose pensively and continued, "Besides, who's to say it's not all for the best? Who will make social revolution, if not the embezzlers, the wretches, murderers, swindlers, all those low-life types shoved down to the bottom with no way out? Or do you think revolution will come from shopkeepers and journalists?"

"Okay, okay—but, while we wait for the revolution, what is that poor man supposed to do? Me, what do I do?"

And grabbing Ergueta's arm, Erdosain burst out:

"Because I am that close to jail. See? I stole six hundred pesos and seven cents."

The pharmacist winked slowly at Erdosain and then said:

"Don't be upset. The times of tribulation spoken of in the Scriptures have come. Didn't I marry the Lame Whore? Has the son not risen up against the father, and the father against the son? The revolution is even closer than we would like to think. Are you not the thief and the wolf who ravages the flock?"

"But, tell me, can't you lend me those six hundred pesos?"

Ergueta shook his head slowly.

"You think because I read the Bible I'm stupid?"

Erdosain looked at him in desperation.

"I swear, that's what I owe."

All at once something unexpected happened.

The pharmacist got up, reached out one arm and snapping his fingers exclaimed, to the astonishment of a nearby waiter:

"Beat it, you creep."

Erdosain, red-faced, crept off. When he got to the corner and looked back, he saw Ergueta gesticulating as he talked to the waiter.

HATRED

His life was bleeding away. All of his pain was unraveling and flooding out toward the horizon, barely visible through the maze of cables and wheels of the trolley cars, and suddenly he had the feeling that he was treading on his own anguish, which lay beneath his feet. Like a horse with its guts torn out by a bull, mucking around in its own viscera, every step he took drained his lungs of their lifeblood. He breathed slowly and despaired of ever making it. Making it to where? In all truth, he did not know.

In Piedras Street he sat down in the entryway of a

vacant house. He stayed for several minutes, then began to walk rapidly; sweat ran down his face as though it were a hot day.

Thus he got to the corner of Cerrito and Lavalle.

Reaching into his pocket, he found a fistful of paper money and then went into the Japanese Bar. Cabbies and thugs were gathered around the tables.

A black with a wing collar and rough black sandals was delousing his armpits, and three Polish pimps, with heavy gold rings on their fingers, spoke in their private language of brothels and madams. In another corner several cabdrivers were playing cards. The black man who was delousing himself peered all around, as though seeking approval for his labors, but no one paid any attention to him.

Erdosain ordered coffee, leaned his forehead against his hand, and sat peering into the surface of the counter.

"Where can I get those six hundred pesos?"

Then he thought of Gregorio Barsut, his wife's cousin.

He stopped caring that Ergueta had told him to get lost. Now he could see before his eyes the taciturn figure of this other man, of Gregorio Barsut, with his shaven head, his bony nose like a bird of prey, his greenish eyes, and pointy wolf ears. He would ask him for money again tonight. Surely at nine-thirty he would come to Erdosain's home as usual. And again he would see the man. He would already be amassing an endless conversation full of vague excuses for coming to see him, torrents of words that stupefied Erdosain like tons of sand rolling over him.

Because now he remembered Barsut's interminable talk, leaping with feverish versatility from one topic to the next with his perverse eyes on Erdosain, who sat dry-mouthed and trembling, not daring to throw the man out of his house.

And Gregorio Barsut must have been aware how
deeply he revolted Erdosain because more than once
he said:

"You don't much care for my conversation, do you?"
which never kept Barsut from coming over to his house
with wearisome frequency.

Erdosain was quick to deny it, and tried to look interested in the man's ramblings, as he went on for hours
and hours, aimlessly, always keeping an eye on the
southwest corner of the room. What was he hoping to
find there? Erdosain would try to feel better about these
unpleasant conversations by thinking that the poor man
must live wracked with envy and certain hellish sufferings which were completely unjustifiable.

One night Gregorio said, in front of Erdosain's wife,
who was rarely on hand for these conversations, staying in the other room with the door closed to avoid
hearing the voices:

"How extraordinary it would be if I should go mad
and shoot you two dead, then kill myself!"

His slanted eyes were fixed on the southwest corner
of the room, and he smiled with a flash of pointy teeth,
as if what he had just said were only a joke. But Elsa
looked at him dead serious and said:

"That's the last time you talk like that in my house.
Otherwise, don't come around."

Gregorio tried to apologize. But she walked out and
didn't appear again all evening.

The two men went on talking, though Barsut was
ashen and his narrow forehead was continually going
into spasms, and he kept running his hand over his
bristly bronze hair.

Erdosain could not understand how he had come to
hate Barsut so much. At first he thought he was just
coarse, but that couldn't be, considering some of the
dreams Gregorio had, which revealed a vague, strange,

delicate inner self, full of the most inexplicable feelings.

At other times his real or imagined coarseness veered over to the downright disgusting, and in front of Erdosain, who squeezed his mouth in a tight line to suppress his indignation, Barsut added obscenity to obscenity, just for the sheer joy of offending his host.

It was an invisible duel, a poisonous, no-win game, so grating that when Barsut left, Erdosain would swear never to let him in again. But a few hours before his nightly visit, Erdosain was already thinking about him.

Often the guest would be talking even before he sat down.

"You know something? I had a funny dream last night."

And with his eyes glued to the southwest corner of the room, unsmiling, with a three-day beard, Barsut continued his slow monologue, revealing the terrors of a twenty-seven-year-old man, the anxieties that planted in his mind a one-eyed, winking fish, and merged the one-eyed fish into the scheming eyes of an aging madam trying to marry him off to her daughter, who contacted the spirits of the dead; he steered their conversation from one absurdity to another until, suddenly forgetting to be annoyed, Erdosain wondered if his visitor was stark raving mad. Elsa, indifferent to all of it, sat sewing in the next room, while Erdosain sat paralyzed with spasms of ill-being.

He felt a sudden tremulous impatience, he clacked his knuckles together, and the effort of hiding his attack of nerves was exhausting in itself. It was even hard to talk, as though his lips were frozen stiff from ice-cold soda.

Leaning one elbow on the table and straightening his pants leg, Barsut would complain that nobody loved him, looking at Erdosain at great length as he said it.

At other times he would make fun of his clairvoyant hunches and of a ghost he claimed to see in a corner of his boardinghouse bathroom, a huge woman with a broom in her hands and thin arms and a harpy's eyes. At other times, he confessed if he was not already mad he would end up that way. Erdosain pretended to be worried about Barsut's health, asked about his symptoms, advising him to rest and stay in bed, and when he said that too often Barsut would ask sneeringly:

"Does it bother you that much, my being here?"

At other times, Barsut would be wild with crazy glee, like an uncommunicative wino who just managed to set off a big oil fire, and prancing around the dining room, clapping Erdosain on the back, he would keep asking him with tiresome persistence,

"How goes it? How's it going?"

Barsut's eyes were glittery, and Erdosain sat there sadly, shriveled, wondering why he shrank back from confrontation with that man who was forever on his chair edge, with his eyes on that one corner of the room.

And they avoided one another's eyes.

Between them there was a dark, unfocused stalemate. One of those no-win situations that two men who hate each other can get locked into and never get out of.

Erdosain loathed Barsut, but it was a gray, complicated loathing, made of bad fantasies and worse possibilities. And what compounded the hatred was the lack of any concrete motive.

Sometimes he would sit inventing horrible revenge ploys, and, scowling, would rain imaginary disasters on his guest's head, but the next time Barsut came to the door, Erdosain would start trembling like an adulteress at her husband's knock, and once he even scolded Elsa for being so slow to open up for Barsut, then rationalized away his cowardly behavior this way:

"He'll think we don't want to let him in. If that's really true, then we should just tell him not to come anymore."

There was no concrete motive, and that inward-turned hatred spread through him like a cancer. Erdosain saw Barsut's every move as a fresh reason to burn with fury and wish horrible deaths on him. And Barsut, as if he were aware of his host's inner thoughts, would seem all the more eager to carry on in the most vulgar, disgusting vein. Erdosain would never forget one especially gross stunt.

One night they had gone out for a drink. Along with the drinks, the waiter brought some potato salad with mustard. Barsut pinioned a piece of potato with such a greedy stab of his toothpick that he splattered the salad all over the tabletop, coated with grime from people's dirty hands and cigarette ash. Then Barsut, sneering, scooped it up bit by bit, and when he got to the last piece, he used it to sop up the mustard smeared over the marbletop and then popped it into his mouth with a nasty grin.

"Why don't you just lick the marble?" asked Erdosain in disgust.

Barsut shot him a funny look, virtually a provocation. Then he put his head to the countertop and used his tongue to wipe the marble clean.

"Is that what you wanted?"

Erdosain turned pale.

"Have you gone crazy?"

And suddenly Barsut all laughing and friendly, seized with that vague frenzy that had been hanging darkly over him all afternoon, leaped up and vainly attempted to make things all right.

Erdosain would never forget it: the close-cropped head, bronze-colored, right down against the marble top with its tongue protruding into the slime on the yellowish stone.

And he often imagined that Barsut thought of him from then on with the hatred you feel for anyone you have let have too close a look at you. But he could not stop exposing himself, and the moment he got to Erdosain's house he would start baring his unhappy soul endlessly, even though he knew Erdosain gloried in his wretchedness.

In truth, Erdosain egged him on; in a seizure of crazed pity, he would play father confessor to Barsut, who would forget he was Erdosain's enemy when he gave him such sober advice. But his hatred would come out with a vengeance when the nasty gleam in Erdosain's eyes showed that his pity was about at an end and a vile joy was appearing at the spectacle of this life coming apart at the seams, since even though Barsut had money enough to live on from his assets, he still was haunted by the fear of going mad like his father and brothers.

All at once, Erdosain looked up. The black with the wing collar finished picking his lice, and now the three pimps were divvying up bundles of money under the greedy gaze of the cabbies who, at the other table, watched from the corners of their eyes. The black, gripped by the sight of money, seemed to be verging on a sneeze as he turned mournful eyes to the toughs.

Erdosain got up and paid. Then he went out saying: "If Gregorio won't cough up, I'll try the Astrologer."

INVENTOR'S DREAMS

If someone had told Erdosain that a few hours later he would be plotting Barsut's murder and would look on with near calm as his wife deserted him, he would not have believed it.

He spent the whole afternoon just wandering. He felt a need to be alone, to forget human voices and

stand apart from his surroundings like a man in a strange
city where he missed his train connection.

He walked past the lonely crossing of Arenales and
Talcahuano Streets, past the crossing of Charcas
and Rodríguez Peña, past the corner of Montevideo and
Avenida Quintana, savoring the sight of magnificently
constructed neighborhoods, forever off limits to the
poor. His feet, on the white sidewalks, squished
the fallen leaves from banana trees, and he looked
up at those great oval-paned windows, like leaded
mirrors with white curtains inside. It was a world
apart, set inside the grimy city he knew, a world
apart to which his heart now beat in slow, heavy
longings.

Stopping, he eyed the ritzy garages that almost glistened and the green-tufted cypresses inside the gardens
defended by rampart walls, or by ironwork solid enough
to halt a charging lion. The red-paved walkway slithered among the ovals of greenery. A gray-hatted gov-
erness was strolling down the street.

And he owed six hundred pesos and seven cents!

He gazed a long time at those balustrades that glowed
against the black balconies with their rounded golden
railings, those windows painted dove gray or the palest
shade of café-au-lait, those windowpanes so thick they
must have made passersby look bent and wavy. The
filmy curtains, so light that their names must have a
lilt like the names of exotic countries. How different
it must be to love in the shadow of that tulle that turns
light to half-shadow and modulates sounds.

But still he owed six hundred pesos and seven cents.
And the voice of the pharmacist rang in his ears:

"You're right—the world is full of wretches, burnt-
out cases . . . so what do we do about it? . . . How can
we share the sacred truths with those of little faith?"

Pain, like a tree forced to grow faster by electricity,

spread through the depths of his chest, creeping up his throat.

Stopping, he felt each spasm of grief hopping like an owl from branch to branch in his misery. He owed six hundred pesos and seven cents, and even though he wanted to push it out of his mind and only think how Barsut and the Astrologer would save him, his thoughts twisted off to a dark street.

Strings of lights seemed to hang from every ledge. A fog of dust choked the street. But he was off to the land of joy, the whole Sugar Company mess forgotten.

What had he done with his life? Was this or was this not the right moment to ask? And how could he walk along if his body weighed seventy kilos? Or was he a ghost, a ghost remembering his earthly existence?

How much seethed in his heart: What about the man who had married a prostitute? What about Barsut, scared of a one-eyed dream-fish and the eldest daughter of the seance lady? And what about Elsa, who wouldn't sleep with him, sending him out on the street? Was he crazy or not?

He had to wonder because at times he was amazed by the strength of hope that welled up inside him.

He imagined, peering through a louver in one of those palaces, there would be a "melancholy and taciturn millionaire" (I use Erdosain's exact words), observing him through binoculars.

And what was really odd was that whenever he thought the "melancholy and taciturn millionaire" could see him, he assumed a careworn, thoughtful expression and stopped watching the rears of passing maids, feigning the utmost paralyzing absorption in some terrible inner struggle. He thought that if the "melancholy and taciturn millionaire" caught him watching the maids' rumps, he might get the idea that he was not troubled enough to be worth rescuing.

And so Erdosain would wait for the "melancholy and taciturn millionaire" to send for him at any moment, just from seeing his face with its muscles stiff with years of bitter anguish.

He became so obsessed with it that afternoon he suddenly felt that an idler in a red-and-yellow striped jacket lounging in the door of the hotel and staring at him with bald curiosity was a scout for the "melancholy and taciturn millionaire."

And the servant called him over. He followed. They went through a garden prickly with cactus into a room where he was left alone for several minutes. The whole building was dark. A lamp in one corner was the only light. On the piano ledge, sheet music wafted the fragrance of continual contact with feminine hands. On a windowsill, draped in violet linen, a marble bust of a woman lay abandoned. Great cushions were upholstered in some Cubist print fabric, and on top of the desk there were black-bronze ashtrays and a multicolored desk set.

Where in his life could he have encountered a room like the one that now grew in his imagination? He could not remember. But he saw a great ebony frame whose sides ran up to the whitest of ceilings, whose pale plaster threw light onto a seascape: a sinister wooden bridge, under whose massive pilings a multitude of blurry men were seething, splotched with reddish shadows, carting great masses of something beside a tumultuous sea, cast-iron and somehow bloody, from which there arose straight up a stone dock jammed with a confusion of rails and cranes and pulleys.

Before their marriage, his Elsa had known just such a fine parlor. Yes, perhaps, but why bring that up now? He was the embezzler, the man with the wornout shoes, with the fraying tie, with grease stains on his suit who went off to eke out a living while his sick wife did laundry at home. That was why the "melancholy and taciturn millionaire" had sent for him.

Erdosain savored his fantasy until he could practically have reached out and touched it, supplementing it with fresh images supplied at the expense of the great invisible lord. He added on a splendid interview with the "melancholy and taciturn millionaire," who offered to finance the building of his inventions, and like those crime novel fans who skip the boring bits to get to the denouement, Erdosain shortcut over some of his own imaginative embellishments and got himself back in the street, even though he really already was on the street.

Then, leaving the crossing of Charcas and Talcahuano or Arenales and Rodríguez Peña, he went hurrying off.

And he set up great spasms of hope inside himself.

He would triumph, yes, he would triumph! With the money from the "melancholy and taciturn millionaire" he would set up his electrotechnical laboratory, he would specialize in the study of beta rays, in the wireless transmission of energy and of electromagnetic waves, and with his youth forever preserved, like the absurd hero of an English novel, he would grow older; only his face would pale to the whiteness of marble, and his flashing eyes, deep magus eyes, would seduce every maiden on earth.

The night began to fall and suddenly he remembered that the only one who could rescue him from his horrible situation was the Astrologer. At this thought, all others fled his mind. Perhaps the man had money. He even suspected him of being a Bolshevik agent sent to spread Communism in the country, since he had a strange scheme for a revolutionary band. Without hesitation, he hailed a cab and told the driver to take him to the Constitution Station. There he got a ticket to Temperley.

THE ASTROLOGER

The Astrologer lived in a building set in the middle of some wooded acreage. The house was built low and its red roof was visible a long way off through the foliage. In the clearings in the greenery, among tangled grasses and creepers, black-bottomed insects zoomed around all day through a perpetual mist of weeds and stray stalks. Not far from the house, a millwheel limped along on three paddles around a triangular, rusted iron axis, and ahead a bit, over the stables, hung the blue and red panes of some half-destroyed glass paneling. Behind the mill and the house, past the walls, a green mountain range of eucalyptus verged off into blackness, sending crests like mountain peaks into the sea-blue sky.

Sucking on a honeysuckle, Erdosain walked across the acres to the house. He felt as though he were in the country, very far from the city, and it cheered him to see the house. Although low, it was two-storied, with a decrepit balcony on the second floor and a peeling row of Greek columns at the entrance, marking the end of an unkempt path edged with palm trees.

The red roof tiles slanted downward, their eaves sheltering the transoms and tiny attic windows, and through the luxuriant greenery of the chestnut trees, over the tops of the pomegranate trees spangled with scarlet asterisks, a zinc rooster stood waving its twisted tail in the shifting wind. All around him the garden burst out in wild profusion, as if trying to become a minor forest, and now, in the still afternoon, in the sun that gave the air a nacreous shimmer, the rosebushes poured out their potent perfume, so piercing that it seemed to fill everything with an atmosphere red and fresh and like a river torrent of water.

Erdosain thought:

"Even if I had a silver boat with golden sails and marble oars, and the ocean were to turn seven splendid colors, and a millionairess were blowing me kisses from the moon, I would still be unhappy . . . But what's all this rot? It's still better to live out here than back there. Here, I could set up a lab."

A faucet dripped into a barrel. A dog dozed by an old-fashioned gazebo, and when Erdosain called from the foot of the stairs, the gigantic figure of the Astrologer loomed in the door, wrapped in a yellow smock with his hat pulled down over his eyes, shadowing his wide rhomboidal face. Stray wisps of hair wandered across his temples, and his nose, which had been broken at midpoint, skewed remarkably far to the left. Under his beetle brows round pupils darted, and that hard-cheeked face, with furrows grooved deep into its surface, seemed sculpted in lead. How that head must have weighed on its bearer!

"Ah! So it's you? Come on in. I want you to meet the Melancholy Ruffian."

Crossing the dark, dank-smelling vestibule, they entered a study with faded greenish wallpaper twisting across the walls.

It was, in all truth, a sinister room, its high ceiling furrowed with cobwebs and the narrow window fortified with a gnarled iron grille. When the bluish light fell on the lock of an antique chest, it fragmented into slivers of half-light. Sitting in an armchair covered in worn green velvet was a man in gray, with a jet black shock of wavy hair across his forehead and wearing light-colored spats. The Astrologer's yellow smock billowed out as he went up to the stranger.

"Erdosain, this is Arturo Haffner."

On another occasion, the embezzler would have said something to the man whom the Astrologer privately called the Melancholy Ruffian, who, after shaking Erdosain's hand, crossed his legs in the armchair and leaned one bluish cheek on three shiny-nailed fingers. And Erdosain looked again at that nearly round face, with its peaceful slackness, where nothing bespoke the man of action except a mocking, skittery spark in the depths of the eyes and a trick of raising one eyebrow higher than the other while listening to conversation. Erdosain made out on one side, between the jacket and the silk shirt the Ruffian had on, the black butt of a revolver. Undoubtedly, in life, faces mean very little.

Then the Ruffian looked toward a map of the United States, which the Astrologer was facing with a pointer in hand. Standing with his yellow arm across the Caribbean's sea blue, he exclaimed:

"The Ku Klux Klan had only one hundred fifty thousand followers in Chicago . . . In Missouri, one hundred thousand followers. They say that in Arkansas there are over two hundred 'caverns.' In Little Rock, the Invisible Empire affirms that all the Protestant pastors are part of the Klan. In Texas it holds absolute sway over the cities of Dallas, Fort Worth, Houston, and Beaumont. In Binghamton, home of Smith, who was Grand Dragon of the Order, there were seven thousand five hundred initiates, and in Oklahoma they got the legislature to remove Walton, the governor, for trying to stamp them out, so in fact the state was under Klan rule until lately."

The Astrologer's yellow smock seemed to be the robe of some Buddhist monk.

The Astrologer continued:

"Do you know they burned several men alive?"

"Yes," said the Ruffian. "I read the telegrams."

Erdosain now began to take a good look at the Melancholy Ruffian. The Astrologer called him that because many years ago the pimp had tried to kill himself. That was a mysterious affair. Overnight, and after years of exploiting prostitutes, Haffner shot a bullet into his chest, right next to his heart. Only the contraction of the organ at the precise moment of the bullet's entry saved him. Later, he went on with his life just as always, only maybe with a little added glamor from this gesture which made no sense to any of his fellow vultures. The Astrologer went on:

"The Ku Klux Klan collected millions—"

In a fit of despair the Ruffian cut in:

"Yes, and their Dragon—and a dragon is the right word for him!—gets hauled into court for theft."

The Astrologer ignored this outburst.

"What in Argentina prevents the formation of a secret sect that could grow just as strong as that one did there? And I'll speak frankly now. I don't know if our group will be Bolshevik or Fascist. Sometimes I think the best thing would be to invent some tutti-frutti that would leave everyone guessing. See, I'm being as open about all this as anybody could ask. What I mean to do is make a big something to be the ultimate focus of human yearnings. My plan is to appeal especially to young Bolsheviks, students, and intelligent proletarians. Besides them, we'll appeal to all the world reformers, clerks who fantasize being millionaires, frustrated inventors—not you, of course, Erdosain—plus anyone who's been laid off or else had some run-in with the law, people who're out on the street not knowing where to turn—"

Erdosain remembered what had brought him to the Astrologer's house, and said:

"I have to talk to you—"

"Just a moment . . . I'll be with you," and he resumed his pitch. "The power of our group will come not from member contributions, but from brothels each cell will set up for funding. When I talk about a secret society, I don't mean the classic setup but some supermodern version, where each member and initiate has an interest and shares earnings, since that's the only way to really get them involved in the projects which only a few will be very informed about. Anyway, that's the business side of it. The brothels will fund the growing branches of the society. In the mountains, we'll build a revolutionary training camp. There, we'll school new recruits in anarchist tactics, revolutionary propaganda, military hardware, industrial planning, so as soon as they get out of training they can set up a new cell anywhere. Do you see? The secret society will have its training institute, the Revolutionary Institute."

The clock on the wall struck five. Erdosain saw there was no time to lose, and burst out:

"Forgive my interrupting. I came on serious business. Do you have six hundred pesos?"

The Astrologer put down his pointer and crossed his arms.

"What's your problem?"

"If I don't show up with six hundred pesos tomorrow the Sugar Company will send me to jail."

Both men stared at Erdosain. He had to be in great distress to go blurting out his plea like that. Erdosain went on:

"You have to help me. Over the past few months, I managed to embezzle six hundred pesos. Somebody turned me in with an anonymous letter. If I don't bring the money in tomorrow, they'll send me to jail."

"And how did you come to steal all that money?"

"It just happened, sort of one day at a time."

The Astrologer fiddled with his beard in dismay.

"But how did it happen?"

Erdosain had to explain all over again. Whenever the retailers got a shipment of goods, they signed a receipt showing they owed whatever the price was. Erdosain, along with the other clerks in his department, got a bunch of those receipts at the end of the month and had thirty days to collect.

The bills which they said they could not collect on just stayed with them until the retailers paid up. And Erdosain went on:

"Just think, the clerk was so lax about it that he never checked back on the bills we said we couldn't collect on, so if we did collect and pocketed the money, we could just enter it as a regular bill paid and then cover for it using money from a bill we collected on later. See how the coverup worked?"

Erdosain was the vortex of the triangle formed by the three. The Melancholy Ruffian and the Astrologer exchanged glances from time to time. Haffner flicked the ash from his cigarette and then, with one eyebrow cocked, kept examining Erdosain from head to foot. At last he put a strange question to him:

"Did you get pleasure from stealing?"

"No, none . . ."

"But why are you still wearing those wornout shoes?"

"I didn't make much money."

"What about all that money you stole, though?"

"It never occurred to me to buy shoes with that money."

That was the truth. His initial glee at getting away with spending somebody else's money soon wore out. One day Erdosain noticed he was full of a restless ache that turned sunny skies soot black in a way that only a wretched soul could perceive.

When he found out he already owed four hundred pesos, the shock plunged him into madness. Then he dashed about in a mad frenzy trying to get the money spent. He bought candy, which he never even liked, lunched on crab, tortoise soup, and frogs in restaurants that charge for the privilege of sitting among the well-dressed, he drank expensive liquors and wines which were wasted on his untrained taste buds, and still he was without the most necessary items for simple comfort, such as underwear, shoes, neckties . . .

He started giving money to beggars and big tips to waiters who served him, just to be rid of the last bits of that stolen money he carried in his billfold and that might be taken away from him at any moment.

"So you never thought about new shoes?" insisted Haffner.

"Really, now that you make me think about it, it does seem strange, but to tell the truth I never thought those things could be bought with stolen money."

"So, what did you spend the money on?"

"I gave two hundred pesos to a family of friends, the Espilas, to buy an accumulator and set up a small galvanoplastics lab, for the production of a copper rose, which is—"

"Yes, I know already—"

"Yes, I told him all about it," said the Astrologer.

"And the other four hundred?"

"I don't know . . . I spent them just in a crazy way . . ."

"And what's your plan now?"

"I don't know."

"Don't you know anyone to help you out?"

"No, no one. I went to a relative of my wife's, Barsut, ten days ago. He said he couldn't . . ."

"So you go to jail?"

"Well, of course . . ."

The Astrologer turned to the pimp and said:

"You know I need to have a thousand pesos. That's for setting up my big projects. So all I can give you,

Erdosain, is three hundred pesos. Still, my friend, you sure manage to look after your affairs!"

Suddenly Erdosain forgot all about Haffner and burst out:

"It's unhappiness. You know what I mean? This fucking unhappiness is what pulls you under—"

"How's that?" interrupted the Ruffian.

"I said, it's unhappiness. You steal, you do all these crazy things because you're unhappy. You walk down the streets under a yellow sun, and it looks like a festering plague sun. . . . Sure. You have to have been down to know. Walking around with five thousand pesos in your pocket, still you're miserable. And suddenly a little idea blooms: to steal. That night you can't sleep for joy. The next day you do your accounts, you're shaking all over but you make it look really good, and so you have to keep on with it—it's just like your suicide attempt."

These words made Haffner sit bolt upright in his armchair and grip his knees with clenched fingers. The Astrologer tried to shush Erdosain. It was no use, for he went on in the same vein:

"Yes, just like your suicide attempt. I've often pictured it to myself. You were sick of pimping. If you only knew how much I've wanted to meet you! I said to myself: that must be one strange pimp. Of course, out of a thousand men like you who deal in women, there's one who's like you. You asked me if I got pleasure from stealing. Now, you tell me if you get pleasure—But, what the hell, I'm not here to give explanations, see? What I need is money, not a lot of talk."

Erdosain had got up, and now he stood clenching his hat brim in his fists. He glared indignantly at the Astrologer, at his hat blocking the view of Kansas on his map, and at the Ruffian, who stuck his hands between belt and pants. Haffner settled back into the armchair covered in green velvet, propped one cheek on his plump hand and with a smirk he said calmly:

"Sit down, here, friend, I'll give you that six hundred pesos."

Erdosain pulled his arms up against his sides. Then, not moving, he stared for a time at the Ruffian. The man insisted, and this time emphasized his words more clearly.

"Relax, sit down. I'll give you that six hundred pesos. What are real men for?"

Erdosain did not know what to say. He was flooded with the same terrible torrent of sadness that had been unleashed in his soul when the pig-headed office boss told him he could go now. So, life was not so bad, after all.

"Let's do it like this," said the Astrologer. "I give him three hundred pesos and you give him the other three hundred."

"No," said Haffner. "You need the money. I don't. I have three women bringing it in." And, turning to Erdosain, he went on: "So see, now, how things have a way of working out? Things okay now?"

He spoke with a smirking calm, with the unshakable cool of a country man who knows that he knows enough about the natural world to cope with any crisis. And it was only then that Erdosain noticed the overpowering rose scent and the tap dripping into the barrel, plunking clearly outside the half-open door. Outside, the roads meandered away, wavy in the afternoon sun, and birds sitting in the pomegranate trees bent the boughs downward in great sagging clusters of scarlet asterisks.

Again a nasty gleam appeared in the Ruffian's eyes. Cocking one eyebrow, he waited for Erdosain to light up with joy, but, when that didn't happen, he said:

"Have you been going on like this for long?"

"Yes, quite a while."

"Do you remember I once told you, even before you had confided in me, that you couldn't go on living the way you were?" the Astrologer objected.

"Yes, but I didn't feel like talking about it. I don't know . . . things that really confuse you are the ones you won't talk about even with people you know you can trust."

"When will you put the money back?"

"Tomorrow."

"Good, then I'll write you a check right now. You'll have to cash it tomorrow."

Haffner turned to the desk. He pulled out his checkbook and wrote the sum firmly, then signed his name.

Erdosain went through a paralyzed moment of utter suspension, as unthinking as someone who is confronted with a dream landscape that stays in his memory later, so that he would swear that sometimes life really operates with an intelligent fatalism.

"Here you go, pal."

Erdosain took the check, and without reading it folded it twice and put it in his pocket. It was all over in a minute. It was more absurd than anything in a novel, and yet it was a real live person doing it. And he did not know what to say. Just a minute before he was six hundred pesos and seven cents in debt. Now he was no longer in debt, and this miracle had been worked by a single move on the Ruffian's part. By all standards of logic it should not even have happened, but it went off without a hitch. He wanted to say something. He peered again into the face of that man lounging in the frayed velvet armchair. Now the revolver stood out visibly under the gray fabric of the suit coat, and Haffner, irritated, propped his bluish cheek on three flashy-nailed fingers. He wanted to thank the Ruffian, but no words came to him. The man understood, and, turning to the Astrologer, who had sat down on a stool by the desk, said:

"So then, your society will be very big on obedience?"

"That and industrialism. We need gold if we want to seize men's minds. So just as there was mysticism in religion and then again with chivalry and knights-errant, what we need is industrial mysticism. Make man see how beautiful it is to head a great foundry, as beautiful as it used to be to discover a continent. My political man, my student, my right hand in the movement will be someone who sets out to win happiness through industry. He will be a revolutionary equipped to speak on fabric processing as well as the demagnetization of steel. That's why I was so impressed when I met Erdosain. He thought along these exact same lines. You remember how often we talked about how many ideas we shared. The creation of a proud, beautiful, inexorable man who will harness the multitudes and show them a future based on science. How else can we have a social revolution? The leader of today must be a man who knows everything. We will create this prince of wisdom. The society will undertake the fabrication and dissemination of his myth. A Ford or an Edison has a thousand more chances to touch off a revolution than a politician. Do you think future dictatorships will be the military type? No, sir, the military man is nothing compared to an industrialist. The most he can be is the industrialist's tool. That's all. Future dictators will be kings of petroleum, steel, wheat. Through our society, we will set the scene for all this. We will familiarize people with our theories. For that purpose, there has to be a thorough study of propaganda techniques. We need to use students, both male and female. Science must be made to seem glamorous, must be made accessible to everybody . . ."

"I'm going now," said Erdosain.

He was going to say good-bye to Haffner when the man said:

"Wait a minute, listen."

The Astrologer and the pimp went out for a moment, then came back in, and as he said his good-byes at the door of the house, Erdosain looked back and saw that giant man with his arms raised in farewell.

THE OPINIONS OF THE
MELANCHOLY RUFFIAN

And once they were around the corner from the house, Erdosain said:

"You know I have no way to thank you for the huge favor you just did me? Why did you give me the money?"

The man, who swaggered a little in the shoulders as he walked, turned to him and replied tartly:

"I don't know. You just caught me in the right mood is all. It's not like I had to do it every day . . . but coming at me like that . . . anyway, look, I'll make it back in a week easy."

A question popped out spontaneously.

"How come, if you already have a fortune, you keep pimping?"

Haffner turned on him, looking feisty, then said:

"Look here, pimping isn't a game any fool can play. You know? So why should I leave three women at loose ends when they can bring in two thousand pesos a month? Would you just let them go? No. So?"

"And you don't love them? None of them especially appeals to you?"

As soon as it was out of his mouth, Erdosain saw what an asinine question he had asked. The pimp looked at him a second, then answered:

"Now listen to this. If tomorrow some doctor came and told me: that Basque woman of yours will be dead in a week on or off the job, then I'd let that woman, who's brought me in some thirty thousand pesos over four years, work six days more and die the seventh."

The pimp was hoarse now. There was some rabid, bitter streak running through his words, a bitter streak Erdosain would later recognize in that whole breed of operators and bored sharpers.

"Pity, huh?" he went on. "Listen, it's idiotic to pity a woman who sells herself. No woman could be harder, more bitter than the one who goes into the streets. Don't be surprised, because I know them. The only way to keep them in line is with the back of your hand. Like ninety percent of all people, you see the pimp as the exploiter and the prostitute as the victim. But tell me: what would a woman do with the money she brings in? What novelists don't mention is that a woman like that without a man goes running all over looking for a man to cheat her, smash her down every so often, and take all the money she makes, because that's what a mutt she is. They say woman is equal to man. What garbage. Woman is inferior to man. Take your wild savage tribe. She does the cooking, the work, everything, but the male goes off to hunt or fight. Same for modern life. The man, apart from making money, does nothing. And believe me, if you don't take a hooker's money she'll think very little of you. It's true, as soon as she starts to grow fond of you the first thing she wants is for you to hit on her . . . She goes into ecstasy when you ask her, 'Ma chérie, could you loan me one hundred pesos?' Then she feels things are okay between you. At last the filthy money she makes is good for something if it makes her man happy. Naturally, novelists leave that part of it out. And people think we're monsters or some exotic creatures, that whole image they get from the pulps. But come live in our world, get to know it, and you'll see it's just like the middle class or aristocracy. The kept woman looks down on the showgirl, the showgirl looks down on the street-walker, the streetwalker looks down on the woman in a brothel and, the funny thing is, just as the brothel girl almost always finds a man to take her for all she's worth, the showgirl finds some little rich kid, or even some crumbbum doctor to exploit her. The psychology of the hooker? You have it in a nutshell in something one told me through her tears when a friend of mine gave her the heave-ho: *'Encore avec mon cul je peux soutenir un homme.'* That's the part people don't know and novelists don't tell them. A French proverb says it all: *'Gueuse seule ne peut pas mener son cul.'* "

Erdosain looked at him stupefied. Haffner went right on:

"Who looks after her like the pimp? Who takes care of her when she's sick or gets busted? What do people know about that? If some Saturday morning you heard a woman say to her 'marlu,' 'Mon chéri, I made fifty pesos more this week than last,' you'd take up pimping, see? Because that woman tells you 'I made fifty more' just in the same tone an honest woman uses to tell her husband: 'Dear, by not buying a new dress and doing the laundry at home, I saved thirty pesos this month.' Believe me, friend, woman, honest or not, is an animal crazed with the idea of self-sacrifice. She's just made that way. Why do you think the Church fathers thought so little of women? Because most of them had sown a lot of wild oats and saw first-hand what a little animal she is. And the hooker is even worse. She's like a child, you have to point everything out to her. 'You can walk past this place, only keep away from that corner, don't say hi to that "operator." Don't go getting into a fight with that woman.' You have to tell her everything."

They walked along under the garden walls, and in the mellow dusk the pimp's words opened Erdosain up to gaping astonishment. He grasped he stood next to a

life considerably unlike his own. Then he asked him:
"And how did you get into pimping?"

"It was when I was young. I was twenty-three and
on the university faculty in math. I'm a professor, see,"
Haffner added proudly. "A math professor. I was living
on my salary when one night in a whorehouse on Rin-
cón Street I met this French girl that I liked. All this
was about ten years ago. Just around then I came into
about five thousand pesos when a relative died. I liked
Lucienne, and I asked if she'd come live with me. She
had a pimp, the Marseillais, a giant brute I saw now
and then . . . I don't know if it was my smooth talking
or good looks, but anyway she fell in love with me and
one stormy night I came and got her out of her house.
It was straight out of a novel. We went to Córdoba in
the mountains, then to Mar del Plata, and when we'd
gone through the five thousand pesos, I told her: 'Well,
that was our fling. It's all over now.' Then she told me,
'No, darling, we'll never again be apart.' "

Now they were strolling under clusters of greenery,
intertwining branches, and clumps of stalks.

"I was jealous. Do you know what it's like to be
jealous of a woman who sleeps with everyone? And do
you know what it is when she pays for the first lunch
with money from some john? Can you picture the joy
of sitting there eating away with the waiter looking at
you and knowing what the deal is with you? And the
joy of walking out with her hanging from your arm and
all the johns trying to get a look at you? And seeing
that she prefers you, you alone, after she's been to bed
with so many men? That's a sweet sensation, pal, once
you get to make a career of it. And she's the one who
recruits a second woman for your stable, brings her
home and tells her 'We'll be sisters-in-law,' she's the
one who keeps the new girl in hand and makes her
turn everything over to you, and the more shy and
squeamish you are, the more she likes to wreck your

conscience, pulling you down to her level, and suddenly—when it's the last thing on your mind you find
you're up to your ears in slime—and then there's no
way back out. And while you have the woman going
you have to work her hard, because one day she'll dump
you, go crazy over another guy, and in the same blind
way she took to you, she'll give everything up for him.
You'll ask me, what does a woman need to have a man
for? But I'll tell you: nobody's going to deal direct with
a woman he wants for his whorehouse. He wants to
go through her 'marlu.' The pimp takes care of business
so the woman can get on with it in peace. Johns don't
harass her. If she's busted, he bails her out, if she's sick,
he gets her to the doctor and gets her fixed up, and he
generally keeps her out of trouble and all kinds of really
useful stuff. Look, if a woman goes it alone she's just
asking for a beating or some kind of con or anyway
something will happen to her. But if a woman has a
man, she just does what she does, and nobody's about
to mess with her and they all have to respect her. And
since it was her decision to earn it that way, it follows
she should be free to spend her money on something
that will give her the security she needs.

"Of course, it all sounds new to you, but you'll catch
on. And if not, tell me this: how do you explain away
the pimp who has up to seven women? Old Repollo
once had eleven in his stable at his peak. Julio the
Galician had eight. Most all Frenchmen have three.
And they get to be friends, they live in peace and each
tries to bring in more than the others, since it's a big
deal to be the favorite of some dude who can make
mobsters cool it with a single glance. And, poor things,
they're all so crazy you don't know whether to feel
sorry for them or sock it to them good."

Erdosain was overwhelmed by the massive contempt
the man had for all women. And he remembered another time when the Astrologer told him: "The Mel-

ancholy Ruffian is a guy who sees a woman and right away he's thinking 'She'd bring in five, ten, twenty pesos on the street.' That's it for him."

Now Erdosain felt revolted by the man. Trying to switch the conversation around, he said:

"Answer me this: Do you believe the Astrologer's plan can work?"

"No."

"Does he know you don't think so?"

"Sure."

"Well then, what are you in it for?"

"I'm in it only more or less, and even that much just from boredom. Life has no meaning, so it's about the same to go off wherever it takes you."

"So for you life has no meaning?"

"Not the least bit. We get born, live, die, without the stars stopping in their tracks or the ants stopping work over it."

"And are you very bored?"

"Average. I have my day compartmentalized like an industrialist. Every day I go to bed at twelve and get up at nine in the morning, do an hour of exercises, take a bath, read the papers, eat lunch, take a nap, at six I have a glass of vermouth, go to the barber, eat dinner at eight, then I go out on the town a bit, and in a couple of years when I'll have gotten two hundred thousand pesos together, then I'll retire and live off dividends and what I've got set up."

"And what's your real part in the Astrologer's group?"

"If the Astrologer can get up the money, I'll help get the women and get the brothels going."

"But what's your deep-down, private opinion of the Astrologer?"

"One of those madmen who just might pull it off, or maybe not."

"But his ideas—"

"Some are a mess, others make sense, and really I don't know what the guy's shooting for. Sometimes it seems like I'm listening to a reactionary, sometimes a leftist and, to tell the truth, I don't think he himself knows what he wants."

"What if he pulls it off?"

"Then God knows what all might happen. Oh, by the way, did you talk to him about growing an Asian cholera bacillus?"

"Yes . . . it would be a terrific weapon to unleash on the army. Just let one culture loose in each barracks. See? Thirty or forty men could destroy the army in one action and then let the proletarian masses make revolution—"

"The Astrologer really admires you a lot. He always talks about you to me like you're somebody who could really have a big success."

Erdosain smiled, flattered:

"Yes, you have to work on some project to sabotage the present system. But about this other thing, what I can't figure out is what your relationship to us is."

Haffner turned around quickly, sized Erdosain up with a cold eye, then, with a smirk, he answered:

"I'm not in any relationship. Understand me good. I have nothing to lose helping the Astrologer. The rest, his theories, for me it's just some talk, see. He's just a friend of mine who wants to get set up in a business, one that even comes under the law, and that's it for me. Now, the money he gets out of it he can use to start a conspiracy or a convent full of nuns, it's nothing to me personally. So, see, my part in this big underground society of his couldn't be more innocent."

"And to you it makes sense that a revolutionary group should live off the exploitation of women?"

The Ruffian glowered. Then, giving Erdosain only a sidelong glance, he explained:

"That's a lot of nonsense. The way the system works now, we exploit men, women, and children all the time. If you want to see real exploitation in this capitalist setup, just go look at the foundries down on Avellaneda, the meat packers, the glassworks, tobacco and match factories." He let out a nasty laugh to go with these remarks. "We, the men who play these games, maybe we have one or two women, but an industrialist has a whole mass of human beings. So what do you call a guy like that? Who's inhuman, someone who has a whorehouse or the stockholders of a company? And, not to get into this business of yours, but didn't they say you should keep honest and pay you a hundred pesos to carry around ten thousand pesos in your billfold?"

"You're right . . . but then, why did you let me have the money?"

"Well, that's a whole different story."

"But it keeps bothering me."

"Okay, well, see you later."

And before Erdosain could answer, the Ruffian was already off down a tree-lined path. He was walking off fast. Erdosain looked at him, and then rushed to catch up with him next to an old house. Haffner wheeled around, irritated, and burst out:

"Would you mind telling me what it is you want?"

"What do I want? . . . I want you to know one thing, see, that I'm not the least bit grateful for the money you gave me. You know? You want your check? Here, take it."

And he pushed it right at him, but then the Ruffian looked at him, this time with total contempt.

"Don't be silly, okay? Go pay up."

Erdosain was seeing the fence like a series of waves. He was obviously not doing very well and turned so pale he was practically yellow. He leaned on a post, sure he was going to throw up any moment now. Haffner, standing in front of him, asked condescendingly:

"Feeling better, now?"

"Yes . . . a little . . ."

"You're not in good shape . . . you should go see a doctor."

They walked on a few steps in silence. The light bothered Erdosain's eyes, so they took a path that lay more in shade. They followed it to the train station. Haffner walked slowly through the station. Suddenly he wheeled and asked Erdosain:

"Have you ever had the urge to be cruel to people?"

"Yes, sometimes . . ."

"That's odd . . . because just now I was thinking about this idea I had a while ago, the idea of having a blind girl to offer my clients . . ."

"Is she still alive?"

"Oh yes, and now she's pregnant. See? Blind and pregnant. I'll take you to see her someday. You can meet her. It really is a strange thing, so be prepared for something strong. See? Blind and pregnant. Oh, she's a wild one, wanders around with needles in her hands . . . besides which she eats like a pig. You'll find it very interesting."

"And you're going to—"

"Right, as soon as the Astrologer gets the whorehouse set up, she'll be our number one girl. We'll keep her on ice and bring her out as the exotic *spécialité de la maison*."

"You're more exotic than she is, you know?"

"How's that?"

"Because you defy explanation. While you were telling me about that blind girl, I was thinking of something the Astrologer told me. You took up with a really pure woman and even when she was right in your house you didn't lay a hand on her. Let me ask you this one thing: if that woman was in love with you and she was a virgin, why did you leave her alone?"

"No big deal. A little self-control, is all."

"What about the necklace story?"

Erdosain had heard this story from the Astrologer, that the Ruffian once asked a dancer for concrete proof she loved him, so with other women watching she took off a magnificent necklace given to her by a lover, an elderly yard-goods importer. It was bizarre, since the old man was sitting nearby. Haffner took the necklace and, to everyone's shock, hefted it jeweler-style, cast an appraising eye on it, then handed it back with a snide smirk.

"That necklace story is easily explained," Haffner answered. "I was a little drunk. But even so I knew my little bit of theater would really raise me in the eyes of that cabaret scum, especially the women, they're all pushovers for that dashing stuff. What's so odd is half an hour later the old guy who gave Renée the necklace came to thank me humbly for not accepting the gift. See? He'd been watching the whole thing from another table and the only reason he didn't do anything about it was he didn't want to make a scene. But the whole time he was quaking in his boots, worried sick about his necklace . . . well, you see what a sordid business it all was . . . but here's the train for La Plata. See you soon, pal— Ah! Be there for the meeting Wednesday at the Astrologer's house. You'll find other people even more bizarre than me."

Erdosain went over to where the trains left for Buenos Aires. It was clear in his mind that Haffner was a monster.

THE HUMILIATED MAN

He got home at eight that night.

"The dining-room light was on . . . But, in point of fact," as Erdosain was to tell it later, "my wife and

I were so dirt poor that our so-called dining room was an unfurnished room. The other room was the bedroom. You may wonder why, if we were so poor, we could rent a house, but my wife had this notion, since she'd known better days she couldn't bear to just 'set up camp' somewhere.

"In the dining room the only furniture was a pinewood table. In one corner our clothes hung from a wire, and another corner was taken up by a trunk with brass fittings, so it always seemed like we were about to take off for someplace else. Later, how often I've remembered how that cheap trunk always gave us that 'bon voyage' look, and it added to my misery when I was somebody who knew he could go to jail overnight.

"As I was saying, the dining-room light was on. When I opened the door, I stopped short. My wife was waiting for me, dressed to go out, sitting at the table. Her rosy little face had a veil down to her chin. To the right of her, by her feet, was a suitcase and on the other side of the table a man stood up when I came in, or rather, when I stood in the doorway paralyzed with shock.

"We were all frozen like that a second: The Captain on his feet, one hand on the table and the other on his sword hilt, my wife looking down and me in front of them, still with one hand on the door frame. Just that second's glimpse, but I'll never forget that man. He was a big guy, a big strapping jock in a green uniform. He looked away from my wife and his eyes were so very hard. I'm not exaggerating when I say he looked at me with insolence, as an inferior being. I kept my eyes on him. His big body went oddly with his little oval face, delicate slender nose, and tight-squeezed, prim little mouth. His chest bore the insignia of an air-force pilot.

"The first thing I said was:

" 'What's all this about?'

" 'Mr . . . ,' then she felt ashamed and started differently. 'Remo,' she said, calling me by my name, 'Remo, I won't be living with you anymore.' "

Erdosain did not even have time to start shaking. The Captain spoke then:

"Your wife, whom I met a while ago—"

"And where did you meet her?"

"Why are you asking about this stuff?" Elsa cut in.

"Yes," the Captain objected. "Surely you can see that there are some things you just don't ask about . . ."

Erdosain turned red.

"Maybe you're right there . . . sorry . . ."

"And since you weren't making enough to support her . . ."

Gripping the revolver butt in his pocket hard, Erdosain looked at the Captain. Then, involuntarily, he smiled thinking how he had nothing to fear, since he could kill him.

"I hardly think what I said is all that funny."

"No, no, I was smiling over a weird thought I just had. . . . So she told you that kind of thing?"

"Yes, and she also told me about how you were a genius, and in a bad way—"

"We've talked about your inventions—"

"Yes . . . about your project to make metallized flowers."

"So why are you leaving, then?"

"I'm tired, Remo."

Erdosain felt fury scrunching his mouth into nasty words. He would have liked to insult her, but remembering the stranger could smash his face in, he held back his abuse and answered:

"You were always tired. At home, you were tired . . . here . . . there . . . up in the mountains . . . remember?"

Unsure how to answer him, Elsa looked at the floor.

"Tired . . . how come you're so tired? All of you

women are tired, and I don't see why . . . but anyway
you're tired . . . You, Captain, aren't you tired, too?"
The stranger looked at him for some time.
"When you say tired, how do you mean?"
"From boredom, from unhappiness. Haven't you noticed that these seem to be the times of tribulation that
the Bible speaks of? That's what a friend of mine says,
a guy who married a lame whore. The lame woman is
the Whore of whom the Scriptures tell us—"
"I never knew that was so."
"Ah, well, I did. It may seem odd for me to be talking
about suffering under these circumstances, but that's
how it goes . . . men are in such a bad way that they
need someone to humiliate them."
"I see nothing of the sort."
"Of course not, considering how much you
make . . . How much do you make? Fifteen hundred?"
"Somewhere around there."
"Making that much it's only logical . . ."
"What's only logical?"
"That you shouldn't feel like a slave."
The Captain was glowering at Erdosain.
"Germán, don't pay him any mind," Elsa cut in.
"Remo's always going on about unhappiness."
"Is that so?"
"Yes . . . but her, she believes in happiness. In the
feeling of 'perpetual bliss' that would descend on her
life if she could spend her days going to parties."
"I detest unhappiness."
"Well, sure, since you don't believe in unhappi-
ness . . . the horrible thing gnawing away inside of us,
inner unhappiness . . . a soul-deep thing that worms deep
into our bones like syphilis . . ."
They fell silent. The Captain, obviously bored, looked
at his nails, buffed to a shine.
Elsa looked out fixedly from behind the rhombus

pattern veil, at the gaunt face of the husband she had once loved so much, while Erdosain wondered why he should be one huge vacuum on the inside, a vacuum in which his consciousness dissolved, finding no words that might howl out his pain to eternity.

The Captain looked up suddenly.

"And how do you plan to metal-coat your flowers?"

"Simple . . . Take a rose, for example, and dip it in a solution of silver nitrate dissolved in alcohol. Then you put the flower under a light that reduces the nitrate to metallic silver, which leaves the rose covered with a fine metal film, a good conductor of current. Then it's treated by the usual coppering process, galvano-plastic plating technique . . . and, of course, at the end of it you have your rose turned into a copper rose. It would be really useful in a lot of ways."

"The idea is original."

"Didn't I tell you how clever Remo is, Germán?"

"He sure is."

"Yes, maybe I'm talented in certain regards, but I don't have life . . . enthusiasm . . . something like some extraordinary dream . . . a great lie always struggling toward reality . . . but anyway, changing the subject again, do you two expect to be happy?"

"Yes."

Once more silence came over them. In the light of the yellow lamp their three faces looked like three wax masks. Erdosain saw that in a few brief moments it would all be over and digging down into his grief, he asked the Captain:

"Why did you come to my house?"

The other man vacillated, then said:

"I was eager to meet you."

"Sounded like it might be fun?"

"No . . . I swear that's not it."

"What, then?"

"I wanted to meet you out of curiosity. Your wife told me so much about you lately. Besides, I never figured on getting into such a weird situation. . . . Well, really, I'm not too sure why I came."

"See? These inexplicable things really happen. I've been trying for some time to think why it is I don't shoot you dead seeing that I've got a gun right here in my pocket."

Elsa looked up at Erdosain, who was at the head of the table . . .

The Captain asked:

"What's stopping you?"

"Really, I don't know . . . or yes, I'm sure that must be it. I believe each one of us bears in his heart a destiny cut to a certain measure. It's like a way of knowing things through some mysterious instinct. This thing that's happening to me now, I feel, must fit within the measure of my destiny . . . it's as though I'd seen it somewhere before . . . where I don't know."

"How so?"

"What?"

"It wasn't that you gave me a motive . . . no . . . I tell you . . . a remote certainty."

"I don't follow you."

"I follow me fine. Look, it's like this. Suddenly you see in a flash how particular things have to happen to you in life . . . so life can be changing and always new."

"And you?"

"You think that's your life?"

Erdosain, ignoring this question, went on:

"And this thing here doesn't surprise me. If you told me I was going to buy you a pack of cigarettes, by the way, do you have a cigarette?"

"Here . . . and so?"

"I don't know. Lately I've been living an incoherent

life, just numb with unhappiness. You see how calm I am talking to you here now."

"Yes, he was always expecting something extraordinary."

"You were, too."

"How's that? You, too, Elsa?"

"Yes."

"But, you?"

"All right, Captain. I see what you mean. You mean something extraordinary is happening to Elsa right now, too, right?"

"Yes."

"Well, you're wrong, isn't he, Elsa?"

"You think so?"

"Tell the truth, aren't you really expecting some extraordinary thing besides this business here?"

"I don't know."

"See, Captain? That's just exactly how it always was with us here. The two of us sitting at this table in silence—"

"Shut up."

"What for? We'd sit here and grasp, with no need to put it in words, what we were, two losers, one too much more passionate than the other, and when we went to bed together—"

"Remo!"

"Mr. Erdosain!"

"What's this absurd prudishness? By some chance, maybe, you two aren't going to bed together?"

"We can't go on in this vein."

"All right, when we separated we'd have this same idea: all the joy of love and life, and now it's come down to this? . . . And, without saying it, we knew we were thinking the same thought . . . but to change the subject . . . do you two plan to stay on in the city?"

Suddenly Erdosain got that cold good-bye–forever feeling.

He envisioned Elsa on a ship's rail, under a line of round portholes, peering off toward the blue horizon. The sun splashed onto the yellow wood of masts and black handles of the winches. Dusk was falling, but they stayed there with their minds in some other clime; while waitresses flitted by, they stayed there leaning against the railing. The salt breeze fluttered the waves and Elsa looked at the water from whose ever-changing interstices her shadow took heart.

At times she would turn her pale face to look back and then both of them seemed to hear a reproach that welled up from the depths of the sea.

And Erdosain imagined it asking them:

"What have you done to the poor boy?" ("Because, despite my age, I was really just a boy," Erdosain was later to tell me. "You see, a man who just stands there while another man takes his wife . . . he's a wretch . . . he's really like a kid, see?")

Erdosain came back up out of this vision. The question that had popped up was then stamped into him quite against his will.

"Are you going to write to me?"

"What for?"

"Yes, of course, what for?" he repeated, closing his eyes. More than ever, he felt he had sunk to a depth that no man had even dreamed before.

"Well now, Mr. Erdosain," said the Captain, getting up. "We'll just be on our way."

"You're leaving? You're leaving already?"

Elsa held out one gloved hand.

"You're leaving?"

"Yes . . . I'm leaving . . . you can see how it is. . . ."

"Yes . . . I can see. . . ."

"Remo, it just wasn't working out."

"Yes, right, sure . . . it wasn't working . . . right. . . ."

The Captain, making his way around the table, took up the suitcase, the very same suitcase Elsa had brought along on her wedding day.

"Good-bye, Mr. Erdosain."

"All right, Captain, only . . . one thing . . . you're leaving . . . you, Elsa . . . are leaving?"

"Yes, we're leaving."

"Excuse me, I have to sit down a bit. Just wait a bit, Captain . . . just a moment, here."

The intruder bit back words of impatience. He had a brutal urge to shout at the husband, "You stupid weakling, get ahold of yourself!" but for Elsa's sake he held it in.

Suddenly Erdosain jumped up from his chair. He walked slowly to one corner of the room. Then, wheeling to face the Captain, he said in a very plain voice, which showed a tremendous effort to keep from yelling:

"You know why I don't just kill you like a dog?"

They both turned around, alarmed.

"Because I'm ice-cold."

Erdosain was pacing back and forth across the room with his hands clasped behind his back. They kept their eyes on him, expecting something.

Finally, the husband, managing a pallid grimace of a smile, went on softly in a voice that struggled to avoid tears.

"Yes, I'm ice-cold . . . I'm all cold inside." Now his eyes grew vague, but he was still smiling that weird, unreal smile. "Listen to me . . . you won't understand, but I have it figured out."

His eyes had an extraordinary gleam in them and his voice grew hoarse from the strain of speaking.

"Look . . . my life has been horribly shat on . . . mangled to bits."

He lapsed into silence, standing in one corner of the

room. His face still bore the strange smile of a man living out a dangerous dream. Elsa, suddenly irritable, bit one corner of her handkerchief. The Captain, standing beside the suitcase, kept waiting.

Suddenly Erdosain took the gun from his pocket and threw it into a corner. The Browning crashed clattering into the wall and clunked hard onto the floor.

"Some good it's doing me!" he muttered. Then, one hand in his coat pocket and his forehead against the wall, he began to speak slowly: "Yes, my life has been horribly insulted . . . humiliated. You better believe it, Captain. Don't be in such a hurry. Here, I'll tell you a story. My father was the one who started my long trail of humiliations. When I was ten and did something wrong, he'd say, 'Tomorrow I'll beat you good.' Always tomorrow, just like that . . . See? tomorrow . . . and so I'd sleep that night, only badly, tortured sleep, waking up at midnight to look at the windowpanes, terrified it might be day already. But when the moon shone through the window bars, I'd close my eyes and say: there's still a long time to go. But then later I'd wake up again when I heard the roosters start to crow. The moon wasn't there anymore, but a bluish light was coming through the panes, and I'd cover my head with the sheets trying not to see it, but I knew it was there . . . but I knew no human force could drive that light away. And finally when I'd slept a long while a hand would shake my head on the pillow. It was him, telling me in a rough voice, 'Come on . . . it's time.' And while I got dressed slowly, I'd hear him setting the chair out on the patio. Then he'd shout at me again, 'Come on,' and I'd walk right over to him like I was hypnotized; I wanted to say something, but it was impossible with his terrifying eyes on me. He dropped a hand on my shoulder and forced me to kneel. I put my chest against the chair seat, he grasped my head between his knees and suddenly the whip slashed cruelly into my buttocks. And when he let go of me, I ran crying to my room. My soul was flung down to the depths of darkness by a vast sense of shame. Because those depths of darkness do exist even if you don't think they do."

Elsa looked at her husband, shocked. The Captain stood there with his arms crossed, listening in a bored sort of way. Erdosain smiled vaguely. He continued:

"I knew most boys were not beaten by their fathers and in school, when I heard them talking about home, I'd be paralyzed with such terrible psychic pain that if we were in class and the teacher called on me, I would just gape at him dumbfounded, unable to make any sense of his questions, till one day he shouted: 'Are you some kind of idiot, Erdosain, don't you hear me?' The whole class burst out laughing, and from then on they called me 'Erdosain the idiot.' And I felt more wretched, more injured than ever, but I kept quiet about it for fear of my father's whip, and smiled at the boys who insulted me . . . only timidly . . . See, Captain? They insult you . . . and you smile timidly like they were doing you a favor jeering at you."

The stranger frowned.

"Later—a moment more, Captain—later they often called me 'the imbecile.' Then suddenly my soul would shrivel away down my nerves, and feeling my soul hiding in shame inside my own flesh destroyed the last bits of my courage. I felt I was sinking farther and farther down and I'd look whoever was insulting me in the eye, then instead of slapping him down, I'd tell myself: 'Can he possibly know how vastly he is humiliating me?' Then I'd go on my way; I grasped that everyone else was just finishing what my father had started."

"So now," replied the Captain, "I'm dragging you under, too?"

"No, hey now, not you. Naturally, I've suffered so

much that all the fight in me has shriveled inward, to hidden places. So I'm outside it all watching myself and wondering. 'When will all that fight inside of me come bursting out?' And that's the thing I'm waiting for. Some day something will explode in me, a monstrous thing, and I'll be a whole changed man. Then, if you're alive, I'll come looking for you and spit in your face."

The stranger looked at him calmly.

"Not from hatred, though, only to try out my fighting spirit, which will be the newest thing in the world for me . . . Okay, you can go now."

The stranger vacillated a moment. Erdosain's eyes were trained on him in a boundless, intense stare. He took the suitcase and left.

Elsa stood in front of her husband, trembling.

"Okay now, I'm leaving. Remo . . . it had to end like this."

"But you . . . you?"

"What would you say to do instead?"

"I don't know."

"So, see? Please, I want you to keep calm. I left your clothes all ready for you. Put a fresh collar on. You're enough to put any wife to shame, always like that."

"But you, Elsa . . . you? And what about the plans we made?"

"Illusions, Remo . . . splendors."

"Right, splendors . . . but where did you get such a lovely word? Splendors."

"I don't know."

"And our life together will be left undone forever and ever?"

"What alternative is there? But still, I tried to do right. Later, I began to hate you . . . but why weren't you the same man you used to be?"

"Ah, yes . . . the same man . . . the same. . . ."

Pain weighed upon him like a tropical day with the

sun beating down. His eyelids drooped. He felt ready to drop off to sleep. The meanings of words sank into his brain as slowly as a stone into half-congealed water. When the word hit the depths of his consciousness, dark forces tore at his pain. And for that instant, at the depths of his heart, they kept floating and scuttling about as if trapped in a mud puddle, amid weeds and strands of suffering. She went on, in a voice still with deep-seated resignation:

"It's no good anymore . . . I'm going now. Why didn't you behave? Why didn't you go to work?"

Erdosain was sure that Elsa was as unhappy as he was just then, and a flood of compassion made him fall back on the edge of the chair, his head flung down on his arm on the tabletop.

"So, you're going? You're going, for real?"

"Yes, I want to see if our life can get better, see? Take a look at my hands," and, taking off her right glove, she showed him a hand cracked by the cold, eaten by lye, pricked by needles, and blackened by sooty pots.

Erdosain stood up, in the grips of a vision.

He saw his unhappy wife in the vile throes of cities of iron and cement, passing under the dark slashes where the skyscrapers threw down oblique shadows, under a looming tangle of black high-voltage wires. A throng of businessmen shielded by umbrellas passed by. Her little face was paler than ever, but he was in her thoughts even though the breath of strangers touched her cheek.

"Where, where is my little boy?"

Erdosain cut in on his own vision:

"Elsa . . . you know this . . . come back anytime you want . . . you can come back . . . only tell the truth, did you once love me?"

She raised her eyes slowly. Her voice filled the room with human warmth. To Erdosain she seemed to come to life.

"I always loved you . . . now, too, I love you . . . why

did you never before speak like tonight? I feel I'll love you all my life . . . that other man is nothing but a shadow compared to you."

"Darling, my poor darling . . . what life has done to us . . . what life has done."

A painful wisp of a smile turned up the corners of her mouth. Elsa looked at him a moment, her eyes warm. Then, she made a solemn vow:

"Look here . . . wait for me. If life is the way you always told me, I'll return to you, see? and then, if you say so, we can kill ourselves together . . . Are you happy?"

Warm blood surged through the man's temples.

"My love, you're so good to me, love . . . give me your hand," and while she, still overwhelmed, smiled, timidly, Erdosain kissed it. "You're not angry, love?"

She lifted up her head, grave with joy.

"Look here, Remo . . . I'll come back to you, see? And if it's true what you say about life . . . yes, I'll be back . . . I'll be back."

"You'll be back?"

"With everything I have."

"Even if you're rich?"

"Even if I have all the millions on earth, I'll be back. I swear!"

"Darling, my poor darling! You're a pure soul, but yet, you never really knew me . . . it doesn't matter . . . what life has dealt us!"

"It doesn't matter. I'm happy. You see what a surprise you're in for. You're all alone . . . suddenly, creak . . . the door opens . . . and it's me . . . I've come back to you!"

"You're all in a ballgown . . . white shoes and a pearl necklace."

"And I came alone, on foot, through dark streets, seeking you out . . . but you don't see me, you're all alone . . . your head—"

"Tell me . . . go on . . . go on . . ."

"Your head sunk into your hand and your elbow on the table . . . you look at me . . . and all at once . . ."

"I recognize you and I say, 'Elsa, is it you, Elsa?' "

"And I answer: 'Remo, I've come home, remember that night? That night is tonight and outside a cold wind may blow, but we feel neither cold nor pain.' Are you happy, Remo?"

"Yes, I swear to you I'm happy."

"All right, I'm leaving."

"You're leaving?"

"Yes . . ."

A swift spasm of pain contorted his features.

"All right then, go."

"It won't be long, my husband."

"What did you say?"

"Remo, I'm telling you: wait for me. Even if I have all the millions in the world, I'll come back home."

"All right . . . good-bye then . . . only kiss me."

"No, when I get back . . . good-bye, my husband."

Suddenly Erdosain, in the grips of a nameless spasm, grabbed her hands brutally hard by the wrists.

"Tell me: did you go to bed with him?"

"Let me go, Remo . . . I didn't think you—"

"Confess it: did you or did you not sleep together?"

"No."

In the doorway stood the Captain. A vast weariness made the nerves of his fingers go slack. Erdosain felt himself falling and saw nothing more.

LAYERS OF DARKNESS

He never knew how he got himself over to his bed. Time ceased to exist for Erdosain. He closed his eyes in response to his aching body's need for sleep. If he had had the strength, he would have thrown himself down a well. Desperation gathered in great bubbles that blocked his throat, making it hard to breathe, and his eyes grew sensitive to light like a wound to salt. At moments, he gritted his teeth to stifle his crunching nerves, bristly stiff inside his flesh, which was washing away loosely into the waves of darkness that crashed down upon his brain.

He felt himself falling into a bottomless pit and clenched his eyes tighter shut. He did not stop falling, who knows how many leagues his physical self was elongated, endlessly stretched out as his awareness went plunging downward in a great vertical swath of desperation! Layers of darkness, denser and ever denser, fell from his eyelids.

The grief knotted inside him wracked up and down, but it was no good. Nowhere in his soul could it find a crack and slip out. Erdosain bore within him all the grief of the entire world, the pain of the world's negation. Searching the earth over, where could one find a man with his skin more withered and furrowed with bitterness? He no longer felt like a man; he was only a barely covered sore that writhed and screamed with each pulsing of his veins. And yet he was alive. He lived as his body stretched away and as it came swinging back. He was no longer an organism with its suffering, but something more inhuman—perhaps that— a monster furled up tight in the uterine blackness of that room. Each layer of dark that came from his lids was yet more placental tissue forming a wall between him and the universe of men. The walls rose tall in climbing rows of brick, and fresh torrents of darkness gushed into the hole where he lay curled and throbbing like a snail on the ocean floor. He was a stranger to himself . . . he doubted he was Augusto Remo Erdosain. He squeezed his forehead with his fingertips and the flesh of his hand and the flesh of his forehead did not recognize each other, as if his body were of two separate substances. How much of him was already dead? All he could feel was something unconnected to what had happened to him, a soul less than a sword's blade long, slithering eellike through his muddy-watered life. Even his self-awareness shrank to a square centimeter of mind. Yes, his body was only kept plugged in by that square centimeter of mind. Everything else floated off into darkness. Yes, he was a square centimeter of man, a square centimeter of existence, receptive to pain, maintaining the incoherent life of a phantom. Everything else in him was dead, mingling in the placental dark that boxed his atrocious reality in.

He saw ever more clearly that he was sunk in a concrete hole. It was like nothing on earth! An unseen sun lit the walls forever, a turbulent orange. A lone bird's wing slashed across the sky in the rectangle formed by the walls, but he was marooned forever in those noiseless depths, lit by a turbulent orange sun.

Then the whole of his life lay in that meager square centimeter of mind. He could even "see" his heartbeat, and had no defense against that horror that pursued him to the depths of the abyss, sometimes black and sometimes orange. If he relaxed in the least, reality would break out and howl in his ears. Erdosain did not want to, he wanted to look—he could not help but look—and there was his wife down inside a blue-carpeted room. And there was the Captain in one corner. Nobody had to tell him they were in a little bedroom, six-sided and almost completely taken up by a wide, low bed. He did not want to look at Elsa . . . no . . . no . . . he wanted to, but under pain of death he could not have torn his eyes away from that man undressing in front of her—in front of his lawfully wedded wife who was no longer with him—who was with another man. His fear was overcome by a need for more terror, for more suffering, and suddenly, covering her eyes with her fingers, she ran to the naked man, firm and taut, pressed against him unintimidated by the rosy virility erect against the blue background.

Erdosain was flattened by his utter and overpowering horror. If they had run him through a sheet-metal press, his life could not have been mashed thinner. Wasn't that how toads were, squashed into cartwheel ruts in the road, pressed into a mushcake of living tissue? He wanted not to look, he wanted not to so much, for he could see clearly how Elsa leaned onto the man's square, hairy chest and he took her chin in his hand to pull her mouth toward his.

And suddenly Elsa exclaimed, "I, too, my darling . . . I, too." Her face was red with desperation, her clothes whipped about the triangle of her milk-white thighs, and gazing in ecstasy on the man's rigid muscle, she showed her nestled curly hair, her erect breasts—ah! why was he watching?

Elsa . . . Elsa, his lawfully wedded wife, could not span in her little hand the massive virility she caressed. The man, desire howling in his ears, threw one arm over his eyes, but she leaned over to stab words like burning iron into his ears: "You are a finer creature than my husband! My God, what a splendid creature you are!"

Had they screwed him down by his head and neck, boring into his deep-pierced soul, implanting that vision of horror, he could not have suffered more. He was in such pain that if it had suddenly stopped, he would have fragmented into shrapnel. How can the soul hold up under such pain? Yet, he wanted to suffer even more. To be quartered like a steer on the butcher's block . . . and if they threw his butchered quarters into the garbage, he would go right on suffering. There was not a square centimeter of his body free of this high-pressure torment.

Every nerve snapped under that tortuous wrenching tension, and a sudden feeling of repose flooded his members.

He no longer wanted anything. His life ran silently downhill, like a reservoir escaping its ruined dam, and he fell into a lucid, closed-eyed trance state, which did more to alleviate his pain than anesthesia.

He felt his heart beat strongly. With effort, he got his head off the hot pillow and simply lay there with no other sensation of life than the cool freshness on his neck and the opening and closing of heart valves like a vast eye opening its sleep-heavy lids to peer into nothing but darkness. Nothing but darkness?

Elsa was so far from his mind that, in his trance state, he felt they had never even met. He doubted her physical existence. Before, he could see her, but now he could barely manage to recognize her. The truth was that she was no longer herself and he was no longer himself. Now his life ran silently downhill, time flowed backward and, a child, he watched a green tree overshadowing a river forever awakening amid its red-veined rocks. He was a flood of living tissue pouring into darkness. How long till he finally bled dry! And all he felt was the opening and closing of heart valves like a vast eye that opened its sleep-heavy lids to peer into darkness. A street lamp down the block sent a silvery offshoot through a crack to splash against the mosquito screen. His mind painfully cleared.

He was Erdosain. Now he knew who he was. He arched his back with great effort. He spotted a yellow bar of light under the dining-room door. He had forgotten to turn out the light. He should—oh, no! Elsa had left—he owed six hundred pesos and seven cents to the Sugar Company—but no, wait, he doesn't owe anything now, if there's that check . . .

Reality, reality!

The slanting parallelogram of light from the street lamp turned the screen to silver and reminded him he was just the same as before, as yesterday, as ten years ago.

He wanted not to see that bar of light, just as when he was little he had not wanted to see the blue light coming in the window, though he knew it was there, though he knew no human force could make that light go away. Yes, just like when his father would tell him he would beat him tomorrow. It wasn't the same now. The light was blue then and this one now was silver, but just as harsh and full of dire truth as the old light. Sweat came to his temples and hairline. Elsa had left, and would she never return to him? What was Barsut going to say?

A Slap in the Face

Suddenly someone was at the door. Erdosain knew who it was and jumped up from the bed. Barsut, as usual, tried to knock without making much noise.

Erdosain shouted in a hoarse voice:

"Come in; why don't you come in already?"

Barsut came in with a backward-leaning stride.

"I'm coming," Remo shouted to him as the visitor came into the dining room.

And when he came in, Barsut had already taken a seat, cross legged, with his back to the door, as usual, and his eyes on the southwest corner of the room.

"What are you up to?"

"How's it going?"

He put one elbow on the table, then leaned his head on that arm and the light made the white fleshiness of his hand copper-red. Under eyebrows slashing upward to his temples, his green eyes, hard and glassy, seemed to harbor a question.

And Erdosain saw that face as if amidst a swarm of lights teeming in the air: his sloped forehead receding to pointy ears, his bony beak like a bird of prey, his chin seemingly flattened to withstand violent abuse, and the oversize necktie that flooded forth from his starchy collar.

In a flat tone, he asked:

"Where's Elsa?"

Erdosain managed to get his wits together.

"She's left."

"Ah . . ."

They fell silent and Erdosain sat contemplating the angle of the gray suit sleeve against the white edge of the table, and the cheek lit with copper-red lamplight to the bony nasal ridge, while the far side of the face remained unilluminated from the hairline to the dimple in the chin, with a special pocket of shadow forming in the bag under the eye. Barsut slowly moved one of his crossed legs.

"Oh!" Erdosain heard, and he responded, "What?"

Erdosain had really only heard that "oh," even though it was uttered a few seconds before.

"Elsa left . . ."

Barsut lifted his head, his eyebrows went up to let more light into his eyes, and with his lips slightly open, he whispered:

"She's gone?"

Erdosain scowled, eyeing the visitor's shoes in a sidelong glance and secretly waiting behind half-closed lids for Barsut's shocked reaction, he let the bomb fall:

"Yes . . . she . . . went . . . off . . . with . . . another man. . . ."

And winking his left eye like Ergueta, the pharmacist, he bent his head over. Under the bronze ridge of his eyebrows, his eyes were wary.

Erdosain went on:

"See? There's the gun. I could have killed them, only I didn't. Man is one weird animal, huh?"

"You stood there while he took your wife?"

Erdosain felt the old hatred inside him, heightened by his fresh humiliation, turned into a source of cruel glee and with his voice trembling in his throat, his mouth dry with rancor, he burst out:

"What's it to you?"

A savage slap in the face knocked him off the chair. Later he remembered Barsut's arm swinging toward him and swinging away, kneading his flesh like dough. He covered his face with both hands, he tried to escape that great mass coming at him like some unleashed force of nature. His head thunked against the wall and he fell.

When he came to, Barsut was kneeling beside him. He noticed his collar was undone and water was dribbling down his face. A ticklish pain ran upward through his nasal bridge and he thought he might sneeze at any moment. His gums were bleeding a little and he could feel the exact shape of his teeth pressing against his swollen lips.

Erdosain managed to scrape himself up off the floor and into a chair; Barsut was so pale it looked like two flames were coming out of his eyes. From his cheeks to his ears, taut muscles were knotted into two quivering arches. Erdosain felt he was reeling through some endless dream scene, but he understood it when the visitor took hold of his arm, saying:

"Look, just spit in my face, if you want, only let me say one thing. I have to tell you the whole story. Sit down . . . There, that's good." Erdosain had gotten up without thinking. "Listen, do me a favor. You see how things are, I could clobber you to death . . . I just let my hand get the better of me—I swear—if you want, I'll get on my knees and beg your pardon. If you want,

I'll do it willingly. Look . . . ah . . . ah . . . if people only knew."

Erdosain spat blood. A band of heat ran across his forehead and inside his skull, emerging again at the nape of his neck. He was bent over so far his chin was resting on the table edge. Barsut, seeing what kind of shape he was in, asked him:

"Want to wash your face? It'll do you good. Wait a minute, don't you go." And he ran out to the kitchen and came back with a basin of water. "Here, wash up. Do you lots of good. Want me to get you cleaned up here? Look, I'm sorry, I got carried away. But why did you wink like you were making fun of me? Come on, get cleaned up, do it for me."

Erdosain arose wordlessly and dipped his face in the basin several times. When he was out of breath, he took his face out of the water. Then he sat down and let the water dry off the hair around his face. He was bone tired. If only Elsa could see him now! Then she'd have to feel sorry for him! He closed his eyes. Barsut brought up his chair next to him and said:

"I have to tell you the whole story. I'd feel like a worm if I didn't. See, I'm cool as a cucumber right now. Look, if you don't believe me, feel my heartbeat. I'm being totally open with you. Okay now, I . . . I . . . ratted on you to the Sugar Company . . . I was the guy that sent the anonymous letter."

Erdosain didn't even look up. Him, or somebody else, what difference did it make?

Barsut looked at him: he waited for him to react somehow, then said:

"Why don't you say something? Look here, I blew the whistle on you. I wanted to have you in jail and then have Elsa to myself and humiliate her. You can't possibly know how I've spent my nights fantasizing how they'd throw you in jail! There wasn't any place you could get that much money so they'd get you for sure. But, why don't you say something?"

Erdosain looked up. Barsut was there, yes, it was him, and he really was saying those things. Bulging knots of muscles trembled imperceptibly under the skin from his cheekbones to his ears.

Barsut looked down, with his knees on his elbows like a man beside his campfire, and insisted slowly:

"I have to tell you the whole story. Who else is there that I can pour out my heart to? They say, and it's true, that sadness isn't literally in your heart, but still I have to wonder: why go on living? If this is what I'm like, what good is life? See? You have to understand, this is the kind of stuff I've been thinking about a lot lately. Look, I shouldn't even tell you this stuff. How can you be a total bastard to a guy, then turn around and pour out your heart to him, and not feel bad over it? A lot of times, I've wondered: why don't I feel bad about what I do? What good is life if we do really rotten things and don't feel bad? In school what they teach is that a crime will sooner or later make the criminal go mad, so how come in real life you commit a crime and go around not feeling anything?"

Erdosain kept an eye on Barsut and now the man's image was engraved on the depths of his mind. With all his vital forces, he was making a life mask of Barsut's pale face, so exact that it would last for all time.

"Look," Barsut went on. "I knew how mad you were at me, that you'd have killed me just like that, and that made me feel good and at the same time bad. The nights I went to bed thinking how to kidnap you! I thought about sending you a letter bomb, or a snake in a cardboard box. Or I'd hire a taxi to run you over. I'd close my eyes and hours would fly by while I'd think about you two. Do you imagine I loved her?" Erdosain later realized that during that whole night's conversation Barsut avoided calling Elsa by name. "No, I never loved her. But what I wanted was to humiliate her, see? Humiliate her for no good reason: to see you dragged down so she'd be on her knees asking me please to bail you out. See? I never loved her. If I turned you in it was only to humiliate her for being so snooty to me. And when you told me how you'd been stealing from the Sugar Company, wild joy burst out inside me. And before you were through telling me about it, I was saying inwardly: okay, now we'll see where that high and mighty attitude gets her."

Erdosain let the question pop out:

"But weren't you in love with her?"

"No, I never loved her. If you only knew what she's put me through! So now I'm supposed to love her, when she never paid me the least attention? Whenever she looked at me it was like spitting in my face. You were married to her, but you never really knew her! You don't know what kind of woman she is! She could just stand there while you died without the least sign of pity. You know? Something I remember. When the Astraldis went broke and you two were out in the cold, if she'd asked me for everything I had, I'd have given it to her. I'd have given her my whole fortune just to hear her tell me 'thank you.' Just that, 'thank you.' Just to hear those words from her I'd have given literally all I had. But when I brought it up she said: 'Remo is man enough to bring home our bacon.' You don't know her, see. She could watch you die without lifting a finger to help. So I thought. My God, the thoughts that go through a man's head! I threw myself down on the bed and fantasized all kinds of stuff . . . you had killed someone . . . she needed somebody to come to your rescue and came to me, and without ever mentioning my great sacrifices to her, I'd turn everything upside down to get you out of it. What a woman, Remo! I remember she'd be there sewing. I'd have loved to sit by her side, see? just to hold up her sewing for her, and I could tell she wasn't happy with you. I could see it in her face, how tired she always was, the way she smiled."

Erdosain remembered the words Elsa had spoken an hour ago:

"It doesn't matter. I'm happy. You see what a surprise you're in for. You're alone . . . suddenly, creak . . . the door opens . . . and it's me . . . I've come back to you."

Barsut went on:

"And of course, I wondered why she would keep on living with you, with the kind of man you are . . ."

"And I came alone, on foot, through dark streets, seeking you out . . . but you don't see me, you're all alone, your head . . ."

Erdosain felt his thoughts whirling wildly around on top of his brain like a surging maelstrom. The vast whirlpool sucked its spiral down to the ends of his limbs. A whirlpool that touched against his soul, leaving it raw and tender. How much virtue and insight Elsa had shown when she said:

"I always loved you . . . now, too, I love you . . . why did you never before speak like tonight? I feel I'll love you all my life . . . that other man is nothing but a shadow compared to you."

Erdosain was sure that these words rescued his soul for all time, while Barsut went on venting his envy and rage:

"And I'd have liked to ask her what it was she saw in you, make her see you for what you were and shove it in her face what a madman you were, what a bastard, a coward . . . I swear, I'm not saying these things in anger."

"I believe you," said Erdosain.

"Like right now, I look at you and wonder: how does a woman really look at a man? That's something we'll never know. You realize that? To my mind, you were a miserable wretch, a zero in the arithmetic of life. But to her, what were you like? That's what we'll never know. Did you ever figure it out? Tell me frankly: did you ever really truly know what it was your wife saw in you? What did she see in you to make it worth suffering with your oddities and putting up with you like she did?"

Barsut went on in all seriousness. He demanded an answer to his hoarse questions. Sitting there with him, Erdosain felt he was not a man but only an exact copy of himself, a phantom self with a bony nose and bronze hair created inside his head, since these were the very things he had asked himself at other moments. Yes, most likely it was necessary to kill him to live in peace, and the "idea" blossomed serenely within him.

"Easy as slicing a bale of cotton with a sword," Erdosain would later say.

Barsut had no idea that at that very moment Erdosain had just pronounced a sentence of death on him. Later, explaining to me how the notion came to flower inside him, Erdosain told me this:

"Have you ever seen a general in battle? . . . But to make it easier to grasp my point, I'll tell you like an inventor would. For a while you've been looking for the solution to some problem. See, you know you have the clue to it somewhere inside you, only you can't get at it, it's hidden under layers of mystery. One day, when you least expect it, suddenly the plan, the complete finished machine, flashes before your eyes, stunning, because it's all there, perfect. It's like a miracle! Think of a general in battle . . . everything's lost, only then, all at once, clear, exact, he gets this flash that solves everything in a way he'd never dreamed he could do it, and still, he'd had it all the time within his reach, someplace inside him. At just that moment, I saw how I had to have Barsut killed, and sitting right across from me spouting useless words, he didn't imagine me, with my swollen lips, aching nose, holding in this terrific joy, a wild flash like discovering something as inevitable as a law of mathematics. Maybe we have an inner mathematics whose terrible laws are less inviolable than the ones that govern the workings of numbers and lines.*

"Because it's funny. My gums were still bleeding from his beating, which battered into my mind as if by hydraulic power the definitive plans for his death. See? A plan is made out of three general lines, three regular straight lines is all it takes. My joy came bubbling up wildly over the new contours of that freshly minted shape, three lines which for me were: kidnapping Barsut, having him killed, and using his money to set up the secret clan the Astrologer wanted. See? The whole crime just came to me like that, while he was going on gloomily about how we were two damned souls. The whole plan was there, inside me, like they stamped it into iron under thousands of pounds of pressure.

"Ah! How can I explain it to you? All at once I forgot everything, sealed in a frozen block of thought, full of joy, like the dawn coming to some night creature, ending his weariness with the morning after an exhausting night. See? To have Barsut killed by somebody who absolutely had to have the funding for a brilliant scheme. And that new dawn was throbbing inside me, so perfect, so distinct, that often, since then, I've wondered what secret could lie in a man's soul that can come to show him new horizons and awaken him to new sensations that amaze even him by leaping out of sheer illogic."

---

* Commentator's note: This part of Erdosain's confessions made me wonder whether the idea of committing a crime might not have already been in his subconscious, which would explain his passive response to Barsut's violent attack.

In the course of this story, I forgot to say that when Erdosain got enthusiastic, he would send a lot of words orbiting around his central idea. He had to try every possible way of expressing it, and a slow frenzy laid hold of him as he spoke and made him see himself as a truly extraordinary man and not some wretch. I had not the slightest doubt he was telling me the truth. What puzzled me was a question I kept wondering about: where did he get the energy to carry on like that for so long? He was always absorbed in self-examination, analyzing everything that went on inside him, as if the sum of all those details could convince him he was really alive. Of this I am certain. Not even a dead man who could somehow talk would have talked more than he did, just to keep up his own belief he was not dead.

Barsut, unaware what had happened inside Erdosain, went on:

"Ah! You don't know her . . . you never knew her. Look, listen to what I'm going to tell you. One afternoon I went to see her. I knew you weren't home, I wanted to be with her, only to see her, even if that was all. I got there all sweaty, I walked I don't know how many blocks in the sun before I worked up to doing it."

"Just like me, in the sun," thought Erdosain.

"And even though I was too poor, you know that, to take a cab, and even when I asked after you, she said to me, 'Sorry, I won't let you in because my husband's not in the house.' See what a bitch?"

Erdosain thought:

"There's still a train to Temperley."

Barsut continued:

"Now me, I could see what a loser you were, so I wondered: what did Elsa see in that man to fall in love with him?"

In a perfectly calm voice Erdosain asked him:

"Does it show on my face I'm a loser?"

Barsut looked up in surprise. For a moment he kept his translucent greenish eyes fixed on Erdosain. The splotch of light falling on him and Erdosain gave everything a dreamlike distance. And Barsut felt as spectral as the other man, because, moving his head painfully, as if all the muscles in his neck had suddenly gone into spasm, he answered:

"No, when I look good and long you're more a guy who has one big obsession . . . but who knows what it is."

Erdosain replied:

"You're a real psychologist. Naturally, I don't yet know what that obsession is but, it's funny, the last thing I thought was that you'd go after my wife . . . and you are so calm telling me this."

"You can't deny I'm being open with you."

"No."

"Besides, I wanted to humiliate her . . . not get her to run off with me, what for? I knew she'd never love me."

"How did you figure that?"

"That's something I don't know. You just do certain things you can't explain. Because I kept on seeing you and you me even when we couldn't stomach each other. I kept coming because my being there made you suffer and me suffer. Everyday, I'd tell myself: 'I won't go anymore . . . I won't go anymore . . .' But soon as it was time, I'd be all jittery. It was like they were calling me from someplace and I'd get dressed quick . . . I'd come over—"

Erdosain suddenly had a weird idea and said:

"Off the subject, you know—I don't know if you know, but this morning at the Sugar Company they told me about the anonymous letter. You're the only one to blame, I think you've pretty well admitted it, for all this happening to me, so you have to get me the money to cover. Where am I going to get that much?"

Barsut sat bolt upright in amazement.

"Hey, what's this? Here I'm cuckolded, messed up, Elsa leaves, and I end up acting like a bastard just now, and I'm supposed to go get the money for you? Are you crazy? What's in it for me if I give you six hundred pesos?"

"And seven cents . . ."

Erdosain got up.

"That's your last word?"

"But lookit, how is it I . . ."

"All right, kid. Hold on now. So would you kindly go now, because I want to get some sleep."

"You don't want us to go out someplace?"

"I'm tired. Just leave me alone."

Barsut hesitated. Then, getting up and grabbing his hat brim, he made a clumsy exit.

Erdosain heard the door shut behind him, waited a minute, scowling, found a rail schedule in his pocket, checked the schedule, then washed up again and combed his hair in the mirror. He had a purple lip, a red splotch by his nose and another around one temple at the hairline.

He peered around looking for something, saw the gun lying there, picked it up and left. But he had left the light on, so he came back and switched off the lamp. Everything was dark as if the tail end of some light had flashed before his eyes and was gone. For the second time that day he was going to the Astrologer's.

"TO BE" BY COMMITTING
A CRIME

One patch of the Temperley platform was lit feebly by the light falling from one door of the telegraph office. Erdosain sat on a bench next to the rail switches in the darkness. He was cold and possibly feverish. Besides, he had a feeling as if his criminal plot were an extension of his body, like a creature of darkness he could thrust out into the light. A red disk glowed at the end of the signal arm; farther on the darkness was studded with other red and green circles and the rails, galvanoplastically fused with the lights, ran off in blue or red arcs into the darkness. Then there was silence; the chain stopping clanking against the pulleys and the noise of metal against stone ended.

He sat submerged in a half sleep.

"What am I doing here? Why do I stay here? Is it true I want to kill him? Or is it really that I want to get up the will to feel like wanting to kill him? Is that the necessary thing? By now, she's romping in bed with him. But what's that to me? Before, when I knew she was home alone, and I was out having a cup of coffee, I felt bad about her. I felt bad knowing she was unhappy with me. They must have dropped off to sleep, her head on his chest. Oh, God! This is what they call life? To be lost, lost for all time! But can I really be who I am? Or am I somebody else? Weird! Lost in weirdness! That's my situation. And his, too! From a distance I see him for what he is, a rat, a loser. He almost broke my nose. But can you believe it! So now it turns out he was the one who was cuckolded and messed up, not me! Me! . . . Really, life is slapstick! Only, still, there's something serious about it. Why does it revolt me to even be near him?"

Shadows intermingled in front of the yellow glass panes of the telegraph office.

"To kill him or not to kill him? What's that to me? Does killing him matter to me? So to me it's all the same if he lives or not. Still, I want to work up the will to kill him. If a god appeared to me right now and asked: Do you want the power to destroy mankind? Would I destroy it? No, I would not destroy it. Because being

able to do it would make it something totally unin-
teresting. Besides, what would I do alone on earth?
Watch dynamos rust away in workshops and horseback
riders' skeletons fall apart in the heat? It's true he slapped
me around, but, what's it to me? What a crew! What
a zoo! The Captain, Elsa, Barsut, the Astrologer, the
Pig-Headed Man, the Ruffian, Ergueta. What a crew!
Where did they ever get so many monsters? And me,
out of whack, I'm not who I am, and yet I need to do
something to be aware of my own existence, to affirm
it. Just that, to affirm it. Because I'm like a dead man,
I don't exist for the Captain or for Elsa, or Barsut. If
they want, they can put me in jail, Barsut can beat me
up again, Elsa can run off with another guy and me
standing right there, the Captain can run off with her
all over again. I'm antilife for all of them. I'm like
nonbeing. A man is not like action, and so he doesn't
exist. Or does he exist despite not being? He is and he
is not. Take those men over there. They must have
wives, children, homes. Maybe they're poor wretches.
But if somebody tried to come into their homes, get
one penny away from them or steal their wives, they'd
be tigers. And so, why haven't I put up a fight? Who
can answer me that? I myself don't know. I know I
exist like that, like antiexisting. And when I tell myself
all this, I'm not sad, only my soul falls silent and my
head goes empty. Then, after that silence and empti-
ness, curiosity about the murder plot creeps up out of
my heart. Just that. I'm not crazy, since I know how
to think, to reason. But this curiosity about the murder
comes creeping up from my heart, a curiosity that brings
me utter sorrow, the sorrow of curiosity. Or, the demon
of curiosity. To find out what I am by committing a
crime. That, just precisely. To see what happens in my
conscience, my feelings as I commit a crime.

"Yet, these words can't make me feel the crime any
more than a telegram about a disaster in China can

make me feel the disaster. It's like I wasn't the one planning the crime, somebody else was doing it. Somebody else like me, a man, only with nothing to him, a shadow of a man, an image on a screen. He has a shape, he moves around, he seems to exist, to suffer, but still, he's only a shadow. He has no life. God only knows if this makes any sense. Okay: what all would the shadow-man do? The shadow-man would watch the crime happening, but not feel the impact, because he has nothing for its force to strike against. He's a shadow. I see the crime, too, but don't feel the impact. This must be a new theory. What would a criminal-court judge say to all this? Would he grasp that I really mean it sincerely? But do those people believe in sincerity? Outside of me, of the limits of my body, people go by, but they could no more imagine what my life is like than they could living on the earth and moon both at once. I'm nothing in everyone's eyes. But still, if tomorrow I throw a bomb or murder Barsut, suddenly I'm everything, the man who exists, the man for whom generations of criminologists have prepared punishments, jails, and theories. I, who am nothing, will start up the whole terrible machinery of police, secretaries, reporters, lawyers, prosecutors, jailers, paddywagons, and nobody will see me as a loser, instead I'll be the antisocial man, the enemy who must be kept apart from society. That's really weird! And yet, only crime can affirm my existence, just as evil is all that affirms the presence of man on earth. And I'd be the one and only Erdosain, the genuine one, who is and ever shall be. Really, this is all so weird. Still, despite everything, there is darkness and mankind's soul is sad. Infinitely sad. But that can't be how life is. If tomorrow I figured out why that can't be how life is, I'd pinch myself and disinflate like a balloon spewing out all these lies I'm filled with, and, from what I seem to be now, a brand-new man would emerge, as strong as one of the primal gods who created all things. But I'm off on a tangent. Should I go to the Astrologer or not? What will he say when he sees me back again? Like me, he's a mystery to himself. That's the truth. He has about as much idea where he's going as I do. The secret organization. The whole thing for him is just exactly that: secret organization. Another case of demonic possession. What a zoo! Barsut, Ergueta, the Ruffian, me . . . If they tried to, they couldn't get such perfect weirdos. And to top it all, that pregnant blind girl! What an animal!"

The guard passed by Erdosain a second time. Remo realized he was attracting the man's attention so, getting up, he headed for the Astrologer's place. There was no moon. The arc lights shone amid the branches arching over the crossings. Piano music wafted from one house, and as he walked along, his heart shriveled smaller yet, reacting to the anguish that hit him at the sight of the happiness he imagined behind the walls of those houses nestled coolly under shade trees with an automobile in front of the garage.

THE PROPOSAL

The Astrologer was getting ready for bed when he heard steps on the path to his house. Since the dog did not bark, he opened the door part way. A parallelogram of light sliced through the dark up to the tops of the pomegranate trees, and now he saw Erdosain coming through that yellow box with light hitting him full in the face.

"Strange!" thought the Astrologer. "I never noticed the kid wears a straw hat! What can he want?" And after checking to see his revolver was tucked in his waistband (it was instinct with him by now), he unlocked the door and Erdosain came in.

"I thought you were in bed."

"Come in."

Erdosain went into the study. The map of the United States was still there with the black flags stuck into the areas the Ku Klux Klan controlled. The Astrologer had been drawing up a horoscope, because the box of compasses lay open on a table. The wind coming through the window grate stirred the papers, and Erdosain, after waiting for his host to put some papers in the cabinet, sat down with his back to the garden.

From his chair, he surveyed the man's broad face, the twisted nose rising from a troubled forehead, the ear doubled back on itself, the massive chest under the black, dull clothing, a copper chain across the jacket, the steel ring with a violet stone on the hand with its gnarled fingers and leathery skin. Now that the man had his hat off his hair turned out to be kinky, tangled, and short. He stretched out his legs and supported his body on the chair arms. With his unshined boots he looked like a mountain man, maybe a gold prospector. "Isn't that what prospectors look like in Patagonia?" wondered Erdosain, and, not grasping how his thoughts had wandered to that, he sat gazing at the map of the United States and repeating to himself the words he had heard the Astrologer say that very afternoon as he pointed out the states to the Ruffian.

"The Ku Klux Klan is strong in Texas, Ohio, Indianapolis, Oklahoma, Oregon . . ."

"What's that you say there, friend? . . . What?"

"Ah, right! . . . I came to see you . . ."

"I was just going to bed. I'd been working out some idiot's horoscope—"

"If I'm in your way I'll go—"

"No, stay. Did you get in some new mess? What's it now?"

"A lot of stuff. Tell me, if you can— You won't be

shocked by my question?— If, to set up your secret society, that is, to get the twenty thousand pesos you need, if to get twenty thousand pesos you had to kill somebody, what would you do?"

The Astrologer sat bolt upright in his chair, his body stiffened into right angles by surprise. And even though his head shot up with the impact of the ideas Erdosain gave him, it seemed to sit terribly heavy on his shoulders. He wrung his hands and peered into Remo's face.

"Why do you ask me that?"

"Because I have just the guy with that twenty thousand pesos. We can kidnap him, and, if he won't sign a check for us, torture him."

The Astrologer frowned. Faced with a proposal so fraught with enigmas, he grew more perplexed and began twisting the ring on his right ring finger around in the fingers of his left hand. The violet stone appeared and disappeared in front of the bronze chain, and though he kept his head lowered, under his knitted brow his eyes searched Erdosain's face. And the skewed nose and chin half-sunk in the black fabric of his tie looked, from that angle, set for a fight.

"Okay now, explain the whole thing to me, because I don't follow at all."

Now he sat up and his face looked ready to take punch after punch if need be.

"It's easy, a brilliant scheme. My wife ran off tonight to stay with another man. Then he—"

"Who's he?"

"Barsut, my wife's cousin—Gregorio Barsut, he came to see me and confess he was the guy who turned me in to the Sugar Company."

"Ah! . . . So he was the guy who turned you in?"

"Yes, and on top of that—"

"But what would make him go turn you in?"

"How should I know! To humiliate me— What it boils down to is he's half-crazy. He has twenty thousand pesos. His father died in a madhouse. He's going to end up there, too. The twenty thousand pesos are an inheritance from an aunt he got from his father."

The Astrologer squeezed his forehead with his fingers. He was more mixed up than ever. The whole thing intrigued him, but he couldn't get it all straight. He insisted:

"Tell me everything in detail, and begin at the beginning."

Erdosain began his story all over. He retold everything we know. He spoke slowly and precisely, since he was over the nervous tension of working up to proposing his plan to the Astrologer.

Now he was sitting on the chair edge, hunched over, his elbows on his knees, his fingers splayed across his cheeks, his eyes fixed on the floor. His yellow skin, taut over the flat bones of his face, gave him a tubercular look. Atrocity after atrocity poured from his throat, endlessly, flatly, as if he were reciting a lesson pounded into his mind. The Astrologer, covering his mouth with his fingers, listened while staring at him dumbfounded. He had imagined quite a lot, but not that much.

Slowed down by the great care he was taking not to get anything wrong, Erdosain piled up bitterness, humiliations, memories, sufferings, nights he spent without sleeping, terrible quarrels. One of the many things he said was:

"You can't believe how I, who've come to propose a man's murder to you, am talking to you about innocence, but, still, I was twenty years old and still a kid. Do you know the kind of sadness that will make you spend all night in a sleazy bar, killing time with trashy talk and cheap liquor? Do you know what it's like to be in a brothel and suddenly have to fight back desperate sobs? You look at me so surprised, sure, you saw a strange fellow, maybe, only you didn't grasp that that strangeness was from the misery I carried around deep inside me. Look, I can hardly believe I'm talking so precisely, like I am. Who am I? What am I heading for? I don't know. I get the feeling you're the way I am, that's why I came to you about Barsut's murder. With the money we'll set up the organization and maybe shake the foundations of this social order."

The Astrologer cut in:

"But, have you always acted this way?"

"That's what I don't know. Why do you want to set up the society? Why does the Melancholy Ruffian keep on pimping and shining his own boots even when he has a fortune? Why did Ergueta marry a prostitute and dump the millionairess? Do you think, by some chance, that I've put up with being slapped around by Barsut and having the Captain there just because? It looks like I'm a coward, Ergueta's a madman, the Ruffian's a miser, you're a man with an obsession. That's what we seem to be, but underneath, on the inside, on a deeper level than consciousness and thought, there's a whole other life, more powerful and vast . . . and if we put up with all this, it's because we believe that by putting up with it or acting like we do we can finally get at the truth . . . that is, get at our own truth."

The Astrologer got up, came over to Erdosain and, putting a hand on his head, said:

"You're right, son. We're all mystics without realizing it. The Melancholy Ruffian is a mystic, Ergueta is a mystic, you, me, her, and them . . . The plague of our time, lack of religion, has blinded our understanding, and so we look outside ourselves for something that lies within the mystery of our subconscious. We need a religion to save us from the disaster that's come over us. You'll say what I'm saying is nothing new. Okay: but remember, all that can change on this earth is the style, the manner; the substance stays the same. If you believed in God, you would never have had such a rough time of it, if I believed in God I would never hear out your proposal to kill a fellowman. And what's really terrible is that the time to get a belief, a faith, has passed us by already. If we were to go to a priest, he wouldn't understand our problems, and all he'd suggest would be reciting an Our Father and going to confession every week."

"So what are we going to do—"

"There you have it. What are we going to do? In the old days we could have taken refuge in a monastery or traveled to unknown and marvelous lands. But today you can eat a morning sherbet in Patagonia and be eating bananas in Brazil in the afternoon. What are we supposed to do? I read a good deal, and believe me, in every book from Europe now I find that same undercurrent of pain and bitterness you describe in your own life. Look at the United States. Movie stars have platinum ovaries implanted and murderers compete for the most horrible crime on record. You've been around, you know this stuff. Houses, more houses, different faces, but the hearts are the same. Mankind has lost its festivals, its celebrations. Men are so low in spirit they've even lost God! And even a three-hundred-horsepower motor can only manage to distract them if some madman at the wheel blows himself to bits. Man is a sorry creature who can only get his kicks by miracles. Or blood and guts. Well, with our organization we'll give them miracles, plagues of Asian cholera, myths, gold strikes, diamond-mine bonanzas. I've noticed this talking to you. You only get excited when the conversation is about miraculous things. And everybody is that way, saint or sinner."

"So then, we kidnap Barsut?"

"Yes. Now we have to see how we can get him and the money."

The wind stirred the leaves. For a few seconds, Erdosain contemplated the bar of light that fell from the half-open window onto the pomegranate trees. The Astrologer had moved his chair next to the cabinet, so he leaned his head against its ocher paneling, and his fingers again played with the steel ring, twisting it and watching himself do so.

"How do we get them? It's very simple. I tell Barsut I've found out where the Captain and Elsa are—"

"Fine, that's fine. Only, how did you find that out? We can be sure he'll ask you that..."

"I'll say I wrote to the Personnel Division of the Ministry of Defense."

"Perfect... very good... sure..."

Now the Astrologer had sat up, almost enthusiastically, and was looking at Erdosain with interest.

"And pretending he's supposed to convince Elsa to come back home to me, we'll lure him here."

"Fantastic. Let me think a little. Everything you propose... of course... is just fine. Ah... tell me this one thing, does he have relatives?"

"Except for my wife, no."

"And where does he live?"

"In a boardinghouse. The landlady has a cross-eyed daughter."

"What will they say when Barsut disappears?"

"We can work this terrific cover-up. We send the landlady a telegram from Rosario, signed by him, saying she should send his trunks to such and such a hotel, where you'll be staying under the name of Gregorio Barsut."

"You've got it. You know you've thought the plan through thoroughly? The plan is perfect. Of course, everything is set up for it, the Captain, the address from the Defense officials, his having no relatives and living in a boardinghouse. It's neater than chess."

Saying this, he started pacing up and down the room. Each time he passed in front of the window grate, the garden went dark or the cabinet sent a shadow up to the roof beams. He and Erdosain were in total agreement that the plan was as well-minted as if they had stamped it into iron under a thousand pounds pressure. And as the Astrologer's boots thunked hard and loud in the room at each step, Erdosain regretted that the "plan" should be so simple, not at all like a thriller. He would have liked a more dangerous adventure, less neatly geometrical.

"Damn it! There's nothing tricky about the plan. If this is all there is to it, anybody can be a murderer."

"There's nothing between Gregorio and the cross-eyed girl?"

"No."

"Then why did you tell me about her?"

"I don't know."

"And you're not afraid you'll suffer from remorse after 'it' happens?"

"Look, I think that stuff only happens in novels. In real life, I've done bad things and good things and not felt the least bit of happiness or remorse in either case. I believe what they call remorse is really fear of punishment. Here, they don't hang people, and only cowards—"

"And you? . . ."

"If you don't mind, I'm no cowardly man. I'm a cold man, which is another matter. Think about it. If I just stand there and let somebody take my wife, if I let myself be slapped around by the guy who turned me in, won't I be even more apt not to have a reaction to his death, so long as it's not done butcher style?"

"True. That makes a lot of sense. Everything you do makes sense. Do you know, Erdosain, you're one interesting guy?"

"That's what my wife used to say. It didn't stop her running off with another man."

"And you say you hate him?"

"Sometimes. It depends. Maybe for me physical repulsion is stronger than hatred. Really, it's not hatred, since we can never hate a person when we know he's willing to lower himself to our level."

"So then why do you want to kill him?"

"Why do you want to set up the organization?"

"And why do you think a crime will make a change in your life?"

"That's what I'm so eager to find out. To find out if my life, how I see things, my feelings change after I watch him die. Besides, I have this need to kill somebody. Even just to take my mind off things, you know?"

"And you want me to do the dirty work for you?"

"Sure! . . . because for you, in this case, doing the dirty work for me means getting twenty thousand pesos to set up the organization and the brothels."

"And where did you get the idea I might not be above carrying 'it' out?"

"How? I've been observing you a long time. But the realization that you were the man to try a dangerous scheme came to me when I met you at the Theosophy Society."

"How's that?"

"I remember like it just happened. A lady coal vendor, on your left, was talking about the perispirit with a cobbler. Haven't you noticed how cobblers have a tendency toward occult sciences?"

"And?"

"That time you spoke to a Polish gentleman who communicated with the spirit of Sobiezki."

"I don't remember . . ."

"I do. The Polish gentleman, you yourself told me this later, was a construction worker . . . You and the Polish gentleman went on from Sobiezki to debate the 'homing instinct in pigeons' issue and you replied, 'For me all the homing instinct in pigeons means is that they would be useful messengers in a blackmail plot,' and you went on to explain exactly how— Well, when you stopped talking, leaving the Pole, the coal lady, and the cobbler dumbfounded, I said to myself: this is one audacious man . . ."

"Ha, ha! You're quite a guy!"

"Right."

"You have to figure in all this: it's a setup that involves three elements that must work in harmony, even though they're independent. Look: the first element is the kidnapping. The second, when you stay in Rosario, and from there send for and receive the trunks under the name Barsut. The third, the murder and the disposal procedure."

"Will we destroy the body?"

"Of course. With nitric acid or else with an oven where—if it's with an oven it has to be four hundred degrees minimum to turn the bones to ash, too."

"Where did you find that out?"

"You know I'm an inventor. Ah, from the twenty thousand pesos we can set part aside to produce the copper rose on a large scale. I have a family I'm friends with working on it. Maybe one of the kids could be part of the organization. Also, the other day I figured out how to switch Stephenson's steam engine over to an electromagnetic system. With my scheme, it's a hundred times simpler. You know what I need? To get away for a while, to stay up in the mountains, to rest and study."

"You could go to the colony we'll have set up—"

"So the plan meets with your approval?"

"Ah! One thing. The money, where did Barsut get it?"

"Three years ago he sold some property he'd inherited."

"And he keeps it in a savings account?"

"No, he can write checks on it."

"So he's not living on the interest?"

"No, he keeps spending it bit by bit. At a rate of about two hundred pesos a month. He says he'll be dead before it's all gone."

"That's odd. What sort of guy is he?"

"Strong. Cruel. The kidnapping will have to be watertight, because he'll defend himself like a wild beast."

"Okay."

"Ah! Before I go. Are you going to mention this to the Ruffian?"

"No. The secret stays with us. The Ruffian will participate by getting the brothels set up, but that's all. Tomorrow you pay back the Sugar Company, right?"

"Yes."

"Now I remember. I know a printer. He'll make up the official bulletin from the Ministry of Defense."

Erdosain paced about the room for an instant.

"The kidnapping is easy. You go to Rosario and send a telegram asking for the trunks. What happens is, when you're faced with actually committing a crime—"

"Well, it won't be the only one we commit."

"How's that?"

"Well, of course. Another thing on my mind is how we keep the society secret. I came up with this: there will be revolutionary cells all over the country. The central committee will be located in the capital. So, this committee will be organized according to this plan: chairman of the provincial capital, member of the central committee, chairman of the principal township, committee member of the head district."

"Doesn't that seem rather complicated to you?"

"I don't know, I'll think about it. Some other details of organization that occurred to me are: each cell must be equipped with a radio setup, and it will be necessary to have one car per ten members, and ten guns, two machine guns, and when we get a hundred members they must buy a war plane, bombs, etc., etc. The system of increments will be worked out by a high council, while lower-level choices will be made by standard voting procedure. But it's time to go to bed. The train will be here shortly . . . or do you want to sleep over?"

Really Erdosain had nothing to do. The clock had already struck three in the morning and the words the Astrologer had said flowed through his mind in a near blur. Nothing interested him. He wanted to go away, that was all. To go far away.

He shook the Astrologer's hand: his host said good-bye to him in the pomegranate orchard, and Erdosain, feeling it was all too much, walked to the boundary of the land. When he looked back into the darkness, the light from the window projected a yellow rectangle out into the dark.

UP THE TREE

Dawn is breaking. Erdosain walks along the path beside a ruined sidewalk past the villas. The morning cool penetrates to the innermost sac in his exhausted lungs. Although the open sky above grows blacker and descending darkness makes things seem closer to his eyes, distant objects are invisible on the horizon. Flowing through the streets, some gray-green streaks take on a reddish tinge.

Erdosain thinks as he walks away:

"This is as sad as the desert. Now she's asleep beside him."*

---

* Commentator's note: Only later was Erdosain to find out that Elsa was then in the care of a Sister of Charity. One gross pass made at her by Captain Belaúnde was enough to alert her to her true situation, and she leaped from the car. Then it oc-

Quickly the watery dawn light fills the street with pale wisps of fog.

Erdosain tells himself:

"But still, man must be strong. I remember when I was little, I thought I saw, on the clouds' crests, big men stride by with kinky hair and angular limbs all agleam. But really they were striding through the land of Happiness within me! Ah! to lose a dream is almost like losing a fortune. What am I saying? It's worse. Man must be strong, that's the only truth. And show no mercy. And even when he's tired, say to himself: Right now, I'm tired, I regret getting involved in this business, but tomorrow I won't. That's the truth. Tomorrow."

Erdosain closes his eyes. A fragrance, which might be spikenard and might be carnations, wafts a mysterious festive scent into the air.

And Erdosain thinks:

"Despite everything, it's necessary to bring some happiness into life. This is no way to live. It's not right. Some happiness must be floating high above our misery, who knows just what, but something more beautiful than the ugly human face, than the horrible human truth. The Astrologer is right. We must usher in the reign of Lies, of magnificent lies. Having someone to worship, making a pathway through this forest of stupidity—only how?

Erdosain continued his soliloquy, his cheeks flushing rosy pink.

"So what if I'm a murderer or a degenerate? Does that make any difference? No. It's beside the point. There's a thing more beautiful than all the vileness of

---

curred to her to turn to a hospital, where the Mother Superior took her in hand, realizing she was a woman at the end of her wits.

all men put together, and that's happiness. If I were happy, bliss would absolve me of my crime. Happiness is the key. And also, to love someone . . ."

The sky tinges green in the distance while the low-lying darkness still swathes the tree trunks. Erdosain scowls. Vaporous wisps of memory flow from his spirit, golden mists, glowing rails trailing away into the countryside of an afternoon canopied with sunshine. And the girl's face, a pale little face, with greenish eyes and black curls escaping from under a straw hat, floats upward from the surface of his soul.

It was two years ago. No, three. What was her name? María, María Esther. What was her name? The sweet little face now shares its inner warmth with a night-dark pocket of fantasy. He remembers so many things: He was sitting beside her, the wind was ruffling her black curls, suddenly he reached out and took the girl's warm, live chin in his fingertips. Where is she now? Where might she be living? If he found her again, would he know her? Three years ago. He met her on a train, talked to her off and on over a two-week period, then disappeared. Only that and nothing more. And she didn't know he was married. What would she have said if she found out? Yes, now he remembers. Her name was María. But what does that matter? No. There was something more splendid in it, the great sweet fever that flowed from her eyes, which were sometimes green and sometimes hazel.

And her silence. Erdosain remembers stretches of railway travel, sitting beside the girl who has rested her head on his shoulder, he intertwines his fingers in those curls and the fifteen-year-old girl is trembling. If she knew now that he plans to kill a man, what would she say? Perhaps she would fail to grasp what it meant. And Erdosain remembers how, timidly, like the school-girl she was, she raised one arm and touched her hand to his stubbled face; and perhaps that joy, the one he lost, might be the very joy we need to smooth away so much ugliness from the human face.

Erdosain now investigates himself with curiosity. Why does he harbor such thoughts? What right does he have? Since when do murderers think? And still, something within him gives thanks to the universe. Is it made of humility or of love? He does not know, but he understands that within the incoherence there is sweetness, he grasps that when some poor soul goes mad, he gratefully leaves behind the sufferings of this earth. And underneath this pity, some implacable, almost mocking force twists his lip to a sneer of contempt.

The gods exist. They live hidden beneath the outer shell of those men who remember life on the planet when the earth was still young. He, too, bears within him a god. Can it be true? He touches his nose, painful from Barsut's beating, and the implacable force insists it is true: he bears a god within him, beneath his aching skin. But is there any provision in the penal code for a homicidal god? What would the presiding judge say if he replied: "I sin because I bear a god within"?

But, isn't it true? This love, this strength that he brings to the breaking day, under the moist trees dripping dew into the darkness, is that not a godlike thing? And again the surface of his soul becomes a contour map of that memory: a pale little oval face with its greenish eyes and black curls that the wind would now and then wrap around her throat. How easily it comes! He has no need to speak a word, so perfect is his delight. Though he could quite conceivably have gone mad with thinking of the schoolgirl under those dew-dripping trees. What other explanation could there be for his soul becoming so different from the soul that tormented him by night? Or, perhaps, can somber thoughts only arise at night? Even so, it doesn't matter. He's a

brand new man. He smiles there under the trees. Isn't
the whole thing magnificently idiotic? The Melancholy Ruffian, the depraved Blind Girl, Ergueta with
his myth of Christ, the Astrologer, all those incomprehensible phantoms, who speak human words, fleshly
words, what do they matter to him, leaning on a post
by a bushy hedge, feeling life pushing forward to meet
and touch him?

He's a brand new man, just from thinking about the
girl who rested her head on his shoulder in a railway
car. Erdosain closes his eyes. The acrid smell of earth
sends a shiver through him. A dizzy spasm courses up
his tired body.

Someone else is coming along the road. A harsh
whistle sounds from the station. Other men in caps or
in twisted, battered hats cross by in the distance.

Really, what the devil is he doing there? Erdosain
winks, feeling he's playing a trick on God, playing at
being the man who couldn't fend God's curse off his
head. Still, waves of darkness pass before his eyes now
and then, and a sort of dulled drunkenness is taking
hold of his senses. He'd like to violate something. Violate common sense. If a haystack had been handy he
would have set it ablaze. Something nasty distorts his
face; it wears the harsh expressions of a madman; suddenly he looks at a tree, leaps up, grabs upward and
catches hold of a branch, and bracing his feet against
the trunk, shoving himself upward with his elbows, he
manages to hoist himself up to the fork in the acacia
tree.

His shoes slip on the smooth bark, twigs whip back
into his face, he reaches out an arm and gets hold of a
branch, plunging his face through the dripping leaves.
The street below him falls away toward an archipelago
of trees.

He is up in the tree. He has violated common sense,
just for the hell of it, for no reason, like murdering

somebody who happened to walk in front of you to see if the police could track you down afterward. To the east, funereal chimneys are silhouetted against the greenish sky; farther on, green hills like monstrous elephant herds stand in the meadows of Banfield, and the same old sadness comes flooding back. It's not enough to have violated common sense to be happy. But still, he makes a try and says aloud:

"Hey! Sleepy beasties! I swear . . . but, no . . . I want to violate the laws of common sense, you smug little beastie-weasties. . . . No. What I want to do is yell out for daring, for new life. I speak from the treetop, but I'm not your partridge in a pear tree, I'm a Remo in an acacia tree; whoo-oo, you sleepy beasties!"

His energy runs out quickly. He looks around, almost surprised to be where he is, suddenly the face of the faraway girl fragments inside him like flower petals, and, terrifically ashamed of his crazy stunts,* he comes back down the tree. He is beaten down. He is a loser.

---

* *Commentator's note: Later Erdosain offered me two explanations for his behavior. The first one is that it gave him great pleasure to fake a state of madness, the kind of pleasure a man gets when he's drunk one glass of wine and then acts drunk in front of his friends to upset them. He smiled sadly as he was explaining it, and told me that when he came down from the acacia, he was ashamed of himself, just like some poor slob who gets himself up in a Carnival costume, shows himself off to a bunch of people and, instead of making the strangers laugh, his attempt to be funny only gets him sneered at. "I felt so disgusted with myself that I even thought of killing myself and was sorry I didn't have my revolver on me. Later, as I was getting undressed at home, I realized that when I was out there I forgot I was carrying the gun in my pants pocket."*

2

INCOHERENCIES

Erdosain spent the remaining days till Barsut's kidnapping holed up in a boardinghouse where he had taken temporary lodgings after paying back the Sugar Company. The thought of going out filled him with dread. He never thought about the planned kidnapping of Barsut, and he even stopped going to see the Astrologer. He spent the whole day in bed with his fists pressed into the pillow and his forehead smashed down against his fists. At other times he would sit staring fixedly for hours at the wall, where he seemed to see slithering mists of dreams and desperation.

During that time, he could never bring back an image of Elsa's face.

Then he would sleep or turn things over in his mind.*
He tried, though it was no use, to occupy his mind with two projects he thought were important: the electromagnetic conversion system for steam engines, and the one for a dog-coloring service which would

---

* Commentator's note: Speaking of those days, Erdosain told me: "I believed my soul had been given to me to enjoy the beauties of the world, moonlight along an orange-tinged cloud crest, a dewdrop trembling on a rose. But, when I was little, I always believed life held in store some sublime and beautiful thing just for me. But when I got a good look at other men's lives, I found out they lived with boredom, as if they lived in a land of perpetual rain, where the rain always pelting down left puddles of water in their eyes and kept them from seeing

put on the market electric-blue dogs, green bulldogs, violet greyhounds, lilac for terriers, lap dogs with three-color prints of sunsets across their backs, little bitches with curlicues like a Persian rug. He was off balance: one afternoon he dozed off and had this dream:

He knew he was the lover of one of the princesses, and this in addition to being his majesty's lackey filled him with glee, because the generals were always hanging around him making smutty innuendos. Mirror-smooth water came up to the very trunks of trees that bloomed in perpetual white splendor, while the willowy princess, taking his arm, asked him in lisping Castilian Spanish:

"Oh, Erdosain, dotht thou love me?"

Erdosain, breaking into a snicker, answered the princess's question with a crude remark; a circle of drawn swords flashed before his eyes and he felt he was going under, cataclysmic forces were ripping the continents asunder, but he had lain sleeping for many long centuries in a lead chamber at the bottom of the sea. On the other side of the porthole, one-eyed sharks were swimming about, vile-humored because of their piles, and Erdosain enjoyed a silent glee, sniggering with the muffled chortles of someone trying not to be heard. Now all the fish in the sea were one eyed, and he was the Emperor of the City of One-Eyed Fish. An endless wall ran along the sandy seaside wastes, the blue sky lay rusting against the brick of the wall, and along the

---

things clearly. And I could see how souls wandered the earth like fish trapped inside an aquarium. Outside of those greenish glass walls was life, all beautiful, singing, soaring high, where everything would be different, full of power and variety, and where the brand-new creatures of a more perfect creation would send their lovely bodies springing through an elastic atmosphere." And then: "It's no good, I have to get away from this world."

walls of the red towers, the waves smashed against myriad fat, one-eyed fish, monstrous big-bellied fish rotting away with sea leprosy, while a dropsied black man threatened them with the butt end of a pagan god made out of salt.

At other times, Erdosain would flash back to past times when he had actually foreseen what was going to happen, just as he had told the Captain that night. Tormenting thoughts attacked all around a reality that now made him exclaim:

"I was right. I saw things the way they were."

Thus, he recalled one night he was talking with Elsa and she, in a moment of frankness, confessed that if she were still single, she would take a lover instead of getting married.

Erdosain asked her:

"Are you serious?"

From the other bed, Elsa answered:

"Yes, yes, I'd take a lover . . . why get married?"

Something strange happened: Erdosain was suddenly aware of the silence of death, a silence stretched out like a coffin entrapping his horizontal body. Perhaps at that moment all the unconscious love man bears toward woman was destroyed within him. And later it would steel him to bear up under terrible situations that would have been insupportable if he had not experienced that moment. It now seemed to him he was at the bottom of a tomb, he thought he would never see the light, and in that weightless, dark silence that filled the room, ghosts stirred, awakened by his wife's voice.

Later, explaining those moments, he remembered that he lay stock still in the bed, afraid of destroying the balance of his boundless unhappiness, which weighed down upon his body, trapping him flat against the surface of an implacable anguish.

His heart pounded heavily. Each systole and diastole

seemed to have to fight against the pressure of an elastic mass of mud. And it was no use to try to work his hands toward the sun above. And his wife's voice repeated again in his ears:

"I'd have taken a lover and not gotten married."

And those words, which had taken no more than two seconds' time to say, would echo within him for the rest of his life. He closed his eyes. The words would stay with him for all time, rooted in his inmost self like some organic growth. And his teeth gnashed together. He wanted to suffer even more, to exhaust himself with pain, bleed himself dry in a slow outpouring of grief. And with his hands pressed to his thighs, stiff as a corpse in its coffin, not looking at her, trying to hold his galloping breathing steady, he managed to spit out the question:

"And would you have loved him?"

"What for? . . . Who knows! . . . Yes, yes, if he was nice, why shouldn't I?"

"And where would you have met? Your family would never allow that under their roof."

"In some hotel."

"Ah!"

They fell silent, but Erdosain could see her in the clear-cut misfortune of his life, coming up the sidewalk of a street paved with river stones. She made her way along the wide sidewalk. A dark veil covered half her face, and as she turned her steps toward that place where she deliberately permitted her desire to lead her, she strode briskly and purposefully onward. And, eager to stomp even more on the last bit of hope he still held onto, Erdosain went on, with a faked smile she could not see in the dark, keeping his voice soft so Elsa wouldn't detect the fury that made his lips tremble:

"See? Isn't it nice when a married couple can tell

each other everything, as close as a brother and sister?
And, tell me, would you have taken your clothes off
in front of him?"

"Don't be an idiot!"

"No, tell me; would you have gotten undressed?"

"Well . . . of course! You don't think I'd keep my
clothes on!"

If they had split his spine down the middle with an
axe, Erdosain could not have gone stiffer. His throat
was as dry as if a fiery wind had parched it. His heart
was barely beating; his brain felt like a fog was streaming out of his eyes and flowing over it. He fell back
into silence and darkness, he plunged gently downward, and the rigid spasm that locked his cubic flesh
relaxed, only to leave it sensitive to deeply graven pain.
He was silent, but yet he would have liked to burst
out sobbing, to fall on his knees, to rise, put on his
clothes and go sleep in the doorway of some house in
a strange city.

Furious, Erdosain shouted:

"But can you see . . . can you see how horrible this
is, the enormity of what you've just told me? I should
kill you. You're a bitch! I should kill you, that's right,
kill you. See?"

"But what's got into you? Have you gone crazy?"

"You've ruined my life. Now I know why you kicked
me out of your bed and sent me off to masturbate! Yes,
that's what you made me do! You've reduced me to
the shell of a man. I should kill you. Any slob can come
up and spit in my face. See? And while I steal and steal
and suffer just for your sake . . . oh, yes, that's what
you're thinking about. How you'd leap in bed with
some fine young man! See? A fine young man, that's
all you need, a fine young man!"

"Have you gone crazy?"

Quickly Erdosain pulled on his clothes.

"Where are you going?"

He pulled his coat over his shoulders; then, leaning over his wife's bed, he answered:

"You want to know where I'm going? Out to some cathouse and catch the syph!"

NAIVETÉ AND IDIOCY

The compiler of this account would never attempt a definition of Erdosain, for so many traumatic events had blighted his life that the disasters he set off after joining up with the Astrologer could be explained by the psychic damage he sustained during his marriage.

Even now, reading over Erdosain's confessions, I can hardly believe I sat through such horror stories, told with no holds barred and riddled with human pain.

I remember how it was. During the three days he was holed up in my house, he poured it all out to me.

We got together in a vast room with no furniture, where hardly any light came in.

Erdosain would be sitting on the edge of the chair, hunched over, his elbows on his knees, his fingers splayed across his cheeks, staring fixedly at the floor.

He spoke flatly, without stopping, as if he were reciting a lesson stamped onto the surface of his darkened mind under infinite atmospheres of pressure. The tone of his voice, no matter what he was talking about, never varied, always steady, even, and regular as clockwork.

If he was interrupted, he didn't get mad, he just started up where he left off, supplying extra details as I asked for them, his head bent always over, his eyes fixed on the floor, his elbows on his knees. His story was slowed down because he was so excessively careful not to get anything wrong.

He told me horror story after horror story without showing any reaction. He knew he was going to die, human justice was out there looking for him, full force, but there he was with his revolver in his pocket, his elbows on his knees, his fingers splayed across his face, staring into the dust of the enormous, empty room, not showing the least emotion.

He had grown extraordinarily thin in just a few days. His yellow skin, stretched taut over the flat facial bones, made him look consumptive. Later the autopsy showed that he really was in an advanced stage of tuberculosis.

The second afternoon he was at my house, he told me:

"Before I got married, I felt this horror at the thought of fornication. To my way of thinking, a man only married to be with his wife and enjoy the pleasure of their shared togetherness all the time, talking to each other, sharing love through looks, words, and smiles. True, I was young then, but while I was courting Elsa I felt I had to watch myself all the more closely."

He talked on.

Erdosain never kissed Elsa, because it was enough to be choked up with the dizziness of loving her and since, moreover, he believed that "you don't kiss a nice girl." And so he made a big spiritual thing out of what was really just the hunger of his flesh.

"We always avoided the familiar pronoun for _you_, since I treasured the distance that the more formal pronouns kept between us. Besides, I believed you didn't go calling a nice young lady by the familiar form. I had this concept of the nice girl, a girl who was all purity, perfection, and lily-white. When I was with her I felt no desire, only the restless longing of a delicious joy that brought tears to my eyes. And I was happy because I was loving, suffering, having no notion where it was taking me, and so I made a great spiritual love out of the body's demands, which were what really had me throwing myself at her feet in rapture over her quiet eyes, clean eyes that cut through slowly to the quivering inmost layers of my soul."

As he spoke, I looked at Erdosain. Here he was, a murderer, a murderer, going on about the subtleties of his ridiculous feelings! He continued:

"And on my wedding night, when we were alone in the hotel room, she unself-consciously took off her clothes with the light on. I was blushing to the roots of my hair and turned away so I wouldn't see her and she wouldn't see my ashamed reaction. Then I took off my collar, coat, and shoes and climbed under the sheet with my pants on. Across her pillow, from amid her black curls, she turned to me and said smiling and laughing an odd laugh:

"Aren't you worried they'll get all wrinkled? Take them off, silly."

Later, there was a mysterious gap between Elsa and Erdosain. She gave herself to him, but in a revolted way as if she'd been cheated out of something, who knows what. And he went on his knees at the head of the bed and begged her to let him have her for just an instant, but she'd turn on him and almost shout, her voice flat with impatience:

"Leave me alone! Can't you see you disgust me?"

Fighting back his fear of some looming catastrophe, Erdosain sank back down onto his bed.

"I didn't get in, I just sat there, almost leaning back against the pillow, staring into the dark, but I imagined that she might be sorry to see me sitting like that, all alone in the dark, and then she'd take pity and tell me, 'All right, come here if you want.' But not once, not once, did she say those words, till finally one night I shouted at her in desperation:

"Maybe you like to think . . . I'll just keep on masturbating forever and ever?"

She kept her cool and replied:
"It's no good. I should never have married you."

THE BLACK HOUSE

And anguish blossomed inside him, so violently that Erdosain gripped his head, crazed with physical pain. It seemed to him his brain tissue had come loose from his skull and banged against it at the least thought.

He knew he was past the point of no return, cast out from the possible happiness that, someday, smiles on the palest cheek; he grasped how fate had aborted him out into the chaos of that ghastly multitude of hostile men who rubber-stamp life with their overload of sin and suffering.

He no longer had any hope, and his fear of life grew stronger when he thought he would never have dreams to live up to, when, his eyes stubbornly glued to a corner of the room, he realized it was the same to him to be a restaurant dishwasher or a servant in some cathouse.

What did he care! His wretchedness brought him to the level of that silent host of terrible men who by day drag around their misery selling handicrafts or Bibles and by night make the rounds of urinals, exposing their genitals to young people drawn to the same by similar urges.

Knowing these things, he was mired in dark broodings. He felt he was screwed down into a massive block from which he would never escape.

This sense of anguish became so chronic that suddenly he found his soul was saddened by the fate that awaited his body in the city, his body that weighed seventy kilos and that he only saw when he walked in front of a mirror.

At other times in his thoughts he placed himself amid all the comforts and luxuries that there were, pleasures unbounded in space and time, while his present misery had only to do with his body, a suffering body, and something Erdosain no longer regarded as his, though he regretted not having made it happy.

The remorse he felt over his neglected physical self ran deep, as deep as the remorse a mother must feel who can never give her child the things it needs.

Because he never gave his body, which would live so short a time, so much as a decent suit or a scrap of pleasure to get it through life; he had done nothing to please his material being, though his soul had access to all things, even the geography of lands which no man-made technology had yet reached.

And often he reflected:

"What have I done for the happiness of this wretched body?"

Because, in all truth, he felt trapped inside something as alien to him as a barrel is to the wine it holds.

Then he had to think how it was his body that held his soul-searchings, fed them off its tired blood; a wretched, poorly clothed body that no woman would look at twice, and felt despised, felt the days weighing down on it, and all because his thoughts had never wanted the kind of fulfillment it longed for timidly, in silence.

Erdosain was flooded with pity, sorry for his physical double, almost a stranger to him.

Then, like a desperate man hurling himself from the seventh floor, he threw himself into the delicious terror of masturbation, trying to drown his remorse in a world from which nobody could exile him, amid all the fine delights that were far from his life, amid striking, splendid bodies, such as could only be enjoyed at the greatest outlay of existences and money.

It was a universe of gelatinous ideas, running off

down corridors where obscenity was got up in silk and brocade and velvet and fabulous laces, a world that emitted a soft, spongy glow. The most beautiful women in all creation streamed by, baring their ripe-apple breasts to him, and offered his mouth, stale from vile cigarettes, their fragrant lips and words charged with sensuality.

Now they were willowy, delicate, glossy young things, now they were decadent schoolgirls, a world of ever-changing femininity where no one could kick him out, him, the poor slob that madams of even the sleaziest cathouses eyed with suspicion as if he might gyp them out of the price of fornication.

He closed his eyes and came into that blazing darkness, heedless of everything, like some opium smoker who enters a disgusting den, where the Chinese dealer smells of dung, and thinks he's regaining paradise.

And for a moment he slithered surreptitiously into that underground joy, ashamed, but with the eagerness of a young man entering his first brothel.

Desire buzzed like a hornet in his ears, but no one could tear him away from that sensual darkness.

This darkness was a familiar house where he suddenly left behind all of his everyday life. There, in the black house, terrible pleasures seemed merely everyday, though if he had suspected that sort of thing in anyone else's life, he would never again have had anything to do with him.

Though this black house lay within Erdosain, he came to it by devious routes, tortuous maneuvers, and once inside the door he knew there was no turning back, for coming down the halls of the black house to meet him, through one special corridor always swathed in shadow, was the fleet-footed woman who one day, on the sidewalk or in a streetcar, had swelled him with desire.

Like someone drawing from his wallet money earned

in various ways, Erdosain drew from the bedrooms of the black house a woman fragmentary and yet complete, a woman made out of a hundred women broken into pieces by a hundred desires, always the same, rekindled at the approach of such women.

Because this woman had the knees of a girl whose skirt had blown high in the wind as she waited for the bus, and the thighs he remembered having seen on a dirty postcard, and the sad, faded smile of a schoolgirl he met long ago on a streetcar, and the greenish eyes of a seamstress with a pale mouth and pockmarked skin who went out Sunday night with a girlfriend to those recreation centers where storekeepers rub their crotches nuzzling-tight against little girls who like men.

This random woman, put together out of bits of all the women he had not been able to have, knew just how far to let things go, like fiancées who may have slipped a hand between their boyfriends' legs but can still count as virgins. She came up to him. Her rump fit snugly into an orthopedic girdle, which let her slightly off-center breasts hang free, and her behavior was beyond reproach like some well-schooled young lady who keeps her head, but not so much that her boyfriend's fingers can't wander into her accidentally unbuttoned blouse.

Then he fell away backward into the depths of the black house. The black house! Erdosain would always recall those days with a shudder; he felt he had lived within a hell and its infernal substance was stuck fast to him for as long as he lived, even a few days before his death, with justice on his trail. When he turned his thoughts back to that time, he grew morose and agitated, a red flame blazed before his eyes, and his painful fury burned so fiercely he would have liked to leap beyond the stars, to be consumed in a great fire that would purge his present of all that terrible, persistent, inescapable past.

The black house! I can still see it now—the taut face of that silent man, who suddenly lifted his face to the ceiling, then lowered his eyes to be level with mine and, with a cold smile, added:

"So now, tell mankind what the black house is like. And that I was a murderer. And yet I, the murderer, have loved everything beautiful and have fought within myself to drown all the horrible temptations that hour after hour came creeping up from deep inside me. I've suffered for what I am, and for other people, too, you see that? for other people, too . . ."

THE OFFICIAL BULLETIN

The kidnapping occurred as planned ten days after Elsa ran off. The fourteenth of August, Erdosain was visited by the Astrologer, but, since he was out, when he came back he found an envelope shoved under the door. Inside was a faked official bulletin from the Ministry of Defense, giving Erdosain the supposed address of Captain Belaunde and an odd postscript that read like this:

"I will wait for you until the twentieth every morning—you bring Barsut along. Knock and come in without waiting. Don't come see me alone."

Erdosain read the Astrologer's letter and was plunged into thought. He had forgotten about Barsut. He knew he had to kill him, then having decided that, he let it fall away into darkness, and the days that passed during that time and streamed by in a daze were gone for all time. "I had to kill Barsut." The reason behind that "had to" could serve as the key to Erdosain's madness. When I asked him to tell me about it, he answered: "I had to kill him, because otherwise I couldn't have any peace in life. To kill Barsut was a precondition for existing, the way fresh air is for other people."

So, as soon as he got the letter, he went to see Barsut. That man lived in a boardinghouse on Uruguay Street, a dark, dingy dwelling place housing a fantastic universe of the most wildly varied human beings. The landlady of the whole place was in contact with the spirit world, had a cross-eyed daughter, and as far as collecting rent went, had no mercy. A boarder who was even twenty-four hours behind with the rent could expect to come home that night and find his trunks and belongings out in the middle of the patio.

He arrived late that day at Gregorio's house. Gregorio was just shaving when Erdosain came into the room. Barsut stood frozen, pale, with the razor in midstroke on his cheek, then looking Erdosain over from head to foot, he exclaimed:

"What do you want, barging in here like this?"

"Anyone else would have been offended," Erdosain commented later. "I gave him a 'friendly' smile because just then I happened to feel like a friend of his, and without saying anything I handed him the official bulletin from the Ministry of Defense. I was all on edge from an unexplainable joy, I remember I only stayed a minute sitting on the edge of his bed, then I was up and pacing nervously all over the room."

"So she's out in Temperley. And you want us to go out and get her?"

"Yes, that's what I want. And you go in after her."

Barsut muttered something Erdosain didn't catch, then he started giving his arm muscles a rubdown and his skin took on a rosy glow. He was going to shave his whiskers; he stopped with the razor in midair and, turning his head, said:

"You know what? I never thought you'd get up the nerve to come see me."

Erdosain took the full force of those streaky green eyes turned on him, really the man had a tiger face, and after crossing his arms he answered:

"I know, I'd never have thought so either, but, you know, things change."

"You scared to go out there alone?"

"No, I'd just like to see how you pull it off."

Barsut clenched his teeth. With his chin slathered in shaving cream and his forehead vigorously furrowed he considered Erdosain and finally said:

"Look, I thought I was a rat, but I think you . . . you're worse than me. Well, God only knows what I should do."

"Why do you say that God knows?"

Barsut stood in front of the mirror, put his fists against his waist, and what he said was no surprise to Erdosain, who took these words without moving a muscle in his face:

"Who's to say that bulletin isn't a phony and you're not leading me into a trap?"

"The human soul is such a mystery!" Erdosain later commented. "I listened to those words and not a muscle in my face moved. How had Gregorio guessed at the truth? I don't know. Or did he share my wicked imagination?"

He lit a cigarette and answered only:

"Do what you like."

But Barsut, who was warming to the subject, argued:

"But why not? Tell me this: why not? Don't you have every reason to want to kill me? It makes sense. I tried to take your wife away from you, I ratted on you, I beat you up, what the hell! You'd have to be some kind of saint not to want to kill me."

"A saint? No, buddy, a saint I'm not. But I swear I'm not going to kill you tomorrow. Some day, maybe, but not tomorrow."

Barsut burst out laughing cheerily.

"You know, Remo, you're really something? Some day you'll kill me. That's funny! You know what I think is the interesting part? To see the look on your face when you kill me. Tell me, are you going to play it straight or have a good laugh?"

It was a friendly question, one that demanded an answer.

"Maybe I'll play it straight. I don't know. I think I will. You know it's no joke to kill another person."

"Aren't you afraid of jail?"

"No, because if I were to kill you I'd take care and I'd destroy your dead body with sulphuric acid."

"You're a savage. . . . Say, my memory's not so good: Did you pay off the Sugar Company?"

"Yes."

"Who gave you the money?"

"A hustler."

"You don't have many friends, but they're true-blue . . . So, when will you come by tomorrow for me?"

"The man goes on duty at eight so . . . so that—"

"Look, I'm not so sure this is on the level, but if I find Elsa I'll give her the back of my hand so she'll taste it for the next few years."

When Erdosain left, he went to the telegraph office and sent the Astrologer a wire.

THE WORK OF ANGUISH

That night he didn't sleep. He was terribly tired. Nor did he think about anything. He tried to define for me how it felt:*

---

* *Commentator's note: Someday I may write the story of Erdosain's ten "missing" days. Right now I can't possibly do it, because there is no room here for another whole book, which is what his account would take up. You'll notice this book only tells what the characters actually did for three days and despite the space I have available I have had to leave out exactly what everyone felt, but their story will be continued in*

"Your soul is like it's a meter outside of your body. It's like your muscles are totally dissolving and your anxiety is boundless. You close your eyes and it's as if your body's dissolving away into nothingness, suddenly you recall some odd detail from one of the thousands of days you've lived; never commit a crime, because it's not so much horrible as it is sad. You feel you're cutting away, one by one, the links that bind you to civilization, that you're going back to the dark barbarian world, that you'll lose whatever it was you steered by; they say and I said it myself to the Astrologer that it's all because we're not educated about crime properly, but, no, that's not the problem. Really, you want to live like other people, be as straight as other people, have a wife, a home, look out the window and see the people going by, and still there's not a cell left in your body that's not contaminated with these fateful words: I have to kill him. You'll say I'm rationalizing away my hatred. So why shouldn't I reason about it? When I get to feel like I'm living in a dream, I can see how I talk so much to convince myself I'm not dead, not because of what happened but because of the state you're left in after you do it. It's like your skin after you burn it. It heals, only have you seen what it's like afterward? All wrinkled, dry, tight, shiny. That's the way your soul is afterward. And sometimes it's got such a shine it burns your eyes. And it's so wrinkled it disgusts you. You know you're carrying around a monster that might get loose any moment and head off in any direction.

"A monster! I've often thought about it. A calm,

another volume called The Flamethrowers. _In the second part, which I am now preparing and which Erdosain gave me a good deal of material for, there will be all kinds of amazing stories such as_ "The Blind Prostitute," "Elsa's Adventures," "The Man Who Walked With Jesus" _and_ "The Poison-Gas Factory."

resilient, indecipherable monster, that would shock even you with its violent drives, with how it seeks out some vantage point in the inner folds of life and spies on your infamies from every angle! How often I've pondered myself, the mystery of myself, and envied the simplest man his life! Ah! Never commit a crime. Look what's become of me. I tell you this stuff just because, maybe because you understand me . . .

"And that night? . . . I came home late. I threw myself down on the bed with my clothes on, I felt a rush like a gambler might feel in my racing heartbeat. Really I didn't think what might happen after the crime, I just went up to the moment of it and wondered how I'd act, what Barsut would do, how the Astrologer would kidnap him, and I saw the crime I'd read about in novels was all tricked up; I grasped how crime is a mechanical business, that it's simple to commit a crime, and it only seems tricky to us because we're not used to it.

"So much so, really, that I remember I just lay there with my eyes fixed on one corner of the darkened room. Bits of my old life, in fragments, streamed before my eyes as if windblown. I never have grasped the mysterious workings of memory, how at key moments in our lives, suddenly the insignificant detail and the image that has lain buried years and years, overshadowed by the present, take on an almost extraordinary importance. We didn't know those inner photographic images even existed and suddenly the heavy veil that shrouds them rips away, and so, that night, instead of thinking about Barsut, I just let myself lie there in that sad boardinghouse room, the way a man would lie when he's waiting for something, that something I've so often talked about, and that, to my mind, should get my life all freshly turned around, wipe away the past, and show me a new version of myself completely different from what I was.

"In truth, I was not much worried about the crime, only I kept puzzling over this: how would I emerge after the crime? Would I suffer remorse? Would I go mad, end up turning myself in? Or would I simply go on living like I had so far, still stuck with that singular impotence that left everything I did in life in that incoherent state you now say is just part of my madness?

"The funny thing is, sometimes I'd feel great surges of joy, feel like laughing like I'd been seized with madness when I hadn't; but when I fought down the urge, I'd try to figure out how we would kidnap Barsut. I was sure he'd put up a fight, but the Astrologer wasn't the sort to go into such a project without due precautions. At other times, I'd try to second-guess how Barsut had hit on the bulletin from the Ministry of Defense being phony and congratulate myself for keeping so perfectly cool, when he turned his lathery face to me and, almost as a joke, said:

" 'Wouldn't it be funny if the bulletin was faked?'

"The truth was, he was a rat, but I wasn't all that much better; maybe the difference was he wasn't eager to understand his low passions the way I'd have been. Besides, it was no big deal to me then. Maybe it'd be me who'd kill him, maybe the Astrologer, but either way I'd thrown my life away down some monstrous hole, where demons played with my senses like dice in a shaker.

"Faraway sounds reached me; weariness seeped through my joints; at moments it felt like my flesh, like a sponge, sucked in silence and repose. I kept getting these twisted ideas about Elsa, unspoken anger knotted my jaw muscles; I felt the wretchedness of my poor life.

"Yet, the only way I could redeem myself in my own eyes was to murder Barsut, and suddenly I'd picture myself standing over him; he was bound by heavy ropes and lying on a pile of sacks; all you could make out clearly was one green eye in profile and a pale nose; I bent over his body gently, brandished a revolver, tenderly pushed back the hair off his forehead and told him very softly:

" 'You're going to die, scum.'

"His arms were writhing even under those heavy bonds, it was a desperate struggle of frightened bones and muscles.

" 'Do you recall, you scum, do you remember the potatoes, the salad that slopped all over the table? Do I still have that loser's face that bugged you so much?'

"But I was overcome with shame for going on at him like such a bastard, so I'd tell him, I mean I wouldn't tell him anything, I took a sack and put it over his head; under the heavy sacking, his head writhed furiously; I tried to steady it against the floor, so the bullet would do its job and the revolver stay steady; and the sacking slipped all over his hair and nothing I could do was any use against that desperate, panting animal, fighting death. If that dream faded away, I'd imagine myself traveling through the archipelago of Malaysia, on a sailing ship in the Indian Ocean. I'd changed my name, I mouthed English words; even if I carried the same weight of grief inside, now my arms were strong and my eyes untroubled; maybe in Borneo, maybe in Calcutta or past the Red Sea, or on past the taiga, in Korea or Manchuria, my life would recharge."

Certainly this was no longer the inventor who was fantasizing, or the man who discovered electric rays that could melt huge chunks of steel like wax strips, or who would preside over the glass-top table of the League of Nations.

At other times terror took hold of Erdosain; he felt he was fettered or that the rotten social order had him straitjacketed and he couldn't get loose. He saw himself in chains, in prison stripes, filing slowly in a long trail of prisoners south to Ushuaia through vast snowdrifts. The sky above was white as plated tin.

This image set him ablaze, blind with slow fury he got up and, pacing the room, he had the urge to pound on the walls with his fists, he'd have liked to thrust his bones clean through the walls; then he stopped short by the doorjamb, crossed his arms, pain slithered up to his throat once more, nothing he could do helped, and in his life there was only one visible, unique, absolute reality. He and everybody else. Between him and everyone else was a gap, maybe from their failure to understand him, or maybe his craziness. But either way, he was no less unhappy because of it. And once more the past thrust its fragments before his eyes; in truth, he would have liked to flee from himself, just jettison forever the life that trapped and poisoned his body.

Ah! To come into a fresher world with great paths through the woods, where the stench of wild beasts would be incomparably sweeter than the horrible presence of man.

And he walked along; he wanted to stretch his body to the limit, exhaust it once and for all, leave it so thinned out and spent that it would be unable to muster even one idea.

THE KIDNAPPING

At nine in the morning Erdosain went to get Barsut.

They left without a word. Later Erdosain thought back upon this odd trip where Barsut went to meet his fate without putting up any fight at all.

Harking back to that trip, he said:

"I went with Barsut the way a condemned man goes

to the wall, with his strength all gone; with a persistent feeling of there being empty gaps between my vital organs.

"Barsut, for his part, was scowling; I grasped how he, as he sat there by the window, with his elbow on the armrest, was storing up fury to discharge against the unseen enemy that his instinct warned him was lurking in the big old house in Temperley."

Erdosain went on:

"From time to time I'd think how weird it'd be if the other passengers had known that those two men, slouching down into the leather seats, were a future assassin and his chosen victim.

"And even so, everything just went on as always; sunshine fell on the fields, we left behind the meat packers' and plastic and soap plants, the glassworks and foundries, the cattleyards with livestock snuffling around the posts, the streets where paving crews had left deep ruts and piles of material. And after Lanús began that sinister spectacle of Remedios de Escalada, monstrous roundhouses of red brick with gaping black mouths, with locomotives maneuvering under their arches, and off in the distance you could see little bands of wretched men shoveling gravel or hauling railroad ties.

"Farther on, among some rickety-looking banana trees poisoned by the soot and gassy fumes, it cut a diagonal swath lined on both sides with red cottages for the company's employees, with their little tiny gardens, window blinds black with soot, and roads strewn with slag and waste."

Barsut was lost in his own thoughts. Erdosain, to be exact, left himself alone. If just then he'd spotted a train heading straight for them, he would not have blinked; he was numbed to either life or death.

That was how the trip went. When they got to

Temperley, Barsut shuddered as if he'd awakened, cold all over after a painful dream, and all he said was:
"Where is it?"

Erdosain lifted his arm, pointing vaguely off in the distance where they should go, and Barsut started out.

Then they went in silence through the streets to the Astrologer's house.

The gentle blue of the morning fell downward to meet the walls along the slanting streets.

Grass and reeds in all shades of green and trees formed great masses of foliage, crested with wavy tufts and sliced through with labyrinthine woody stems. The gently rippling breeze seemed to set these fantastic creations of nature's whimsy afloat in a golden aura, glassy and clear as a crystal paperweight, its roundness entrapping the strong effluvia of the earth.

"Nice morning," said Barsut.

And that was all they said till they were in front of the house.

"This is it," said Erdosain.

Barsut leaped back and looking at him, incredibly shrewdly, said:

"How can you know it's it if there's no number on it?"

Speaking later about what happened, Erdosain said:

"You could say there's a crime instinct, an instinct that has you lying, lightning-fast, not worried you'll contradict yourself, an instinct like self-preservation that comes into play at the key moment and lets you lie your way out of it in an uncanny way."

Erdosain looked up and, so unexpectedly cool he would later be amazed, answered:

"Because I was here yesterday to look around. I thought I might see Elsa."

Barsut looked at him warily.

He would have sworn Erdosain was lying,* but he was too proud to back out, and so, while Erdosain called out, he clapped his hands to announce their arrival.

His face half-hidden by a wide-brimmed boater, in shirtsleeves, the Man Who Saw the Midwife came to the red-painted meshwork fence gate.

"Is the lady in?" asked Barsut.

Bromberg, without deigning to answer, unbolted and opened the garden gate; then he headed off down a meandering path through the eucalyptus grove to the house, and the two men followed. Suddenly a voice called out:

"Where are you guys going?"

Barsut's head jerked around. Bromberg wheeled around on his heels, and as if a spring had snapped in his arm, it shot out like a lightning bolt.

Barsut's mouth gaped frantically after air, and he doubled over instantly. He was about to grab his belly, but Bromberg's arm came at him from a new angle, and the impact to his jaw made his teeth bang together hard.

He went down and lay like a dead man in the grass, his legs crumpled under and his lips slightly parted.

The Astrologer appeared, and Bromberg, gravely, almost sadly, leaned over the fallen man.

The Astrologer got a hold under his arms, hooking his fingers into the armpits, and so they lugged him over to the abandoned coach house. Erdosain rolled the ocher-painted stable door open, and a smell of dry grass and a swarm of insects escaped from the blackness within. They put the unconscious man into one of the

---

* *Commentator's note: When Barsut was talking with the Astrologer, he said the night before the kidnapping he thought it might be a death trap, and that at the very last only pride kept him from backing out.*

stalls; a heavy chain hung from one of the posts, secured by a padlock.

The Astrologer took one end of it to chain up Barsut by the ankle, tied several knots with the links, and fastened it all with a padlock which opened with a creak, and Erdosain, getting up from over the fallen figure, said, looking at the Astrologer:

"Wouldn't you know? The checkbook's not on him."

It was ten in the morning. The Astrologer looked at his watch and said:

"I have time to take the express that gets to Rosario at six. Want to go with me as far as Retiro?"

"How's that, you're going to Rosario?"

"How else do I get the telegram to his landlady? Do you have the address?"

"Yes, everything's set."

"It's the best way to get hold of Barsut's things without arousing suspicion. That's all he keeps in his boardinghouse?"

"Yes, the trunk and two suitcases."

"Great. Let's stop yakking and get to it. At six I'll reach Rosario, I send the telegram to the old lady, you appear at her door tomorrow morning and play dumb, ask if Barsut has gotten into Rosario yet, and since I'm not there yet, you add that you know they've offered me an important job, etc., etc. How does that sound to you?"

"Great."

At twelve the Astrologer was boarding the train.

3

THE WHIP

The job Erdosain thought up and the Astrologer pulled off was a success, and the Astrologer set up a meeting the next Wednesday for the "heads" to get acquainted.

On Tuesday afternoon at four, the Astrologer went to see Erdosain and tell him that on Wednesday of that week, at nine in the morning, the heads would get together in Temperley.

The Astrologer stayed to visit with Erdosain a few minutes, and as he was going back down the stairs, he got a shock when he checked his watch and told Erdosain:

"Hey—it's four, I have to go a lot of different places. I'll expect you tomorrow at nine. Ah! I've been thinking you're the one logical candidate for Head of Industry. Well, we'll talk tomorrow— Ah! don't forget to present . . . I mean, to draw up plans for hydraulic turbines, the kind for a mountain factory site, simple types. It would be for the training camp and electrometallurgy projects."

"How many kilowatts?"

"I don't know—that's your department. We'll have electric furnaces—anyway, you figure it. Besides, the Gold Seeker is here, tomorrow he'll give you more concrete details. Get set to hear something really big. Damn, it's so late . . . see you tomorrow," and settling his hat on his head, he hailed a cab and got in.

The next day, Erdosain, walking the sidewalks of

Temperley, was amazed to find he was finally feeling things might be all right.

He walked slowly. Walking under overbranching arches, he felt enclosed in a vast, oddly built structure. He took pleasure in the inlaid garden paths that sent their red streamers out to the meadowlands, green cloaks bespangled with violet, yellow, and red flowers. He looked up to find the sky full of great fluid depths and felt he was falling dizzily, for suddenly the sky was gone from before his eyes and there remained only a blackness like blindness, and then his thoughts focused on a furtive flutter of silvery atoms, which evaporated away into harsh, dry, terrible blue shades, arching high like caverns of methyl violet. And the joy the morning had given him, the fresh-made pleasure, unified the bits of his personality that his earlier crises and sorrows had pulled apart, and he felt his body all set to spring into any adventure.

"Augusto Remo Erdosain," as if by pronouncing his name he obtained a physical pleasure, paralleling the energy that brisk movement had given his members.

Through slanting streets and cones of falling light, he walked on, feeling the strength of his new-won personality: the Head of Industry. The freshness of the overgrown streets bestowed on him mental riches of every sort. And this fulfillment provided him with balance weight, like a dummy with lead-weighted feet. He thought he would sit through the meeting ironic and scornful, and he felt a wicked disdain for all weaklings on earth. The planet was only for the strong, it belonged to the strong. They would sweep it all clear and stand proudly before that quivering subrace with secretary's butt, armored in grandeur, like cruel and solitary emperors. He saw them in his mind's eye, in a vast room walled with glass and containing a round table. His four secretaries, carrying papers and with pens behind their ears, would come up and consult him, while the workers' delegates stood off in some corner, hats in hand, white old heads bowed low. And Erdosain, turning to them, told them simply: "Tomorrow you be back at work or we'll shoot you." That was it. He spoke few words, quietly, and his arm was exhausted from signing decrees. All that kept him going with the ruthlessness of the age that called for a tiger's savagery, a tiger who could make each dawn resound with gunshots bespeaking nothing good.

Now he strode right up to the Astrologer's house with his heart surging with enthusiasm, repeating the words of Lenin, which lilted a voluptuous refrain:

"What the hell kind of revolution is this if we don't shoot anyone?"

When he got to the house and opened the door part way, he saw the Astrologer coming to meet him, shrouded in a long gray smock and wearing a straw hat.

They shared a friendly, firm handshake as the Astrologer said:

"Barsut's being cool, you know? I don't think he'll give us much trouble about the check-signing. The others are here already, but first let's check on Barsut. Hell, they can wait! See what this means to me? With that money, the world is ours."

Now they were in the study and the Astrologer, twisting his ring with its violet gem and looking at the map of the United States, went on:

"We'll conquer the world, put our 'idea' in action. We can set up a brothel in San Martín or Ciudadela, and for the training camp, Los Santos in the mountains. Who's better for running the bordello than the Melancholy Ruffian? We'll name him Great Patriarch of Brothels."

Erdosain went over to the window. The roses gushed forth sharp, potent scent, filling everything brimful of red fragrance, cool as streamwater. Glassy-winged in-

sects swarmed amid the scarlet spangles on the pomegranate trees. Erdosain just stood there a few seconds.
The sight took him back to an afternoon just like this
with him in the very same spot. And yet, that night
he was in for a shock: Elsa's leaving him.

Endless varieties of green flooded his eyes, but he
did not see. In the depths of his being, her cheek against
the violet nipples of a square male chest, was his wife,
languid, soft-eyed, her lips parting to meet the other
man's obscene mouth.

A bird flew past his eyes, and Erdosain turned to the
Astrologer and said in the calmest voice he could muster:

"I mean, look, it's up to you, you know?" Then,
sitting down, he lit a cigarette and, eyes on his host,
who was using a compass to make a circle on the blue
map, he asked: "But what is your plan? Is it okay with
the Melancholy Ruffian to handle the brothels?"

"Sure, there's no problem there and Barsut won't
give us trouble."

"Is he still in the coach house?"

"I thought we should stash him away. I chained him
up in the stables."

"In the stables?"

"It's the only safe place to keep him. Besides, the
Man Who Saw the Midwife sleeps in a room over the
stables—"

"What?—"

"Sometime I'll tell you. He saw the midwife, now
he can't sleep nights. So, anyway, I thought you'd—"

"I'm the one who . . . ?"

"Let me finish. You see him and see if he won't sign
and, see, try to get across our ideas to him—"

"You're going to force him to sign—"

"Did I say that? Now, of course, I'm antiviolence,
but you know what I mean. Our plan shouldn't fail
over some sentimental squeamishness, you have to get

Barsut to see, well, how much we'd hate to resort to applying the hotfoot or even something worse . . . all over a check-signing."

"And you'd do it?"

"Sure, we'd do it because we can't blow this once-in-a-lifetime chance. I was counting on your copper-rose invention, but that's so long-term. We can't go asking the Melancholy Ruffian for money. If he doesn't have it, we put him on the spot, and if he does and won't give it to us, we lose a friend. Just because he was generous to you doesn't mean he'll be the same way with us. Besides, the guy's so messed up there's just no telling."

Erdosain gazed through the diamond-shaped windowpanes at the scarlet bursts spangled across the pomegranate treetops. A yellow swath of sunlight sliced the wall high up in the room. Massive sadness flooded his heart. What had he made of his life?

The Astrologer noticed his silence and said:

"Now, look here, Erdosain. We have no choice: it's either go in all the way or just give up. That's life, it's too bad . . . but what can we do? Don't you think I'd rather not have to make any sacrifices, too?"

"Only here it's another guy making the sacrifices—"

"And us, Erdosain, we're doing stuff that could send us to prison for who knows how long. You never read Plutarch's *Parallel Lives*?"

"No . . ."

"Then I'll give it to you so you can read it and see how human life is worth less than a dog's when you have to snuff out that life to get society headed a new way. You know how many murders it takes to bring in a Lenin or a Mussolini? People don't think of that. Why don't they? Because Lenin and Mussolini made it to the top. That's the crux, the thing that justifies any cause, just or unjust."

"And who's going to murder Barsut?"

"Bromberg, the guy who saw the midwife."

"You didn't tell me—"

"No point in it; it was all set."

A burst of fragrance flooded the room. The plunking of water into a full barrel stood out clearly.

"So far the people in on this are—"

"You, me, and Bromberg—"

"Too many to be in on a secret."

"No, because Bromberg's my slave, he's enslaved to himself, the worst kind of slavery."

"Fine, only you give me a signed document where you and Bromberg confess that you two committed the crime."

"And what do you want that for?"

"To be sure you're not trying to trap me."

The Astrologer straightened his hat automatically, held his Oriental face in his great thick fingers and walked to the middle of the room like that, with an elbow cupped in his other hand, and said:

"I can give you what you're asking for easy enough, only bear this in mind. I live only to carry out my plan. Extraordinary times are at hand. I can't tell you about all the amazing things that will happen because I have no time and don't care to go into it now. Beyond any doubt, new times are coming. Who will see them coming? The chosen few. The day I find a man who can replace me and my idea is set in motion, I will go away to meditate in the mountains. Meanwhile, all who stand by me owe me absolute obedience. You should grasp that if you don't want to end up like that guy out there—"

"Hey, what kind of talk is that?"

"The right kind, because I'll sign the statement you're asking for."

"I don't need it—"

"Will you need money?"

"Yes, some two thousand pesos to—"

"Don't tell me— You'll have them."

"Another thing: I want nothing to do with this brothel business—"

"Fine, you'll keep the books, but, you know what we need now? To hit upon some symbol blatant enough to have real mass appeal—"

"Lucifer."

"No, no, that's a mystic symbol . . . too intellectual . . . We need something gross, stupid . . . something that grabs hold of the masses like Mussolini's black shirts—that devil knows his stuff. He figured out the Italian mass mentality was right at the level of the barbershop and operetta star. . . . Anyway, let's see, I have a system mapped out . . . interesting stuff . . . some other day we'll talk about it . . . might turn out to be—"

"The thing is to be self-supporting."

"Forget it—the brothels will fund us—but are you going to see Barsut? Know what you're going to say?"

"Right . . ."

Erdosain headed for the coach house, where the stalls were. It was a big thick-walled structure with an upper story full of empty rooms with rats running about.

In one of these, the sinister Bromberg, whom Erdosain had seen the day of the kidnapping, lived, or rather, slept.

He grasped he was going deliberately under, not knowing what battered version of himself might re-emerge, and, grasping this as well as lacking the slightest enthusiasm for the Astrologer's plans, he felt he was staging an act, setting up an absurd situation just gratuitously. "I was all bankrupt inside," he was later to say; but fighting off his weariness and indifference, he walked out to the coach house. His heart beat hard at the thought of the "showdown" to come. He scowled fitfully and looked like an angry man.

He undid the padlock and chain, and, eager all of a sudden, he pushed back the door.

The prisoner was getting ready to eat, his bare arms showing in a circle of yellow light the kerosene lamp cast on the pine table.

Barsut sat under a metal feed chute, in a wooden horse stall, and when he saw the scowling Erdosain, he froze just a moment in the midst of sprinkling oil on his meat and potatoes; then he put his entire effort into the task at hand. Reaching out and grabbing a pinch of salt, he sprinkled his potatoes. He kept his dignity even though his black armpit was showing through a hole in his pink shirt.

Barsut kept his eyes on his meat to show he cared more about food than he did about Erdosain, who was just three steps off. The rest of the stable was sunk in darkness. The cracks in the walls let in slanting darts of light that made porous golden circles in the dust.

Barsut still wouldn't look up. He braced the bread against the table, vigorously cut himself a slice, poured some soda, fizzing some onto the floor first to clean the bottlemouth, and then bent over to read some old book beside his plate while chewing a mash of meat, bread, and potatoes.

Erdosain leaned on a pillar that held up the roof, feeling queasy from the dry-grass smell, and through half-closed lids could make out Barsut, whose face was half lit by the green light filtering in, while his jaws chomped away in the harsh light the lamp cast onto them. Just then he turned and caught sight of a whip hanging from the wall.

Erdosain reacted visibly to that whip. It had a long handle and short lash, and when Barsut checked to see what had caught Erdosain's eye, he silently sneered at it. Erdosain looked at the man, then the whip, and smiled again. He went to the corner and unhooked the whip. Now Barsut had got up and with his eyes turned full blaze on Erdosain, charged out of the stall. The veins in his neck were terrifically swollen. He would have said something, but pride made him hold it in. The whip cracked drily. Erdosain had whapped it against the wood of the stable to test its flexibility, then he shrugged and the sunbeam slanting through the darkness was streaked with black and the whip fell into the grass.

Erdosain paced around the stables in silence. He thought of that life, now in his hands, nobody could take that away from him, but the thought gave him no pleasure. Barsut was looking over the stall divider at the sunny countryside, through a gap in the door.

Things were no longer the same. And that was all there was to it. He looked angrily at Barsut:

"Are you going to sign the check or not?"

Barsut shrugged and Erdosain didn't ask again. Perhaps some day at that very hour he would sit in some dark cell and see again in memory a tennis court laid out in brick-red dust, beside a river, the rackets' woven mesh across the sky, girls at play. Unable to hold it in, he burst out, not so much to Barsut as to himself:

"Remember? For you, I had a loser's face. Shut up. You couldn't know how much I suffered. Not you, not her, either. Shut up. You think I want your lousy money? No way. It's just that I'm so miserable. You and her, you've dragged me down to this. What's the point in even talking. I only know I'm tired. But why bother talking." And he was all set to leave when the Astrologer came in. Barsut checked to see what was in his hands and the Astrologer, settling his hat, took the lamp, blew it out, and, sitting on a box, began:

"I came to see you to arrange this business of the check. You know that's why we kidnapped you. Of course, I wouldn't come to you like this, except in the notebook we found in your pocket and Erdosain tried to burn,* I read a truly stunning thought: 'Money makes a god of man. Thus Ford must be a god. If he's a god, he's able to destroy the moon.' "

None of this was true, but Barsut had no reaction.

Erdosain watched the impenetrable rhombus-shaped face of the Astrologer. The whole thing was clearly just a put-on that Barsut hadn't fallen for, sure the man was out to hoodwink him.

THE ASTROLOGER'S SPEECH

The Astrologer went on:

"At first, I dismissed this thought as just one more of your crackpot ravings. But then, I had to stop and ask myself why money makes man a god. And suddenly I realized you had hit on an essential truth. And you know how I figured you were right? Because I could see how Henry Ford with his millions could buy enough explosives to blow a planet like the moon to bits. So, your assertion was valid."

"Of course it was," said Barsut snootily, but inwardly flattered.

"Then I realized that of all of our ancients, of all our authors down the ages, nobody but you, who had written that truth without knowing its uses, nobody else grasped that men like Ford, Rockefeller, or Morgan could destroy the moon . . . they had so much power . . . power that, as I said, in myths they could only attribute to some god the creator. And your discovery has a great implication: the beginning of the rule of the superman."

Barsut turned his head to look at the Astrologer more

---

* Commentator's note: In the second part of this work we will quote a passage from Barsut's notebook.

closely. Erdosain realized the man was speaking in earnest.

"So see now, when I concluded that Morgan, Rockefeller, and Ford were some kind of gods because of the power they got from money, I realized social revolution was impossible on earth because a Rockefeller or Morgan could wipe out with one flick of the hand a whole race, like you'd wipe out an anthill in your yard."

"If, that is, you had the guts to."

"Guts? I had to wonder if a god has any choice but to use his powers. . . . I wondered if a copper king or oil baron could stand by and let them take his fleets, his mountains, gold, wells, and I saw that to give up that fabulous world he'd have to be as otherworldly as Christ or Buddha . . . and that the gods who wield all this massive power will never let go of it. So it follows that something really enormous would be needed."

"I don't see that at all. When I wrote that, I was thinking something totally different."

"So who cares! This is the great thing: Humanity, the multitudes roaming the great vast spaces, have lost all religion. I don't mean official Catholicism. I mean any theological creed. So then men will wonder: 'What good is our life to us?' No one can want to keep on with a robotlike existence after science has ruined all faith. And just when that starts to dawn on people, a terrible plague will be visited on earth . . . the new plague of mass suicide. . . . Can you picture a world full of furious people with dried-up minds, milling about in the subways of the giant cities, howling at the concrete walls: 'What have they done with our god?' And little girls and schoolgirls joining secret clubs set up for the new sport of suicide? And men refusing to have any more children even after a distinguished population expert says we'll feed them all with synthetic pills?"

"Now that's getting a bit carried away," said Erdosain.

The Astrologer turned around, startled. He had forgotten all about Erdosain.

"Well, sure it's not going to happen unless mankind figures out just why he's so wretched. That's what's always gone wrong with economically based revolutionary movements. Judaism let itself get stuck on Credit and Debit as if that were the whole world and said: 'Happiness is bankrupt because man has no money to buy the essentials . . .' when what they should have been saying was 'Happiness is bankrupt because mankind has no gods or faith.' "

"Now you're contradicting yourself! Before you said—" Erdosain objected.

"Shut up, what do you know? . . . And when I thought hard I came to the conclusion that this was man's terrible metaphysical sickness. The only way to shore up man's happiness is with metaphysical lies. . . . Take away those lies and he reverts to a lot of economic illusions . . . , then I remembered the only ones who could give man back his lost paradise were the flesh and blood gods: Morgan, Rockefeller, Ford—and I conceived a scheme some mediocre mind would think was just crazy—I saw the dead end where society ends up has just one way out . . . and that's to go backward."

Barsut, crossing his arms, had sat down on the edge of the table.

He kept his greenish eyes on the Astrologer, who, with his smock buttoned up to his chin and his hair all messed up, after taking off his hat, was pacing the length of the stable shoving aside with the point of one shoe the odd clumps of dry grass littering the floor. Erdosain, leaning back against a post, watched as Barsut's face took on an ever more wary and mocking look, almost nasty, as if the Astrologer's speech was something to sneer at. The speaker, as if listening to his own talk, would walk along a bit, stop short, and sometimes muss his hair. He said:

"Yes, there will come a day when mankind, grown skeptical and crazed with pleasure-seeking, cursing the gods in impotent frustration, will run amok and have to be shot like a rabid dog—"

"What are you saying? . . ."

"The human tree will be pruned . . . and only the millionaires, with science at their beck and call, can be the ones to prune it. The gods, sick of reality, no longer hoping science may bring happiness, will arm themselves with tiger slaves, unleash great wild disasters, set plagues upon the land. . . . For decades, the great task of the supermen and their slaves will be to destroy man in every way possible, till the world is bled all but dry . . . and only a handful of survivors will live on, alone on an island, the kernel to grow a whole new society."

Barsut had got up. With a nasty scowl and his fists thrust into his pockets he shrugged and asked:

"But do you take this crap you're talking seriously?"

"No, it's not just crap, because it's exactly what I would say to myself."

And he went on:

"A few losers believe what I say . . . that's enough. . . . But here's my idea: the new society will have two castes, with a gulf between them—that is, an intellectual difference of thirty centuries. The majority will be kept plunged in the darkest ignorance, in a world of trumped-up miracles, which are always more interesting than real miracles, and the minority will be the sole possessors of all knowledge and power. That way the happiness of the many is guaranteed, since the members of that caste will feel like part of a divine world, which today they don't believe in. The few will dole out pleasures and miracles for the masses, and the Golden Age, the days when angels wandered down the twilight paths and gods appeared in moonbeams, will exist on earth."

"But that's atrocious. That could never happen."

"How come? I know it could never happen, but we have to keep on as if it were workable."

"But with everything controlled by so few . . . all knowledge—"

"Ho, now it's knowledge! What good is scientific knowledge? Tell me that. You yourself make fun of researchers and call them 'masters of the totally useless fact.'"

"I see you've read my trash."

"Of course. You have to have something concrete to shove in people's faces. And the elite setup you're talking about in my scheme exists here and now in our society, only it's all backward. Our knowledge, by which I mean our metaphysical lies, is in diapers, but our scientific knowledge is a giant . . . and weak, pathetic mankind is the one who bears the brunt of this atrocious imbalance. . . . So here he's supposed to know everything, but in another way he knows nothing. In my scheme the big thing will be fine metaphysical lies, a god you can know and feel—and all this data about mere objects, which can't give us happiness, will be only a means to our goal: total control. And let's not argue that point, any idiot can see it's true. By now man has invented practically everything, only he hasn't found any form of government better than Christ's or the Buddha's teachings. No. Of course, I don't deny you're entitled to be skeptical, but that's a luxury only our elite can be entitled to. . . . For the rabble we'll serve up happiness à la carte and just see how they'll eat it up."

"You think any of that could happen?"

The Astrologer froze for a moment. Then he twisted the steel ring with the violet stone, took it off his finger and peered inside it; then, advancing on Barsut, but with a faraway look, as if his mind had left reality, he answered:

"Yes, anything the mind can picture can eventually

come true. Didn't Mussolini impose religious school-
ing in Italy? That's my idea of hitting people over the
head and then getting them in line. The thing is to grab
hold of a whole generation. . . . The rest is easy."

"And your grand scheme?"

"Now we get to it. My plan is to set up a secret
society, not just to spread my ideas but to train the
future kings of mankind. I know what you're going to
say, that there've been lots of secret societies—true
enough—they've all failed because they were based on
nothing solid, depended on some vague emotional or
religious or political ideas, never anything real and concrete. But our setup will be based on a more solid modern concept: industrialism, that is, our formula will be
one part fantasy, if that's what you'd call what I've
been talking about, and one part reality: industry, which
brings in gold."

His voice was raspy. His eyes blazed so fiercely they
seemed to have slipped out of focus. His great woolly
head jerked right and left, as if extraordinary feelings
were discharging in his brain, he put his hands behind
his back and went back to his pacing, repeating:

"Ah! gold . . . gold . . . you know what the early Ger-
mans called gold? Red gold. See? Shut up. Satan. But
just imagine, never before has a secret group tried to
fuse together such an amalgam. Money will bind it all
together, give the mixture enough weight and violence
to pull people into it. We'll appeal most to the young,
since they're dumber and more enthusiastic. We'll
promise them anything. See? We'll give them fancy
uniforms, spiffy tunics . . . helmets with rainbow
plumes . . . sparkling gemstones . . . an exotically named
set of ever-more-secret echelons, inner circles. . . . In
the mountains we'll have a cardboard temple—used
only as a movie set— No. After our triumph, we'll
build a temple with six golden doors. It will have pink

marble pillars and inlaid copper paths. And all around we'll have gardens . . . and mankind will flock there to worship the god we've invented."

"But the money . . . the money to do all that stuff . . . millions . . ."

While the Astrologer was speaking, Erdosain had been caught up in his enthusiasm. He had forgotten all about Barsut, even though he was standing right in front of him. He couldn't help imagining a great, fresh new world. Mankind would live in perpetual simple celebration, fireworks would spangle the night sky with showering red stars, an angel with pale green wings would skim the cloud crests, and under the leafy arches of the woods men and women would wander about in white tunics, their hearts free of all the vile slime that now coated his own. He closed his eyes, and Elsa's face went streaming by in his memory, but before it could strike a responsive chord the Astrologer's savage reply filled the stables:

"So you want to know where we'll get the money? No problem. We'll run brothels. The Melancholy Ruffian will be the Great Patriarch of Prostitution . . . every one of our group members will have a share in the deal. . . . We'll live off usury . . . off women, children, workers, the provinces, madmen. In the mountains—out in Campo Chileno—we'll set up gold processors, we'll extract ore with electricity. Erdosain has a five-hundred-horsepower turbine worked out. The nitric acid will come out of the nitrogen in the atmosphere, drawn out with a spinning voltaic arc, and we'll have iron, copper, and aluminum by electric processing. See? We'll lure the workers in with false promises and whip them to death if they won't work. Isn't that just what goes on now in the Gran Chaco, with the production system for tea, rubber, coffee, and tin? We'll fence our setup with electric wire and keep all the cops and bureaucrats in the South paid off. It's just a matter of getting started. The Gold Seeker's here already. He's been having a wild time, wandering around in the Campo Chileno with some prostitute they call The Mask. But we have to start somewhere. And to play god, we'll pick some adolescent. . . . Or better yet, handpick some especially beautiful child and raise him up to play the part of god. We'll let word get out . . . then it'll spread via the grapevine, only getting to be more and more mysterious till word-of-mouth blows him out of all proportion. Can you picture the reaction of those idiots in Buenos Aires once it gets around there's an inaccessible temple of gold and marble in the mountains of Chubut, with an adolescent god living there . . . a wondrous creature who works miracles?"

"You know your ravings are sort of interesting?"

"Ravings, huh? Didn't they swallow that hoax about the plesiosaur that was found by some drunken Englishman, the only guy in Neuquén Province the cops wouldn't let use a revolver because he had such lousy aim? . . . Didn't people in Buenos Aires believe in the supernatural powers of the Brazilian quack who miraculously cured Orfilia Rico of paralysis? That was a shabby trick, also totally lacking in imagination, all those idiots blubbering away when that quack held up his patient's arm, and her as paralyzed as ever, which goes to show that for people today and always there's this urgent need to believe in something. Making use of some newspaper, believe me, we'll work wonders. There are several newspapers dying for some sensational stuff to cash in on. And we'll give them all this miraculous god to feed their craving for marvels, embellishing it a bit with stories we can get out of the Bible—I have it; we'll proclaim the boy the Messiah prophesied by the Jews. . . . That needs some working out. . . . We'll take pictures of the Jungle God. We can make a movie showing the cardboard temple in the depths of the forest and the god conversing with the Spirit of the Land."

"Are you up to something or just plain crazy?"

Erdosain looked at Barsut angrily. How could he be so idiotic, so unable to see the beauty of everything the Astrologer had devised? And he thought, "That animal, he's just jealous of the man's magnificent madness, that's the truth. Nothing for it but to kill him."

"I'm up to something and crazy both, and we'll cook up something halfway between Krishnamurti and Rudolph Valentino . . . only more mystic, a child with a strange face symbolic of the world's suffering. Our movies will show him in slum neighborhoods, the real hellholes. Can you imagine what it's going to be like when the masses get a look at our pale god reviving the dead, an archangel like Gabriel supervising gold processing, and terrifically dolled-up prostitutes waiting to marry the first poor wretch who goes out there? We'll be flocked with people applying to go staff the city of the King of the World and enjoy the fruits of free love. . . . Out of those losers we'll take the least educated—then really beat the hell out of them, work them twenty hours a day panning gold."

"I thought you were pro-labor."

"When I talk to a laborer, I'm a socialist. Now I'll tell you something: my organization is based on one started up at the beginning of the ninth century by a Persian bandit named Abdala-Aben-Maimun. Naturally, without the industrial part I have in mind, the part that will make it work. Maimun attempted a coalition of freethinkers, aristocrats, and believers from two races as different as the Persians and the Arabs with a whole elaborate setup of secret initiate rites and mysteries. They lied to people right and left. They promised the Jews the Messiah's arrival, the Christians the Paraclete, the Moslems the Madhi . . . so a bunch of people with totally dissimilar opinions, social backgrounds, and beliefs were all working for this big scheme but very few knew what the point of it was. That was how Maimun was going to win total control over the Moslem world. I should tell you the movement's leaders were complete cynics, they didn't believe in anything. We'll follow their scheme. We'll be Bolsheviks, Catholics, Fascists, atheists, militarists, depending on where you are in the echelons."

"You're the most shameless huckster I've ever seen. . . . It'd be funny if you brought it off."

Barsut took special joy in insulting the Astrologer. It was mostly because he hated to admit he was outclassed. Besides there was something that really rankled, it sounds odd, but he was furious thinking Erdosain should get to be so close a friend of such a man. And he was fuming: "How come this idiot gets to be friends with a man like that?" And that was the reason he felt so sure that everything the Astrologer said could be proven wrong.

"We *will* bring it off, with gold as the lure. The proof our scheme is really working will be there in black ink on the bottom line. Those brothels will rake it in for us. Erdosain has come up with a device to standardize the number of men a woman gets per day. Then also there's input from donations and a new industry we're going to launch: the copper rose, Erdosain's invention. Now maybe you see why we kidnapped you."

"What good does that do me if I'm still your prisoner?"

Just then, Erdosain thought how odd it was that Barsut had never once threatened to get back at the Astrologer once he was free, which made him say to himself: "You really have to watch it around that rat, he might blow the whistle on us, not for money, just for spite."

The Astrologer went on:

"With your money we could start a brothel, get our little band together and buy the metal and telegraph hookup and other things to process gold with."

"Have you thought you could be wrong?"

"Sure . . . I've thought that, only I just keep on as if I were dead right. Anyway, a secret organization is like a boiler. It gets up enough steam to run a big crane—"

"And what do you want to run?"

"Get some life running in those inert bodies. We happy few want, really, need, the greatest powers on earth. So we're justified in using any means to keep the weak cringing and the strong going strong. And for that, we need to build up our strength, get people's minds turned around, sell them on barbarism. The thing that gives us this mysterious energy, enough to keep the whole thing in motion, is our organization. We'll bring back the Inquisition, burn people at the stake in the square if they won't believe in God. It's necessary, believe me, it's totally necessary for a great, awesome religion to rekindle mankind's heart. To have people falling to their knees as a saint goes by, for the most insignificant priest's prayer to ignite wonders in the evening sky. Ah, if you knew how I've got it thought out! And how I keep going is by seeing how out of whack civilization and the twentieth century have got people. All those crackpots with no place to fit into society are so much waste energy. Go to the tackiest corner café, pick out two numbskulls and a cynic, and I'll show you three geniuses. Those geniuses don't work, don't do anything—I admit that so far they're only geniuses on paper. But there, on paper, is the energy that could be tapped to power a new and dynamic movement. And that's the energy source I want to plug into."

"Director of Madman Energy—"

"But that's it exactly. I want to harness the madman

power, those numberless crackpot geniuses, the un-
settled types who get thrown out of séances and communist party cells. . . . Those idiots—and I have firsthand
experience to talk from—if carefully bamboozled and
hyped-up, can carry out schemes that would stand your
hair on end. Drugstore poets. Neighborhood inventors,
the local prophet, street-corner politicians, and the phi-
losopher down the street, those will be the cannon
fodder for our setup.''

Erdosain smiled. Then, not looking at the man in
chains, he said:

"You don't know how when you get to the fringes
of genius you find the most boundless insolence—''

"Right, not unless you understand those fringes, eh,
Barsut?''

"I don't care about any of that rot.''

"Well, you should, since you'll be in this with us.
This is how I feel about it. If you tell somebody on that
outer fringe that he's no genius, you have all that insolence and raw energy turned against you for not ap-
preciating the guy. But if you carefully praise one of
those incredibly conceited weirdos, then this same guy
who might have killed you for the smallest put-down
is at your beck and call. The secret is in knowing just
how many lies to feed them. If there's enough, you can
have an inventor or poet for your slave.''

"And you think you're a genius, too?'' Barsut burst
out angrily.

"Yeah, I think I'm a genius. . . . Of course I think
so—only for five minutes each day and that's it—after
that I don't much care if I'm one or not. Those labels
don't mean much if you're the guy who can make people's dreams come true. It's just out on the fringes of
genius that empty words are so important. I've been
working it out, and not because I'm worried whether
I'm a genius or not. Can man be made happy? And so

I start by going to those losers, giving them something to focus in on, a lie to make them happy by shoring up their egos . . . and those pathetic weirdos, who by themselves would never have gotten anyone to appreciate them, will blossom into valuable resources, will be our power source . . . our steam power."

"You do go on. I asked you one specific question, what you yourself want to get out of setting the whole scheme up."

"Well, that's a pretty stupid question. What did Einstein go and invent his theory for? The world could get by without Einstein's theory. Do I happen to know if I'm a tool of higher forces, in which I don't even believe? Don't ask me. The world is a mysterious place. Maybe I'm only the servant, the hireling who's setting up a beautiful house where the Saint, the Chosen One, will come to die."

Barsut smiled imperceptibly. There the man was, talking rot about the Chosen One, with his cauliflower ear, mad shock of hair, and carpenter's smock, and the total impression was one of irony and something ungraspable. How much of it was that weasel faking? And what was funny was that he couldn't be mad at him, something about the guy had taken hold of him, even though he had nothing new to say and just seemed to keep saying the same things and in the same tone of voice he had heard before, sometime long ago, somewhere off in the gray landscape of a dream.

The Astrologer's tone grew less commanding.

"Believe me, that's the way it is in times when people feel restless and uprooted. A few people get a feeling like something big is coming. Those who have their nose in the wind, and I'm one of those waiters and watchers, think it's up to them to start stirring society up . . . to do something even if it turns out to be nonsense. So, as it turns out, my something is the secret conspiracy. I mean, God! Does any man know in advance how what he does will turn out? When I think how I'm setting a world of puppets in motion . . . and how there'll be more and more puppets, I shudder to think, I even wonder if maybe the whole thing is as totally out of my control as some electrician who suddenly runs amok in a factory is to the plant owner. And even so, I have a compulsion to set the works in motion, to harness all that waste energy dissipating away inside a hundred heads, to get it all coordinated together by buttering up people's vanity, ego, longings, dreams, with lies for my basis and gold for reality . . . red gold—"

"You're on the right track . . . you're bound for glory."

"Yeah, now, what do you want out of me?"

"Like I said. Sign over a check for seventeen thousand pesos. You'll have three thousand left over. Take it and go to hell, for all we care. The rest we will pay back in monthly installments out of what the brothels and goldworks bring in."

"And do I get out of here?"

"Soon as we cash the check."

"How do I know you're being straight with me?"

"Some things you just take on faith. . . . Only if it's proof you want, let me tell you this: if you won't sign the check, I'll have you tortured by the Man Who Saw the Midwife and when you do sign, I'll kill you. . . ."

Barsut raised his dull, gray eyes, and now his face, three days unshaven, looked out through a coppery mist. Kill him! It had no impact. Right then it meant nothing to him. Life meant so little to him, anyway. . . . He had long been expecting some disaster; here it was, and instead of the icy fingers of terror, he felt full of a vast, burned-out numbness that didn't much care anymore whatever might happen to him. The Astrologer went on:

"But I don't want to have to do that. . . . What I'd like is to ask for your personal help—have you get involved in our projects. Believe me, we're living through terrible times. Anyone who can find the great lie the herd needs will be King of the World. Men live lives of anxiety. . . . Catholicism doesn't work for anybody anymore. . . . Buddhism's no good for people like us who believe in satisfying our desires. . . . Maybe we'll tell them stuff about Lucifer and the Morning and Evening Star. You can supply the poetry we need to get into our dreams, and we'll appeal to the young— Oh! This is going to be very big . . . very big indeed. . . ."

The Astrologer dropped wearily onto a box. He was exhausted. He wiped his sweaty forehead with a worker's checked hankie, and all three sat silently for a moment.

Suddenly, Barsut said:

"Yes, you're right, it is big. Let me go and I'll sign your check."

He had thought that everything the Astrologer told him was a lie, and that had almost proved his undoing.

The Astrologer got up, still wary.

"Sorry, I'll let you go after we cash the check. This is Wednesday. Tomorrow at noon you can get the run of the house, but you can't leave the grounds for two months still." He put that part in because he could see the man still didn't believe in his projects. "You won't need anything this afternoon?"

"No."

"Okay then, be seeing you."

"But are you leaving? Stay here—"

"No, I'm tired. I need some sleep. Tonight I'll come back and we can talk a little more. You want some cigarettes?"

"Yeah, good."

They left the stables.

Barsut lay back on his bed of dry grass and, lighting up, blew some smoke puffs that went swooping in curlicues through a slanting sunbeam, splendid steel blue spirals. Now he was alone, his thoughts got sorted out, and he even told himself:

"Why not help the guy? His scheme to set up a training camp sounds interesting, and now I can see why that jerk Erdosain thinks so much of him. Maybe I'm coming out of this a loser . . . maybe I'm doing myself a favor . . . but things end up one way or another." And he half closed his eyes to reflect on the future.

The Astrologer, with his hat pulled over his eyes, turned to Erdosain and said:

"Barsut thinks he's got us fooled. Tomorrow, after we cash the check, we'll have to execute him—"

"You mean you'll have to execute him—"

"Okay by me . . . only what do we do with him? If he gets free he'll turn us in first thing. And he thinks we're crazy! Well, we would be to let him live."

They stood beside the house. Jagged, chocolate brown clouds scudded quickly across the sky above them.

"So who'll murder him?"

"The Man Who Saw the Midwife."

"You know, it's rough to die with summer just coming in. . . ."

"Well, that's how it goes . . ."

"And the check?"

"You cash it."

"You don't worry I'll cut out on you?"

"Not for the moment, no."

"How come?"

"Because I don't. You're the one who needs the society to get going because you don't know what to do with yourself. That's how come you're in it with me . . . not knowing what to do with yourself, being out of whack."

"Maybe so. What time do we meet tomorrow?"

"Um . . . nine at the station. I bring you the check
and say, Do you have the right identification?"

"Yes."

"Nothing to worry about, then. Ah! One thing. I
suggest you don't say much in the meeting, be cool,
even cold."

"They're all coming?"

"Yes."

"The Gold Seeker, too?"

"Yes."

Shoving back the twigs that whipped into their faces,
they walked out to the summerhouse. It was a round
structure with diamond-latticed wood where a honeysuckle twined its green stems and masses of white and
purple blossoms.

THE FARCE

The entire round table got to its feet when they
came in, but Erdosain stopped short in surprise
when he saw one of its members was an army officer
in a major's uniform.

The Gold Seeker, Haffner, some stranger, and the
Major were there. The first two sat with their elbows
on the table. Haffner was going over some papers and
the Gold Seeker was studying a map. A stone paperweight held down the map. The Ruffian shook hands
with Erdosain and they sat together, Erdosain eyeing
the Major, terribly curious as to what he was doing
there. Really the Astrologer was a master of surprise
moves.

Still, the stranger didn't much appeal to him.

He was quite a tall fellow, pale, with eyes black as
coal. There was something repellent about him, and it
was his lower lip, curled in a perpetual sneer, together
with his long hook nose with three furrows right at the

bridge. A silky mustache brushed his rosy lips and he scarcely deigned to look at Erdosain, and as soon as they were introduced he flopped into a hammock, where he lay back against the headrest, with his sword between his legs and one lock of hair clinging to his flat forehead.

And for a few minutes they all sat there silently, eyeing one another uneasily. The Astrologer, sitting by the summerhouse entrance, lit a cigarette without taking his eyes off the "heads." That was what they were called at a later meeting. Suddenly, he looked right at the other five men around the table and said:

"I see no point in us going over what we all know and have agreed on in private . . . , that is, to start a secret organization funded by business schemes, moral or immoral. We're all set on that, right? How do you men feel (I have a fondness for geometry) about the term 'cells' for the subunits of our setup?"

"That's what they call them in Russia," said the Major. "People in one cell never meet the members of another."

"What—won't the heads know each other?"

"No, no, the people who never meet are the rank and file, not the heads."

The Gold Seeker cut in:

"That way nothing will get done. What ties the members of different cells together?"

"But we six are the real organization."

"No, sir . . . I am the real organization," objected the Astrologer. "But, seriously, we're all the organization . . . except for certain areas because of my position."

The Major cut in:

"I think this is a moot point, since, from what I've been given to understand, there'll be a standardized hierarchy. At each promotion, the cell member will come under a new head. There'll be as many promotions possible as there are heads of cells."

"So how many cells are there right now?"

"Four. I'll be in charge of everything," the Astrologer went on. "You, Erdosain, Head of Industry; the Gold Seeker"—a young man at the corner of the table nodded—"you'll run Training Camps and Mines; the Major will work on infiltrating the army, and Haffner will be Head of Brothels."

Haffner got up and burst out:

"Just a minute, I'll be head of nothing. For me, this is just another business deal. All I'm doing for you is setting up a cost analysis, and that's it, period. If my being here bothers you, I'll go."

"No, stay," the Astrologer urged him.

The Melancholy Ruffian sat down again and went back to scribbling on his papers. Erdosain admired his open rudeness.

But, beyond a doubt, the focus of attention and curiosity was the Major; his uniform was so impressive and his being there so very odd.

The Gold Seeker turned to him:

"How's that? You think you can infiltrate our setup into the army?"

Everyone sat bolt upright in his chair. That was the big surprise of the meeting, the thing the Astrologer had been waiting to spring on them. Undeniably, the man was a born leader. The bad part of it was that he always played his cards so close to his chest. But Erdosain felt flattered to be in on things with him. Now they were all sitting up in their seats to listen to the Major. The Major looked carefully at the Astrologer, then said:

"Gentlemen, I speak to you of weighty matters. If they were not grave, I would never have come among you. Here is what is happening: our army is seething with dissatisfied officers. No point in my giving you the whole how and why of it, which wouldn't interest you, anyway. The notion of 'absolute rule' and recent military actions, I refer to Chile and Spain, have got many of my fellow officers wondering if this country might not be ripe for dictatorship, too."

They sat gaping in astonishment. This was a real surprise.

The Gold Seeker replied:

"But do you think the Argentine army . . . I mean . . . the officer corps, will accept our ideas?"

"They most certainly will . . . so long as you can show them an organized program. I can tell you right now there are more officers than you think fed up with democratic theories, including legislative representation. Don't interrupt, sir. Ninety percent of this country's elected officials are less educated than a first lieutenant in our army. A politician accused of having a hand in a governor's murder put it very aptly: 'Running the country is no big deal—no trickier than running a big ranch.' He hit it on the head, as far as this continent's concerned."

The Astrologer wrung his hands in visible delight.

The Major went on, the focus of all eyes:

"The Army represents an elite grouping within an inferior society, since we're the country's real strength. And yet, we're at the beck and call of the government . . . and who's the government? . . . the legislative and executive branches—that is, men chosen by some half-baked political party—and look at the people they pick! You know as well as I that to land a seat you have to go the whole route of double-dealings, starting out as a ward politico, smoke-filled rooms, wheeling and dealing with shady characters, trade-offs, buy-offs, till your whole life is nothing but lawlessness and lying. I don't know if it's that way in countries more civilized than ours, but it's sure that way here.

In our two houses of congress we have accused loan sharks and murderers, people on the take from foreign companies, and people so grossly ignorant that legislative representation here is the biggest farce that could possibly disgrace a nation. The whole presidential race is funded by American corporations in return for promises to make it easy for them to come in and exploit our national resources. I'm not overstating it when I say that what party politics in our country really boils down to is a contest to see who can sell out the country and get the best price for it."*

They all sat there gaping at the Major. Through the diamond latticework and blossoms the clear morning sky was showing, but nobody bothered to look at it. Erdosain told me later that none of them had come there that Wednesday expecting anything half so interesting to happen. The major wiped his mouth with a handkerchief and went on:

"I'm glad to see you take an interest in this. There are many young officers who share my views. Even some of the younger generals would back us up. . . . The best plan, and don't be shocked at what I'm telling you here, is to make it look like a totally Communist plot. The thing of it is, there's no real Communism here, unless you want to count some bunch of sorehead carpenters who sit around pseudosociologizing and being rude on principle. I want to make my meaning very clear. Every secret plot is a cancer on the host society. Its hidden workings disrupt the whole system. So now, as the people who run the cells, we'll make sure they look like a Bolshevik scheme." It was the first time anyone had used that word there, and everyone had to check out the others' reactions to it.

---

* Author's note: This novel was written in 1928–29 and published by Rosso in October 1929. It would be ridiculous to suppose that the Major's remarks were based on the revolutionary movement of September 6, 1930. Undeniably, there is

"That façade will make it attractive to crackpots and that will swell the ranks. So then we'll have a fictitious revolutionary organization. In particular, we'll stage terrorist attacks. A halfway successful attack can stir up echos in all the dark, twisted minds out there. If we stage a fresh series of attacks a year later, this time with antisocial calls to action, leaflets urging workers to set up 'soviets.' . . . You know what we'll have accomplished? Something very clever and utterly simple. We'll have the country all roiled up in a prerevolutionary state.

"When I say 'a prerevolutionary state' I mean a widespread kind of agitation that isn't yet really out in the open, everybody feels the change, they're all worked up, newspapers keep things stirred up, and the cops do their bit by arresting innocent people and giving them such a hard time they come out of it as revolutionaries; people wake up in the morning eager for some fresh outbreak of violence, hoping it'll be worse than the last and not let them down; people will get all worked up over police brutality to somebody else, some hothead is sure to run out and shoot a policeman, then labor gets all lathered up, calling strikes right and left, and all this loose talk of revolution and Bolsheviks keeps everyone wild with fear and hope. So then after all these bombs go off all over the city and people have read all these wild leaflets and the prerevolutionary state is just right, that's when we step in, the military. . . ."

The Major moved his boots out of the sunlight and went on:

"Right, the military steps in. We'll say that, given the government's inability to defend the Nation, Free Enterprise, and the Family, we're taking over the reins

---

a startling degree of likeness between the declarations of the September 6 group and the Major's, and both bear similar fruit, as shown by the events following the September coup.

and declaring a temporary dictatorship. All dictatorships are temporary, it has a reassuring sound to it.
Bourgeois capitalists and, especially, conservative foreign governments, will immediately salute the new
state of things. We'll say it's all the fault of the Soviets
that we have to crack down and shoot a few poor slobs
who've confessed and been found guilty of bomb making. We'll disband the legislature and make big cut-
backs in the nation's budget. The running of the state
will be placed in the hands of the military. The nation will be on its way to unprecedented heights of
glory."

The Major concluded there, and in the flower-laden
summerhouse the men broke into applause. It startled
a pigeon into flight.

"Your concept is splendid," said Erdosain, "but it
has it so we'll all be working for you people—"

"But didn't you want to be in power?"

"Well, yes, only we'll be getting the crumbs from
your banquet—"

"No, sir . . . you haven't grasped . . . the thing is—"

The Astrologer cut in:

"Gentlemen . . . we haven't come here to argue over
matters we haven't even come to yet—we have to get
the activities of the cell leaders mapped out. So, if you're
ready, let's get to it."

A sturdy young fellow who had been silent all this
time joined in the discussion.

"May I say something?"

"Go ahead."

"Well to me we have just one big question: do you
or don't you want a revolution? The organizational
details should come later."

"Right . . . right, later on . . . yes, sir."

The stranger went on to explain:

"I'm Mr. Haffner's friend. I'm a lawyer. Because of
my opposition to the capitalist system, I've chosen not

to practice my profession for personal profit. Am I or am I not entitled to speak my mind?"

"Yes, sir, go right ahead."

"Well then I'd like to point out that what the Major proposes would turn our organization into something completely different."

"No," objected the Gold Seeker. "We can use his plan as a starting point without sacrificing our principles."

"Of course."

"Right."

It was about to break out all over again. The Astrologer got up:

"Gentlemen, we'll leave this for later. Now we need to get the business end of it worked out—not the ideas. So let's table all other business for now."

"That's dictatorship," the lawyer burst out.

The Astrologer looked at him a moment, then said parsimoniously:

"You think you're a born leader, I see . . . I think you're right. If you're smart, then, you'll go off and start your own conspiracy someplace else. It'll be another blow against the status quo. Here you do as I say or leave."

The two eyed each other an instant; the lawyer got up, looked hard at the Astrologer, bowed, and smiled like a strong-willed man, and left.

The Major was the first to break the silence:

"You handled that very well. Discipline is everything here. We'll hear you out."

Diamond patches of sunlight created a golden mosaic on the black earthen floor. The anvil of some far-off blacksmith clanged away, innumerable songbirds filled their throats with music in the branches. Erdosain sucked on a white honeysuckle blossom and the Gold Seeker, elbows on his knees, gazed keenly at the floor.

The Ruffian was smoking and Erdosain observing the Astrologer's Asian face, which surmounted a gray smock buttoned up to the chin.

An uncomfortable silence followed these words. What did this new fellow want? Erdosain, suddenly angry, got up, exclaiming:

"You can have as much discipline here as you feel like, but all this talk about military dictatorship is absurd, for us. All we care about is if the military can go Red."

The Major sat up in his seat and, looking at Erdosain, said with a smile:

"So I'm convincing in my role, then?"

"In your role?"

"Right—I'm no more a major than you are."

"Now you see how powerful a lie can be?" said the Astrologer. "I dressed up this friend of mine as an officer and here you thought, even though you were practically in on the secret, that we had a revolution underway within the ranks."*

"So?"

"This was just a dress rehearsal . . . since some day we'll stage the real farce."

It sounded so threatening that the four men sat eyeing the Major, who said:

"Really I've never made anything above sergeant," but the Astrologer cut in on his explanations:

"Let's see if our friend Haffner can give us the projected costs."

"Right . . . here they are."

The Astrologer spent a few minutes leafing through the much-revised pages of numbers and explained to the gathering:

---

* Commentator's note: Later it turned out that the Major was no fictitious officer, but the real thing, and that he lied when he said he was playing a part.

"The most solid basis for financing our organization is the chain of brothels."

The Astrologer went on:

"This gentleman has analyzed for me the costs involved in setting up a ten-girl bordello. Here are the projected figures":

And he read:

10 bedroom suites, used	$2,000
Monthly rent on house	400
Three months' deposit	1,200
Additional bathrooms, bar & grill	2,000
Payoff to police chief	300
Payoff to doctor	150
Payoff to local ward boss	2,000
City tax per month	50
Electric piano	1,500
Madam	150
Cook	150
TOTAL	9,900

"Each girl puts up fourteen pesos a week for board and has to buy her tea, sugar, kerosene, candles, stockings, makeup, soap, and perfume from the house supply."

"Total net proceeds should be two thousand five hundred pesos a month minimum. In four months we get our initial investment back. Then fifty percent of that total net proceeds will be plowed back into setting up brothels, twenty-five percent will be to cover debts, the third part to fund the cells. So do I have the go-ahead on ten thousand as an initial outlay?"

Everyone nodded assent except the Gold Seeker, who said:

"Who's the auditor?"

"After it's done we'll choose one."

"Okay."

"Okay with you, too, Major?"

"Yes."

Erdosain looked up and eyed the pseudo-sergeant's pale face, its keen eyes watching a white butterfly flutter amid the leaves, and he couldn't help but wonder how the Astrologer got people to act out all these schemes of his. But the Astrologer cut in by asking:

"You, Mr. Erdosain, how much do you need to set up your galvanoplastics works?"

"A thousand pesos."

"Ah! You're the inventor of the copper rose?" asked the Major.

"Yes."

"My congratulations. I think it will really sell. Of course, you need to metallize the flowers on a large-scale basis."

"Right. I thought of doing that along with our photography lab. That way it would be twice as cheap."

"You know best about that."

"Besides that, I have a practical friend lined up to do the galvanoplastics," he said, thinking of the Espila family, who could fit into the organization, but the Astrologer broke in on his thoughts, saying:

"Now the Gold Seeker will fill us in on the proposed location of our training camp," and the man got up.

Erdosain could hardly believe it when he saw what the man looked like. He had imagined the movie stereotype of a towering fellow with a great bushy beard smelling of strong drink. But what he saw was a far cry from that image.

The Gold Seeker was young, just about his age, his skin stretched taut over flat facial bones, very pale, with lively jet black eyes. His huge barrel chest looked like it should have been on some big burly fellow twice his size. His legs were spindly and bowed. Between his belt and pants a revolver butt was showing. His voice was ordinary, but he seemed like someone from a strange continent, cobbled together out of bits and pieces of different types of men. His face was from a shifty-eyed cardsharp, his chest was from a boxer, and his legs were from a jockey. And he really was a bizarre mixture; he just gave off an unfocused, alien aura. He had lived in the country till he was fourteen, then he shot a rustler dead, and later, fear of tuberculosis exiled him once more to the open plains, and he galloped for days and nights across unbelievable distances. Erdosain felt an immediate kinship.

The Gold Seeker took some rocks out of their wrappings. They were chunks of gold ore. Then he said:

"Here you have a certified analysis from the Mining and Hydrology Department."

The chunks passed quickly from hand to hand. A greedy gleam lit up the men's eyes and their fingers drank in the feel of quartz veined and speckled with gold. The Astrologer, slowly rolling a cigarette, could see on every face a soul-deep impact—the stones were triggering a spasm of temptation all around. The Gold Seeker sat down and said to them all:

"There's a lot of gold down there. Nobody knows about it. It's in Campo Chileno. I went down to Esquel first—all this mining equipment lying around from an old operation that went bust, then I got to Arroyo Pescado . . . I kept going . . . there, I don't know if you understand how it is, whole days count for nothing there, and I entered Campo Chileno. Jungle, sheer rainforest stretching over square kilometers. The Mask was my companion there, a prostitute from Esquel who wanted to go there because she'd been out that way before with a miner who got murdered when he got back. Down there they'll kill you over the least thing. So she had syphilis and stayed out in the jungle. The Mask. I'll never forget her! Twenty years she'd spent wandering those wild parts. From Puerto Madryn she'd go to Comodoro, then Trelew, then Esquel: She knew all the prospectors. First we went to Arroyo Pescado—that's forty leagues south of Esquel—but there was only a little sprinkling of gold dust in the sand . . . we went on for two weeks and came through the mountains to Campo Chileno."

In a clear voice, eager to make his point, the Gold Seeker told of his southern odyssey. Erdosain, as he listened, felt that he, too, was making his way through great, overlooming, icy black mountains, accompanied by The Mask, only to find they were trapped behind more triangular, purple mountains. Whole plateaus lay buried under an avalanche of forest, reddish trunks, dark green foliage, and so, abandoning all sense of reality, they plunged on under the endless, soaring sky, unfurled like a stretch of tundra across the heavens.

Very carefully, indifferent to the amazement his story had triggered among his listeners, the Gold Seeker told of his months-long adventure. They sat listening, rapt.

Then, one morning, he entered the tortuous crack that snaked through those looming mountains. On every side it was hemmed in by towering, jagged, basalt cliffs, and stalagmites rose in dark, uneven forms, while the blue sky above was tinged with infinite sadness. Stray birds flew against the great stone masses, which lay in the shadow of higher, encircling mountains. And at the lowest depths lay a lake of golden water, fed by little streamlets that trickled down from the heights.

The Gold Seeker never had known such a sinister wasteland. He stopped short when he saw that bronze-colored water mirroring tall black cliffs. The stone walls fell perpendicular there, veined with a greenish sarcoma, long streaks of malachite, and in those golden depths his pale, thick-bearded face was mirrored with its eyes turned up to the heavens.

All at once it hit him that the water held true gold,

but he rejected the thought as absurd, because he'd never read or heard of anything like that, and then, he continued:

"But when I got back, one day I was in a dentist's waiting room in Rawson, I just picked up a magazine called *Medical Weekly* which was on one of the tables and started leafing through . . . and then, lightning struck. I just opened it up at random and the first thing I see is an article entitled: "Gold Water, or Colloidal Water in the Treatment of Lupus Erythematosus." I started reading it and then I found out that gold can be suspended in water in microscopic particles—this thing which was completely new to me had been discovered by the alchemists who called it "gold water." They got it by the most simple process you could imagine: throwing a glowing-hot chunk of gold into rain water. Right away I thought of that lake which before I had thought must be full of gold-colored organisms. Without realizing it, I had been right beside a lake full of colloidal gold that might have taken centuries to accumulate as water trickled down over those cliffs veined with ore. You see now what comes of ignorance? If fate hadn't put that journal in my hands, I'd never have known about that important discovery—"

"And did you go back?" the Major cut in.

"Of course. I went back eight months ago, that was when I wrote you—but I was going about it all wrong—I have to know more about extracting the gold. Besides there are solid seams of it, too . . . it needs working on still . . . send down a guy in a diver suit, because the gold is all at the bottom and the water itself is colorless."

Haffner said:

"You know all this business is interesting? Even if there's no gold, it's still got this crappy city beat."

The Major added:

"If we set up a training camp in Campo Chileno, we'll need a telegraph hookup."

Erdosain answered:

"In that case, we could put a portable station up with a wavelength of forty-five to eighty meters. It would cost five hundred pesos and have a range of three thousand kilometers."

"I think the training camp should get high priority because we could set up the poison-gas factory there. You know something about that, Erdosain."

"Right, we can make Aristol by electrolysis, which is something I need to look into, though poison gas and germ warfare should be top priority with us. Especially the lab for bubonic plague and cholera culture. We have to get hold of a typical strain of each, since we can save a lot by growing our own cultures."

The Astrologer cut in:

"I think we'd best leave the organization of the training camp for later. Right now let's just stick to setting up Haffner's scheme. We have to have those funds coming in before we assemble the first recruits to send out there. You were saying something to me about a family, Erdosain?"

"Right; the Espilas."

Haffner burst out:

"What's all this crap! I think this whole thing is sounding like some kind of a joke. If it's true I'm only to be a consultant to your society, then I think it's high time you guys figured out what you're doing."

The Astrologer looked at him and replied:

"Are you willing to put up the money to get us going? No. So? Wait till we get up some money, which we will in a few days, and then you'll see some action."

Haffner got up and, looking at the Gold Seeker, said:

"All right, pal; when the camp is all set to go, let me know; if you need guys to run it, just let me know and I'll send you all kinds of guys who've been finding Buenos Aires a little, shall we say, too hot for comfort," and, putting on his hat, he was going to leave with no more of a good-bye than a vague general wave, when, remembering something, he exclaimed to the Astrologer:

"If you can get up some money fast, there's a terrific cathouse up for grabs. First-rate facilities, bar and grill, a big nightly turnover. The owner's an Uruguayan and he's asking fifteen thousand pesos cash up front, but I think he'll come down to ten thousand now and the other five in a year."

"Can you come here Friday?"

"Sure."

"Okay, check with me Friday, I think we can swing it."

"Cheers." With that, the Ruffian left.

THE GOLD SEEKER

After Haffner left, Erdosain, who had been eager to talk with the Gold Seeker, said good-bye to the Astrologer and the Major. Erdosain was getting uneasy again. Before he left, the Astrologer took him aside to say:

"Be sure to come at nine tomorrow, the check must be cashed."

"That" had slipped his mind. Erdosain looked all around as though he had been stunned, hit hard. He had to talk to someone; to forget the part he had to play, which loomed up blackly and made his heart pound in the blazing noonday sun.

The Gold Seeker had somehow struck a responsive chord in him. So he went up to him and said:

"Can we talk a bit? I want to talk with you about those places down South."

The man checked him over with glittery eyes and said:

"Sure. Fine. I've been impressed with you."

"Thank you."

"Especially from what the Astrologer told me about you. You know, your plan to use plague bacilli for the revolution is really fine?"

Erdosain looked up. It almost shamed him to be praised so much. Could someone possibly be all that taken with the theories he thought out?

The Gold Seeker persisted:

"That and the poison gas are first class notions. See? Put a cannister right at Police Headquarters when we know the number one bastard is in there. Poison them all like the rats they are!" And he laughed so hard three birds took flight from out of a nearby lime tree. "Yes, Erdosain my friend, you do think of things. Plague and chlorine. You see how we'll spark the city to revolution? I can see the day already, scared businessmen trying to beat it out of their moleholes, we'll be cleaning up the planet with a machine gun. Not bad. With a thousand pesos you can get a good machine gun. Goes off two hundred fifty times a minute. Not bad. And then the cannisters of gas . . . Ah! They ought to print your plans in the papers, believe me—"

With this question Erdosain cut short the panegyric:

"But you did find gold? . . . the gold—"

"Surely you don't take that story at face value."

"A story? So the gold then . . . ?"

"Exists, it exists all right—only it has to be located."

Erdosain was so disappointed the Gold Seeker added:

"Hey, now, look, I talked to you because the Astrologer told me you could be the one to do it."

"Yes, but here I thought—"

"What?"

"That in all those lies, the part about gold was true."

"It is true, in a way. The gold exists—it just needs finding. You should be glad it's all set up to go after it. Or do you think those animals would take action without fancy lies being dangled in their faces? Ah! I've given it thought. That's the beauty of the Astrologer's theory: you can only get people moving with lies. He makes up lies as convincing as truths; guys who would never have gotten off their duffs, who'd lost their last hopes, are like new men after a dose of his lies. What more do you want? Look, that's how most things work anyway and who objects? Everything's done for show— look, nobody says it but society needs little lies to keep running. So what's so sinful about the Astrologer's plan? He just has instead of dull little lies a big, eloquent, transcendental lie. The Astrologer, with his stunts, doesn't seem all that extraordinary and he isn't—and then again he is; he is—because he has nothing to gain from his lies, and he isn't because all he does is use the same principle as any other bamboozler or rainmaker or reorganizer of mankind. If one day they write up his life, people who can read it dispassionately will say he had greatness, since to implement his ideals all he used was the means available to any charlatan. And what looks to us excessive and disturbing is just the reaction of weak, mediocre spirits who only have faith in programs carried out complicatedly, mysteriously, never simply. And yet you can see how great actions really are simple, like Columbus using an egg to make his point."

"The truth of lies?"

"But that's it. The thing is we're not bold enough to start enormous undertakings. We have to think it's more complicated to run a country than a household, and we want events to be as thrilling as our silly romanticism demands."

"But in your heart of hearts, I mean, do you have much hope of the plan really succeeding?"

"Absolutely, and believe me, at the very least we'll run the country . . . if not the world. We'll have to. What the Astrologer has mapped out is to save the souls of men crushed under the mechanization of our civilization. No ideals are left intact. No symbols exist for good or evil. The Astrologer last time talked about colonies founded in the old days by misfits who were marginal in their own countries. We'll be like that, but making the Society a sort of vigorous workout—stuff to seduce the shopkeepers who go faithfully to Westerns. Do you know what kind of havoc we can bring about? . . . As a last resort we can do spot bombings, sit back and watch people quake in their boots. What do you think gang warfare was? Some men who didn't know what else to do with their excess adrenaline. So they got it out working over some poor slob in the street.

"Look . . . Comodoro . . . Puerto Madryn, Trelew, Esquel, Arroyo Pescado, Campo Chileno, I know the roads and places where no roads go . . . really . . . we'll organize a wonderful youth corps"—he was getting excited—"you don't think there's gold? You're like a kid you say has eyes bigger than his stomach at the dinner table. In our country, everything's gold."

Erdosain felt sucked into the man's ardor. The Gold Seeker was speaking convulsively, his eyes and brows were atwitch with tics, and he kept a friendly hand on Erdosain's arm.

"Believe me, Erdosain . . . so much gold—more than you could imagine—but that's not the point. The point is: time's awasting. Esquel, Arroyo Pescado, Río Pico . . . Campo Chileno . . . leagues . . . days and days on the road, and, you know, to register a horse not worth ten pesos you ride for weeks, time's meaningless there. It's so big . . . enormous . . . eternal there. There, you have to see it's true. I remember when The Mask and I went through Arroyo Pescado. Not just gold—

red gold. There's the cure for civilization-sick souls.
We'll send our people to the mountains. Look, I'm
twenty-seven, and more than once I've looked at death
down a gun barrel." He took out his revolver. "See that
sparrow?" It was fifty paces off; he raised the revolver
to chin level and squeezed, and with the detonation
the bird plunged straight down off its branch. "See?
That's the death I've looked in the face. Nothing to
grieve about there. Look, I'm twenty-seven. Arroyo
Pescado, Esquel, Río Pico, Campo Chileno . . . we'll
claim those great wild stretches . . . we'll form the
campaign of New Joyfulness. The Order of the Knights
of Red Gold. You think I'm raving. Not a bit! You have
to have been there to see. And then you grasp the necessity, the utter necessity, of a natural aristocracy. To
laugh at solitude, risk, sorrow, sun, wasteland as far as
you can see, you're a new man—above those slaves
withering away in the city. You know, don't you, about
the anarchist, socialist proletariat of our cities? All
cowards. Instead of pitting themselves against mountains or wilderness, they prefer keeping cozy and en-
tertained in the city to the heroic solitude of the desert.
What if all the factory workers, seamstresses, all the
cogs in the parasitic mechanism of the city took off for
the desert—if each pitched a tent down South? Now
do you see why I'm with the Astrologer? We young
people will make a new life; we'll be the ones. We'll
be an outlaw aristocracy. We'll shoot the Tolstoy-
idealist intellectuals and put the rest to work. That's why
I admire Mussolini. He found Italy playing a mandolin
and gave it a club; he turned an operetta kingdom into
Europe's watchdog, overnight. Cities are cancer in this
world. They annihilate men, make them cowards, wily,
envious, then envy and cowardice structure society
around their needs. If those sheep had any fight in them
they'd tear it down. To put faith in the herds is like
trying to catch the wind. You see how Lenin fared with

his Russian peasant. But now it's organized and I can only say: people who don't fit into today's cities should head for the desert. That's the Astrologer's point. He's right. When the first Christians couldn't take city life they took to the desert. There they made their own happiness. But in today's cities, those at the bottom of the pyramid form committees."

"You know, I like the way you speak of the desert?"

"Of course, Erdosain. The Astrologer says: People who can't take the city shouldn't bother the ones who enjoy it. Malcontents and misfits from the city have the mountains, plains, the banks of great powerful rivers."

Erdosain never expected such violence from the Gold Seeker. As though reading his mind, the man went on:

"We'll preach violence, but not accept any theoretical-violence types into the cells, we'll demand a proof of obedience to our society from whoever wants to show us how he hates civilization. See the point of the colony? Hard work will make him a superman. Then he'll be given power. Don't monastic orders run like that? Isn't that the army system? Stop gaping, I'll tell you how in business . . . for instance at Gath and Chaves, at Harrods, the employees tell me personnel is under discipline that makes the army's like a toy. See, Erdosain, we have nothing new here. We just put a splendid goal in place of the petty one."

Erdosain felt little in front of the Gold Seeker. He envied him his violence and was irritated at how he kept laying down undeniable truths, and would have liked to contradict him, but said inwardly:

"I'm a dull character next to him, one more sordid, cowardly city man. Why can't I be so aggressive, so full of hate? He's right. And I smile at what he says, prudently, as if afraid he'll slap me down, and really his violence scares me and his courage annoys me."

"What are you thinking?" asked the Gold Seeker.
Erdosain kept looking at him, then:
"I thought, how sad to have been raised a coward."
The Gold Seeker shrugged it off.

"You may think you're cowardly if you've never had
to stake your life on anything. When your life hangs
from a trigger pull, I'll see if you're a coward or not. In
the city you don't get a chance to be brave. You know
if you smash someone's face, the cops will come around,
so it's easier to leave justice up to the authorities. A
matter of realities. You grow used to giving in, you
knuckle under. . . ."

Erdosain looked at him. "You're quite a fellow."

"Look, don't worry about courage. You'll pick it up
fast—you'll be a brave soul before you know it . . . just
a matter of getting started."

At one o'clock they parted.

THE LAME WHORE

That same day, just as Erdosain was nearly up the
spiral staircase, he saw standing on the landing a
woman in a fur coat and green hat talking with his
landlady. He heard a "Here he is now" which meant
they were waiting for him, and as he stopped, the stranger
turned to him and asked:

"You're Mr. Erdosain?"

"Where have I seen that face?" wondered Erdosain
as he responded affirmatively to the stranger, who went
on to introduce herself.

"I am Mr. Ergueta's wife."

"Ah! You're the Lame Woman?" but suddenly, realizing this clumsy slip had the landlady so curious she
had to inspect the stranger's feet, Erdosain apologized
in embarrassment:

"Sorry, I'm just not . . . See, I wasn't expecting . . . won't you come in?"

Before opening the room to her, Erdosain apologized all over again for the condition the guest would find it in, and Hipólita, smiling ironically, replied:

"That's quite all right."

Still Erdosain did not much like the cold way she looked out of her transparent verdigris eyes. And he thought:

"One of those perverse types," since he had noticed under her green hat her red, red hair was drawn smoothly down either side of her face to cover her ears. He looked again at her unblinking red eyelashes and her lips that seemed inflamed against her face with its plague of freckles. And he thought—how very unlike the woman in the photograph.

She stood facing him, observing him as if thinking:

"So he's the man," and he, next to the woman, felt her presence as incomprehensible, as if she didn't exist or at some inner level was miles off. But yet she was there and something had to be said, and since it was all he could think of he said, after turning on the light and offering the woman a seat while he sat on the sofa:

"So, you're Ergueta's wife? Very good."

He couldn't fit the sudden appearance of this being in with his own chaos. He felt filled with curiosity, but he wanted to feel something else, a familiarity with the woman's face, its oval shapes suggesting the red of copper, like the sunbeams through rain that in holy pictures are always breaking into a thousand rays from behind the clouds. And he said to himself:

"Here I am, but where is my soul?" And so he said again,

"So you're Ergueta's wife. Very good."

She had crossed her legs and was tugging her skirt

well down over her knee, so that the cloth bunched in her bright pink fingers, and raising her head as if it were hard to do so under unfamiliar circumstances, she said:

"You must do something for my husband. He's gone mad."

"Even that doesn't arouse my curiosity," thought Erdosain, and satisfied he had stayed as emotionless as the stereotype tycoon, he added, secretly pleased to play the uncaring man, "So he's gone mad, has he?" but all at once, realizing he couldn't keep up the role, he said, "You know what? You just gave me this stunning news and yet I have no reaction. I don't like being empty of emotion like this; I want to feel, but I'm like a sack of potatoes. You must forgive me. I don't know what it is with me. You forgive me, don't you? Yet I wasn't always like this. I remember I was happy as a lark. Bit by bit I changed. I don't know, I look at you, I want to feel like your friend, and I can't. If you were dying, maybe I wouldn't even hand you a glass of water. See? And yet. . . . But where is he?"

"He's a patient at Las Mercedes."

"But that's odd! Weren't you living in El Azul?"

"Yes, but we've been here for two weeks."

"And when did it happen?"

"Six days ago. Even I can't figure it out. It's what you were saying only about me. Sorry if this is wasting your time. I thought of you, you knew him, he was always telling me about you. When did you last see him?"

"Before he got married. . . . Yes, he told me about you. He called you the Lame Whore."

To Erdosain Hipólita's soul seemed to be filling her eyes with beauty. He felt he could speak to her about anything. The woman's soul stood there without moving, as if in receptive anticipation. She rested her folded hands on her skirt above the knee, and the very way she sat invited his confidences. What had happened that morning at the Astrologer's house seemed far removed, only some branches against the sky flashed across his memory at times, and the flow of fragmented images somehow gave him an unjustified sense of peace. He wrung his hands with satisfaction and said:

"Please don't take this as an offense . . . but I think he was crazy when he married you."

"Tell me . . . did you know him before he married me?"

"Yes . . . besides, I remember he used to pore over his Bible, because among other things he would talk to me about new times to come, the fourth seal and things along those lines. Besides, he gambled. He always intrigued me because he was like a man in a nonstop frenzy."

"Exactly. A frenzy all the time. He once even staked five thousand pesos on a poker game. He sold my jewels, a necklace a friend had given me—"

"What? But didn't you give that necklace to the maid right before you married him? That's what he told me. That you gave her the necklace and the silverware—and the check for ten thousand pesos that other man gave you—"

"Do you think I'm mad? Why would I give my maid a pearl necklace?"

"Then he lied."

"So it would seem."

"But how odd!"

"It shouldn't surprise you. He lied all the time. Besides, toward the last he was a lost soul. He was working out a system to win at roulette. You would have laughed to see him. He worked out a book of numbers nobody but him could understand. What a man! It kept him awake nights; he neglected the pharmacy; sometimes I'd be just about to fall asleep, the lights would be out, then there'd be this bang on the floor; he had leaped out of bed, turned the light on, and was writing numbers down before they got away from him . . . But, he told you I'd given my pearl necklace away? What a guy! What he did was to pawn it before we got married. . . . Well, as I was saying, last month he went to the Real de San Carlos—"

"And, of course, he lost—"

"No, with seven hundred pesos he won seven thousand. You should have seen him coming in . . . without a word . . . I thought: So! he lost—but the odd thing is he was frightened by his own good luck—but I was just sure something would happen. At ten that night he still wasn't back and I went to bed; at one or so his footsteps in the room woke me up, and I was about to turn on the light when he just leaped over and grabbed my arm, you know how terribly strong he is, he got me out of bed in my nightgown and dragged me through the halls to the hotel door."

"And you?"

"I didn't scream because I knew it would drive him wild. At the hotel door he stood looking at me like he didn't know me, his forehead all full of wrinkles and his eyes all huge. There was this wind that bent the trees right over, I covered myself with my arms, and he kept his eyes on me, when a patrolman came up to us, while the doorman grabbed his arms from behind, the noise woke him up. He was shouting so you could hear clear down the block: this is the whore—the one who loved the ruffians whose flesh is as the flesh of mules—"

"But how do you remember those words?"

"It's like I can see it all over again. There he was trying to get back in the door, the patrolman trying to pull him into the street, the doorman with a stranglehold on him, trying to weaken him, and I just hoping things would somehow come to an end, because people were gathering and instead of helping the policeman they were staring at me. Luckily I always wore a long nightgown. . . . Finally with the help of all those other patrolmen that someone inside the hotel had summoned, they got him down to the station. They thought he was drunk but it was an attack of insanity—that's what the doctor said. He was raving about Noah's Ark—"

"I see . . . and what can I do for you?" Again Erdosain felt that character looming up in his life like an element in a novel you have to keep straight, the way you have to keep your tie straight at a dance.

"Really, I came to bother you hoping you might help me. His family is no help at all."

"But didn't he marry you right at home?"

"Yes, but when we got back from Montevideo after getting married, we went to visit—just think—they were people I'd worked for as a servant!"

"I bet that was something."

"You can't imagine how indignant they were. One of his aunts . . . but, why should I inflict all their pettiness on you! Right? Anyway, that's how it goes. They threw us out and so we went. So, what else is new?"

"The odd thing is your having been a servant."

"Nothing so odd about that—"

"You don't seem the type—"

"Thank you. So when I left the hotel I had to pawn a ring—and I really have to watch it with what money I have left—"

"And the pharmacy?"

"They've got a substitute running it. I sent him a telegram asking for money, but he answered he's under orders from the Erguetas not to let me have a cent. And so . . ."

"So what will you do?"

"I can't decide . . . if I should go back to Pico or wait here."

"What a mess."

"I'm sick of the whole thing."

"The thing is today I have no money. Tomorrow I will—"

"You know? I have to hold onto those few pesos, because you can never tell—"

"And while you're getting it sorted out, the whole mess . . . if you like you can stay here. In fact, there's an empty room right in through there. What else do you want?"

"To see if you might get him released."

"How can I get him released if he's crazy? We'll see. Okay, you sleep here tonight. I'll make do with the sofa . . . probably won't get much sleep here."

Again that malevolent green gaze came filtering out from behind her red lashes. It was as if she were pouring her molten soul over his ideas to make a cast of his intentions.

"All right, I accept—"

"Tomorrow, if you like, I'll give you money, you can stay at some hotel unless you'd rather stay on here."

But all at once, annoyed with Hipólita because of something that had just come to him, he said:

"Well, you can't really love Eduardo."

"Why?"

"It's obvious. You come here, tell me the whole drama, amazingly calm about it all . . . and naturally then . . . how does that make you look?"

During this speech, Erdosain had begun to pace in what space there was in the room. He felt nervous and surreptitiously examined the freckled oval face, its thin red eyebrows under the green hat, the inflamed-looking lips, the coppery hair drawn smoothly down either side of her face over her ears, and the transparent eyes that poured forth their steady gaze.

"Why, she hardly even has breasts," Erdosain thought. Hipólita looked around her; suddenly, with a friendly smile, she asked: "So what did you expect, kid?"

Erdosain was irritated by that "kid" with its slutty ring, on top of her hard as nails "So what else is new?" Finally he said:

"I don't know . . . I guess I'd imagined you wouldn't be so cold . . . sometimes you really seem to have something perverse about you . . . I may be wrong, but . . . anyway . . . you can just . . ."

Hipólita got up.

"Look, kid, I don't go in for a lot of theatrics. I came to you, but just because I knew you were his best friend. What do you want? You want I should produce tears to order for the situation? No, I've cried enough. . . ."

He had also stood up. She looked him right in the eye, but the hard lines rigid under her skin like an armor of will melted with fatigue, her head drooped a little to the side, she reminded Erdosain of his wife—and she could well have been—she stood in the door of a strange room—the Captain, uncaring, he watched her walk out forever and did nothing to stop her . . . there was the cold city street . . . maybe she'd find some filthy hotel, and then, seized with pity, he said:

"Forgive me . . . I'm a bit nervous. But do feel welcome to stay. I just don't have any money. But tomorrow I will."

Hipólita got back in the chair and Erdosain took his pulse as he paced. It was going fast. Worn out from the afternoon with the Astrologer and Barsut, he said bitterly:

"Life is hard . . . eh?"

The stranger regarded the toe of her shoe in silence.

She looked up and a fine wrinkle shot across her freckled forehead. Then:

"You look really worried. Is something happening to you?"

"No, no . . . tell me, did you suffer much with him?"

"A little. He is violent."

"How odd! I try to picture him in the mental ward and get nothing. All I get is a bit of face and one eye. . . . I should tell you I could see it coming. I met him one morning, he told me everything, and all at once I just knew you would be unhappy with him . . . but you must be tired. I have to go out. I'll tell the landlady to bring you supper here."

"No, I don't want any."

"Well, then I'll see you. Here's the screen. Make yourself at home."

The Lame Whore watched Erdosain's departure with the strangest gaze, a sort of fan that opens up to slice a man through from head to toe, then folds into itself the whole interior geometry of his life.

INSIDE THE CAVERN

Once in the street, Erdosain noticed it was raining, but he kept on walking, impelled by a dry rancor, annoyed he was not able to think.

It was getting complicated. And he, meanwhile, was he being processed through a big machine that cut off his escape, pulled him further into life and thrust him into the mud, leaving him bereft of hope? Besides, there was that . . . that impotence of mind, his thoughts refused to follow clean lines, like a chess game, and his mental incoherence left him angry at everyone.

Then his irritation turned on the animal contentment of the shopkeepers who from the doors of their grottoes spat into the slanting rain. He imagined their weaselings while in the back rooms their saggy-bellied wives could be seen spreading tablecloths over wobbly tables, scrounging together the stew that, when the lid came off, stank up the street with grease and peppers and stringy bits of leftover veal.

He scowled as he walked, with slow fury he investigated what thoughts must breed behind those narrow foreheads, staring those livid-faced merchants right in the face, as from recessed eyes they watched customers in the shops across the way. At moments Erdosain had an urge to insult them, he longed to call them cuckolds and thieves and throw in something about their mothers, to say they were puffed up like advanced cases of leprosy except for a few thin ones who were consumed with envy. Inwardly putting them on trial, he made vile accusations, imagining those merchants staggering to bankruptcy under a pile of debts, and the misfortune that plunged him into desperation would also be visited on their grimy wives, who, with the same fingers that had pulled out their menstrual rags a moment before, would cut the bread they devoured, cursing at their competitors.

And though he could not say why, he felt the best of that slimy lot was a vile toad, all of them oozing envy and showing as much fair play as a snake-oil salesman.

Walking past enterprises devoted to the sale of goods, he thought these men had no high aim in life, that they spent their lives in voyeuristic vigilance over their neighbors' intimacy, neighbors as low as themselves, inwardly rejoicing as they mouthed polite distress over others' misfortunes; gossip mongering right and left out of sheer boredom, and suddenly the whole thing made him so angry he felt he had better get away to avoid creating a nasty scene with one of those animals, under whose hardened crusts you could see the soul of the city rising, as low, harsh, and ruthless as themselves.

He had no specific plan; he realized his spirit was soiled with revulsion toward life, and suddenly spotting a streetcar heading out to Plaza Once, he sprinted over to catch it. He bought a round-trip ticket to Ramos Mejía. He could equally well have gone any other route. He was tired, and distressed at the certainty he had cast his soul down a gulch from which it would never emerge. And there, waiting, was the Lame Whore. How nice it might have been to be a ship's captain, to command a superdreadnought. A chimney would vomit torrents of smoke, and there on the bridge he would stand in conversation with one of his subordinates, while in his heart there would remain the image of a woman who perhaps was not his wife. But why was his life always the way it was? And other people's, too, as if that "way it was" was a stamped-on misfortune that only came out clearly on the surface of one's own being, but looked blurry in others.

What had become of that surge of life that courses through some men like the blood of a lion? That surging life that can make a whole existence open up without having had to work away at it and everything fall into place cinematically. Wasn't that what you saw looking at pictures of great men? Who kept around a picture of Lenin arguing in some backstreet room in London, or Mussolini wandering the back roads of Italy? But there they were, presto, haranguing the masses from a balcony or among the broken columns of recent ruins, in casual shoes and a straw hat which did nothing to dim the conquerer's aura about them. And he felt his own life came with quite a different set of images: the Lame Whore, the Captain, his wife, Barsut, all existences that, once removed from his sight, were reduced to the tiny size physical distance confers on objects.

He leaned his head against the windowpane. The car pulled up and came to a stop, then with the second whistle blast it pulled out again; the governing mechanism clanked into place and metal strained angrily against metal.

The red and green lights of the tunnel flashed into his eyes for a moment, then he closed them again. At night, the train communicated its trepidation to the rails, and their combined mass, multiplied by the velocity, stamped onto his thoughts the dizziness of a march that would be just as merciless and dizzying.

Clack . . . clack . . . clack . . . the wheels caught at every juncture in the rails, and this flat, imposing monorhythm eased his anger, lightened his spirit, while his flesh sank back into the half-sleep speed induces in one's senses.

Then he thought Ergueta was surely mad to start with. He remembered how when he was on the brink of ruin Ergueta had said, "Beat it, you creep," and, nestling the back of his head into the seat, he thought about past times, closing his eyes to make out clearly the images of a memory. He was a bit surprised, because it was the first time he had noticed how in a memory certain images appear life-size while other images are like tiny tin soldiers or only appear in profile, with no depth to them. So, next to a corpulent black whose hand wandered up the rear of a small boy, he saw a tiny table on which some weary thieves had lain their heads, while the roof, of regal height, gave it all an air of the most extraordinary desolation against the gray of memory. A dark crowd flowed through the inside of his soul; shade fell like a cloud to cover his pain over with fatigue, and next to the table where the little grownup thieves were sleeping, looming up like a huge ox skull, was the café proprietor, digging his fingers into his bulging arm muscles.

And another memory showed him how correct he

had been when he had had a presentiment of his imminent downfall, back when he had not yet even thought of embezzling from his company, but now he was going through those gray stretches searching for an image of his own possibilities.

How many paths branched off through his brain! But now he set off on the path to that diner, that vast diner that occupied the entire space from his forehead through to the nape of his neck, pushed its taciturn mass like a butcher shop sloping at a twenty-degree angle through the inner recesses of his brain. One would expect the tables with the grownup little thieves to go sliding across the floor, but when he thought about it the mass somehow righted itself as though by a counterweight, and his flesh, by now accustomed to the mass of the train times its velocity, settled back into dizzy inertia. Now memory had seized hold of every cell in his being, and the diner appeared before his eyes, a perfect quadrilateral. It seemed to thrust its lines deep into his chest, almost as if were he looking head on into a mirror, he would have seen his body as a narrow room sloping back in perspective. And inside, he walked along a sidewalk filthy with gobs of spit and sawdust, while the frame around this self-portrait edged out into other nearby sensations.

And he thought if the Lame Whore had been sitting beside him, he would have explained to her:

"That's me before I became a thief."

Erdosain imagined the Lame Whore looking over at him and added in a bored voice:

"Next to the building where they used to publish *Crítica*, on Sarmiento, was a diner."

Hipólita looked at him as though asking a question, while the cars clattered infernally as they cut across the Caballito runs. Erdosain imagined he was a character who had renounced a life of crime and reformed, and went on talking to his invisible seatmate:

"Newspaper vendors and thieves gathered there."

"Ah, really?"

The proprietor, concerned lest his motley crew of patrons might smash the windows one day, kept his metal curtain drawn all the time.

The light came into the room through blue-tinted panes so that in that grotto, its walls painted the horrible gray of an immigrant's butcher shop, there floated a shadow that turned the cigar smoke a milky color.

In that shadowy place, with great exposed beams running across the ceiling, and filled with the effluvia of stew and cooking fat, was a dark assortment of what were clearly veteran thieves, their faces shadowed by the visors of their caps and bandannas tied loosely around their throats.

From eleven to two in the afternoon they huddled around the greasy tables, eating rotten clams or playing cards and drinking wine.

In that malodorous fog faces twisted into vile sneers, great globs of spit flew as though someone were being strangled to death, jaws hung slack and lips dangled loosely like funnels, blacks with porcelain eyes and teeth gleaming from between tumescent lips, reaching for the rears of young boys with teeth-gnashing crudity, the human debris of the city, with tiger faces, sunken foreheads, and fixed stares.

Those little clots of benchsitters and others at counters filled the air with their harsh voices. A breed of characters known as "lancers" wandered among them, instantly recognizable by their unstarched collars, gray jackets, and bowler hats costing seven pesos. Some of them were fresh out of jail and carried news of or messages from recent prisoners, others wore eyeglasses to make them look trustworthy. As they came in, they ran an expert eye over the gathering, missing nothing. They spoke in low voices, smiling convulsively, buying strangers beer, and making several mysterious trips in and out in the space of fifteen minutes. The owner of this grotto was an enormous fellow with a huge face like an ox, green eyes, a nose that belled out at the bottom like a trumpet, and thin tight lips.

When he grew angry his roars were enough to scare the sewer rats there, who were afraid of him. He knew how to keep them in hand through a sort of unfocused violence. If someone surpassed the acceptable level of disorder, suddenly the proprietor strode over, the offender knew he was about to get clobbered, but he waited in silence, and then the giant let loose great whacks, using the edge of his fist on the man's skull.

The punishment was meted out in joyful silence, the unfortunate recipient of it was kicked out into the street, and the voices started up again, more nasty and resounding than before, pushing clouds of smoke over toward the glass-paneled door. Sometimes street musicians would wander into this den, frequently a concertina and a guitar.

As they tuned up, an expectant silence seized the animals huddled in corners and an invisible wave of sadness washed through the atmosphere.

The instruments poured forth a plaintive jailhouse tango, and then those wretches would work into its rhythms their own rancors and misfortunes, unconsciously. The silence was like a many-handed monster raising a dome of sound over the heads drooping onto the tabletops. What must have been going through those life-scarred heads! And that dome, tall and somehow terrible, penetrating their very beings, multiplied the languor of the guitar and the concertina, making a divine matter of the suffering of a whore and the horrible boredom of jail that oppresses the heart when one thinks of friends on the outside, taking care of business.

Then in the most scarred-over souls, under the grime

life had deposited, flowered an unfamiliar tremor; then it was over and every hand reached out to toss a coin into the musicians' caps.

"I went there," Erdosain said to his hypothetical seatmate. "I sought more anguish, and to be yet more certain I was lost, and to think of my wife who was alone at home, who suffered because she had married a loser like me. How often, in a corner of that diner, did I imagine Elsa running off with another man. And I sunk deeper, and that café was only a taste of what worse things would happen to me later on. And often, looking at those wretches, I thought: Won't I end up just like one of these? Ah, I don't know how, but I've always somehow known what would happen before it did. I've never been wrong about it. You see? And there, in that grotto, one day I found Ergueta lost in thought. Yes, Ergueta. He was alone at a table and some paperboys were looking at him in amazement, although surely others thought he was just an especially well-dressed thief."

Erdosain imagined the Lame Whore now asking him:

"What, my husband was there?"

"Yes, and with that dogcatcher's face of his he was chewing on the head of his cane while a black man massaged a young boy's rear. But he didn't notice a thing. It was like he was nailed down to the café floor. It's true he told me he had come to wait for his connection to give him hot tips on the next race, but really he just was there as though he'd felt lost and wandered in looking for the meaning of life. Maybe that's just what did happen. Looking for the meaning of life by immersing himself in that ratpack. That was when I first found out he was determined to marry a prostitute, and when I asked about the pharmacy, he said he had left the substitute manager from Pico running it, and I could see he was a hardcore gambler. I don't know if you know they threw him out of his club for cheating. They even said he forged tickets, but they never did prove anything. He only talked about you when I asked about his girlfriend, a millionairess from Cacharí who was really in love with him.

" 'I broke that off a while ago,' he said.

" 'Why?'

" 'I don't know . . . I just stopped giving a shit . . . I got bored.'

" 'But why did you leave her?' I insisted.

"A harsh light showed in his eyes. He waved the flies off the rim of his beer glass and insisted grouchily:

" 'How should I know! . . . Bored, is all . . . just because I do weird things. And the poor girl loved me. But what would she have done with me. Besides, the thing's done.' "

"So Ergueta said that it was irremediably done?"

"He sure did, he said, 'The thing's done, because tomorrow I'm marrying someone else.' "

The electric train left Flores behind. Erdosain, huddled into his seat, remembered that he looked seriously at the pharmacist, at the shifting movements of the muscles under his face that made him look so malevolent.

"So who are you marrying?"

Ergueta's face went white. He leaned over toward Erdosain winking one eye while the other, immobile, tried to gather in all the surprise Erdosain would show in just a moment:

"I'm marrying the Whore." Then he raised his head and rolled his eyes up. Erdosain just sat there.

The pharmacist had on his face an expression of ecstasy like a holy picture, where a saint always appears clasping his hands against his chest.

And Erdosain remembered how in that place, the black who had hold of a child's rear, now pulled the youth's hands toward his pudenda, while a circle of newspaper vendors were shouting about something and the gigantic proprietor strode across the floor with an order of soup in one hand and one of meat in the other for a couple of sneak thieves off in one corner.

Nonetheless, this decision did not surprise Erdosain. Ergueta was apt to take such resolves, like all frenzied souls who follow the dictates of their obsessions with slow fury, a deep-seated explosion which they never hear go off, but which sends out shock waves that intensify their instincts a hundredfold. Nonetheless, feigning calm:

"The Whore? . . . Who is this Whore?" he asked.

A deep flush rose in Ergueta's face. His eyes were smiling.

"Who is she, you ask? . . . An angel, Erdosain. Right in front of me, I was right there, she tore up a thousand-peso check a lover gave her. She gave the maid a pearl necklace worth five thousand pesos. She gave the doormen at her apartment house her silverware. 'I'll enter into the marriage naked,' she told me."

"But it's all lies!" he heard Hipólita say in his memory.

"At the time I believed him. And he went on:

" 'If you knew what all that woman's been through. Once, after her seventh abortion, she was in such despair she was all set to leap out the fourth floor window. Suddenly this terrific thing—Jesus appeared to her on the balcony and blocked her way.' "

Ergueta was still smiling. Suddenly he reached into his pocket for a picture which he showed Erdosain.

The delicious creature in the image stirred him somehow.

She was not smiling. In the space behind her grew palm trees and ferns in profusion. Sitting on a bench, she kept her head slightly bent over, looking at a magazine that rested on her knees, since her legs were crossed. It made her dress hang like a bell suspended above the level of the grass. Her high-rising hairdo and her hair pulled back off her temples made her forehead seem wider and lighter, like a moon. On each side of her delicate nose, her eyebrows arched, their thin line well suited to eyes that were slightly slanted in a delicately oval face.

And looking at her, Erdosain realized that Hipólita's presence would never arouse him sexually, and that certainty cheered him somehow, so that he began to imagine the delight of caressing with his fingertips the chin of the unknown young woman and hearing the sand crunch under the soles of her shoes. Then he murmured:

"How lovely she is! . . . She must be very sensitive."

How different she turned out to be!

The train was passing through Villa Luro. Among piles of coal and gas meters half seen through the fog the arc lights gleamed sadly. Great black gaps loomed in the sheds that harbored the trains, and the red and green lights, hanging at irregular distances, made the signals of the trains more gloomy yet.

How different the Lame Whore had turned out to be! But still, he remembered how he had said to Ergueta:

"How lovely she is! . . . she must be very sensitive."

"Yes, she is; also she's got a very pleasing manner about her. The whole thing with her is really nice from my point of view. Wait till those guys who didn't think I was a real Communist find out. I gave up this fancy virgin to marry a prostitute. But Hipólita has a soul that transcends all that. She likes this wild thing we're doing, great deeds from noble hearts. We'll do great things together, because the times are ripe."

Erdosain took up the pharmacist's phrase:

"So you think the times are ripe?"

"Yes, terrible things must come to pass. Don't you remember you once told me President Roosevelt had spoken in praise of the Bible?"

"Yes . . . but a long time ago."

Erdosain answered vaguely because he really did not recall having quoted anything like that to the pharmacist. The man continued:

"Besides which, I have read the Bible extensively—"

"It doesn't seem to have affected the way you live—"

"That's not for you to judge," said Ergueta severely.

Erdosain looked at him, annoyed, the pharmacist smiled his puerile smile and as the café owner placed one more half liter of beer on the counter, he said:

"See the mysterious words one finds in the Bible: 'And I will save the lame woman, and bring in the woman who has gone astray, and I will give them a place of honor in every country of confusion.' "

An amazing silence was occurring in the diner. All one could see was heads bending over and groups absorbed in the comings and goings of the flies on café tables. A thief was showing a diamond ring to a colleague and both kept their heads bending over the stones in question.

A ray of sun came in a half-open milk-glass door like a streak of sulphur slicing through the blue fog of the café.

The other man was saying again: "And I will save the lame woman, and bring in the woman who has gone astray," insistently and with a malicious wink as he said again, "and I will give them a place of honor in every country of confusion—"

"But Hipólita is not lame—"

"Well, no, but she has gone astray and I am the fraudulent man, the 'son of perdition.' I've wandered from brothel to brothel, from grief to grief in my search for love. I thought it was physical love I sought and only reading that book was I able to see the light: my heart was looking for divine love. See? A heart knows where to go. You're messed up, you need to carry out your will, but you fail . . . and why do you fail . . . a mystery . . . then one day, all of a sudden, no way of knowing how, the truth appears. And look, see what my life has been. 'Son of perdition' is my life for you. Papa, before he died in Cosquín, wrote me the worst letter, he was coughing blood and raining reproaches on me, see? And he would not even sign his name, all he put was 'Your father, as I am cursed to be.' You see?" and again he winked convulsively and raised his eyebrows, making Erdosain wonder:

"But surely he's gone mad."

They left the diner. Cars ran up and down Corrientes sending back flashes of sun, crowds went by making their way to work, and under the yellow awnings women's faces seemed rosier than usual. They went inside the café Ambos Mundos. Around the café tables sat sharpsters, playing cards, dice, or shooting pool. Ergueta looked all around, then, spitting, he said aloud:

"All pimps here. Ought to hang them all without looking at their faces."

Nobody seemed to take it personally.

Erdosain, somehow, was left pondering some words Ergueta had said.

"I was seeking divine love." Ergueta was living a frenzied, sensual life. He was always to be found in gambling houses or bordellos, dancing, drinking heavily, becoming involved in awful fights against deadbeats and pimps. Some impulse was always pushing him into dreadfully rough scenes.

One evening, Ergueta was in Flores Plaza, by Niers's Confectioners. The perpetually drunken Delavene was alongside, having become a lawyer a month before, and also some more unsavory individuals from the Club de

Flores. They were harassing passersby. Suddenly Ergueta saw a Spaniard approaching and unzipped his fly so when the man passed, he urinated onto him. He was a prudent enough individual to merely walk off complaining. Then the pharmacist said looking straight at Delavene who was given to bragging:

"All right . . . could you piss on the next to come by?"

"Sure."

Everyone was happy, because Delavene was likely to do anything. A man came around the corner and Delavane began urinating. The stranger moved a bit over, but the "Basque," nearly knocking him over, drenched him.

Something awful happened.

Wordlessly the man came to a halt; the gang was whistling and laughing at him, but then suddenly he pulled out a revolver, everyone heard a bang, and Delavene fell to his knees grabbing at his abdomen. He lay dying for a long, terrible time. Before he died, he nobly admitted he had been the one to start up the scene, and when Ergueta was drunk and heard Delavene's name, he would kneel and make a cross on the dusty floor with his tongue.

While rolling a smoke, the pharmacist answered Erdosain concerning Delavene.

"Yes, he had a noble heart . . . a friend like him is rare. Someday I'll make somebody pay for him," but coming back to more immediate concerns, he said, "Ah! I have been pondering so much lately. And I wondered how appropriate could it be for a sterile, diseased, vice-ridden, immoral man to marry a virgin—"

"So Hipólita . . . knows?"

"She knows everything. Besides, a virgin deserves a virgin name. A man whose soul and body are virgin. So it will be some day. Can you imagine a handsome, virginal, macho youth?"

"Yes, so he should be ideally," whispered Erdosain.
The pharmacist looked at his watch.
"Do you have something to do?"
"Yes, in a moment I'm going home to see Hipólita."
"I was dumbfounded," Erdosain later told the com-
piler of this chronicle. "His family lived in a big, fancy
house and you could nearly feel souls creeping around
like snails, absolutely conservative and in a rut." Er-
dosain asked him:
"What? . . . She is in your house already?"
"I had worked out a fictionalized version of her life.
She was opposed, or really, she said she would go only
if she could go as who she really was."
"So she would have gone as herself?"
"She would have, but I finally managed to change
her mind. I told Mama I had whisked her away when
she was leaving for Europe with an uncle and his wife—
a made-up episode, of course."
"And so Mama . . ."
Erdosain was inclined to ask if his mother swallowed
such a lie, as if looking at Hipólita was sufficient to
inform an observer about her disordered life.
"And how did Mama react when she found out?"
"She made me get her out immediately. When I introduced her, she hugged her and said: 'Has he been
respectful with you, my dear?' And she, lowering her
eyes, said, 'Yes, Mama.' Which was true. You have to
see that Mama and my sister Sara were won over by
Hipólita."
Erdosain had a feeling these poor losers had all em-
barked on a disaster course. Nor had he been wrong,
and now, in the train, recalling how his hunch had been
borne out, he pondered while passing through Liniers:
"How odd, first impressions never lie," and when he
had asked Ergueta when he would be married, he had
answered:
"Tomorrow we're leaving for Montevideo. We'll be

married there, so if we need a divorce, we can have one." When he said those words, again he winked, smiling cynically, and added: "I'm no dummy, I keep myself covered in case."

Erdosain was shocked by such careful planning. He was unable to hold back, and said:

"Hey—you're not even married and already you've got a plan for divorce under Uruguayan law. Is this some kind of communist garbage? You know, you're as much a cardsharp as you ever were."

The pharmacist was as impervious as a loan shark who no longer cares what he is called, as long as he is paid as well as cursed. Coolly, he replied:

"Look, you screw the world or you get screwed."

Erdosain was amazed by such crudity.

He thought of the delicious creature bearing up under such massive brutishness, under a lowering sky full of dust clouds set ablaze by a ghastly yellow sun. She would wilt like a fern placed in a field of volcanic rocks. Now Erdosain looked the pharmacist over again, this time with fury.

The gambler noticed his friend's malevolent glare and said, "Look, kid, you have to do something against this society. Some days I suffer unbearably. It seems as if all men had become animals. You want to go out and preach extermination or set up a machine gun at every intersection. You see? Terrible times are coming.

"The son will rise up against the father and the father against the son. One must do something against this accursed society. That's why I'm marrying a prostitute. The Scriptures put it well: 'And you, son of man, you will judge the bloodthirsty city and you will show it all its abominations.' And then this other passage, listen to this other bit: 'And she loved the ruffians whose flesh is as the flesh of asses, and whose outpourings like the outpourings of horses.'" And gesturing toward the pimps who were playing cards around the tables he said: "There they are. Just go to the Royal Keller, the Morzzoto, the Pigalle, the Maipú, they're all over the place. Dissipated energy. Even those rats are bored, in the last analysis. When the revolution comes, they'll hang them or send them to the front lines. Cannon fodder. I could have been like them but I gave it up. Now terrible times are coming. That's why the Book says: 'And I will save the lame woman and I will take in the woman who has gone astray and give her a place of praise and renown in all the land of confusion.' Because today the city has fallen in love with its ruffians and they dragged down the lame woman and the woman who has gone astray, but they will have to humble themselves and kiss the feet of the lame woman and the woman gone astray."

"But do you love Hipólita or not?"

"Of course I love her. Sometimes it's like she'd come down a staircase from the moon. Wherever she is, everyone will feel happy."

And for a moment Erdosain could believe that she had come serenely down from the moon so that all men might flock to bathe in the sunshine of her simplicity.

The pharmacist went on:

"Now the days of blood are coming, kid, days of vengeance. Men are weeping inside their souls. But they don't want to listen to the weeping of their angel. And the cities are like prostitutes, in love with their thugs and bandits. It can't go on like that."

He looked at the street an instant, and then, apparently absorbed in listening to some sound from within, the gambler said in a voice resonant with pathos in that café of boredom:

"A man shall come, an angel, I don't quite know. He will kneel in the middle of the Avenida de Mayo. Cars will stop, bank managers and people from swanky hotels will come rushing out to their balconies and gesticulating angrily say:

" 'Hey, what do you want, punk? Don't bother us here.' But he'll rise up, and when they see his sad face and the fever ablaze in his eyes, their arms will fall to their sides, and he'll turn to those pigs, he'll talk to them, he'll ask them why they did evil, why they neglected the orphan and stomped man underfoot and made an inferno of life, which was so beautiful. And they won't know what to answer, and the voice of the last of the angels will resound, giving them goose bumps, and the greatest bastards will be in tears.''

The pharmacist's huge mouth was contorted with anguish. He seemed to be chewing on some bitter, rubbery poison.

"Yes, it's necessary for Christ to come again. The dregs, the barrel-scrapings of humanity are still suffering. And if he doesn't come, then who will save us?''

THE ESPILAS

The train pulled into Ramos Mejía. The station clock said eight at night. Erdosain got off.

A dense blanket of fog lay over the muddy streets of the town.

When he found himself alone on Calle Centenario, hemmed in fore and aft by walls of fog, he remembered they were to murder Barsut the next day. It was true. They were going to kill him. He would have liked to be in front of a mirror so he could see his own body, a murderer's body, it was so odd sounding to be the very "I" who with such a crime would cut whatever linked him to the rest of mankind.

The streetlights shone sadly, pouring cataracts of cottony light dribbling down into the grime of the paving stones, and one could scarcely see two steps ahead. An enormous unhappiness within Erdosain made its way along, sadder than a leper.

He now had the feeling that his soul had separated forever from all bonds of affect with earth. And his anguish was that of a man with a sinister cage inside his head, where elastic-muscled, blood-stained tigers yawned amid the bones of sins, with a certain jungle pounce about them.

And Erdosain, as he walked along, thought about his life as though it were someone else's, trying to comprehend those dark forces that crept up from the roots of the body and whipped against the window grilles with a whistling sound.

Immersed in the fog that extended its heavy wetness down to the innermost sacs of his lungs, Erdosain came to Calle Gaona, where he stopped to wipe the sweat off his brow.

He knocked on a wooden door, the only opening in a vast expanse of factory brick, with a kerosene lamp hanging at one side. Suddenly a hand opened the door and a young man, cursing, followed a path twisting alongside a wall, the bricks sinking into the mud with each step. He came up to a door with light shining through its panes, knocked and a hoarse voice shouted out:

"Come in."

Erdosain entered the house.

An acetylene lamp poured its fiery light onto the five heads of the Espila family, who had just looked up from their supper plates. They all greeted him with smiles and cheery voices, while Emilio Espila, a tall bony youth with a good deal of hair, ran over to pump his hand.

Erdosain greeted, one by one, first the old Señora Espila, bowed with age and all dressed in black, then the two young sisters, Luciana and Elena, then old deaf Eustaquio, a grizzled giant of tubercular build, who, as always, ate with his nose buried in his plate and his gray eyes trained on the hieroglyphs of a magazine, deciphering them as he chewed.

A bit of life crept back into Erdosain at Luciana and Elena's friendly smiles.

Luciana was long-faced and blond, with a retroussé nose and long, fine, sinuous lips, blushing pink. Elena was nunlike, with a wax-colored oval face and chubby pale hands.

"Want some supper?" asked the old lady.

Erdosain, seeing how little there was to go around, said he had already eaten.

"You really have, now?"

"Yes . . . I'll have a little tea."

They made room for him at the table, and Erdosain took a seat between deaf old Eustaquio, who kept his eyes glued to his hieroglyphs, and Elena, who was ladling out stew to Emilio and the old lady.

Erdosain observed them with pity. He had known the Espilas for many years. At one time the family lived in relative ease, then a chain of disasters had reduced them to utter misery, and Erdosain, who one day ran into Emilio on the street, visited them. He had not seen them for seven years and was shocked to find them living in such a hole, when before they had had a maid, a front parlor, and a main parlor. The three women slept in that room cluttered with old furniture that at mealtime became the dining room, while Emilio and the deaf man took refuge in a little zinc-plated kitchenette. To make ends meet, they found the oddest bits of work: they sold society guides, home ice-cream crankers, and the two sisters were seamstresses. One winter they grew so poor they stole a telephone pole and sawed it up for logs one night. Another time they stole all the posts out of a fence, and the scrapes they got into to keep body and soul together both amused and horrified Erdosain.

The first time he went to see them was a real shock. The Espilas were living in a big building near Chacarita, a three-level affair subdivided into metal compartments. The building was like an ocean liner, with children popping in and out like a community of cubicle dwellers. For some days Erdosain roamed the streets, thinking of the sufferings the Espilas had to overcome to feel resigned to their catastrophe, and later, when he invented the copper rose, he thought how in order to cheer them along he must give them an infusion of hope, and with part of the money he stole from the Sugar Company he bought a used accumulator and amp meter and the other elements to set up a crude galvanoplastics lab.

And he convinced the Espilas that they should dedicate themselves to that work in their spare time, because if it worked they could all be rich. And he, whose life was devoid of consolation or hope, he, who had gone around for so long as one lost, was the one to fill them with such hopes that the Espilas started in on the experiments, and Elena applied herself seriously to the study of galvanoplastics, while the deaf man prepared the chemical baths and became handy at setting up the amp meter and controlling the resistance. Even the old lady participated in the experiments, and nobody had any doubt but that once they figured out how to copper-plate a tin slat, before long they would be rich if the copper rose did not fail.

Erdosain also talked to them about gold stitchery, silver curtains, coppered veils and even worked up a project for a metallic necktie that astonished them all. They would make shirts with metal cuffs, collars, and fronts, taking cloth, bathing it in a saline solution and then in a galvanoplastic bath of copper and nickel. Gath and Chaves, Harrods, or San Juan's could buy the patent from them, and Erdosain, only half convinced of such practical uses, wondered if he had not been overstimulating their fantasy lives, since now, although they never paid their bills and were about to starve, they saw themselves acquiring at the minimum a Rolls-Royce and a townhouse, which unless it could be on the Avenida Alvear they wouldn't consider. Erdosain bent over his cup of tea, and then Luciana, blushing a little, responded to Emilio's petulant smile with a signal, but he, who for almost total lack of teeth had a terrible lisp, said:

"Lithen . . . we made the rothe—"

"Yes, thank God, we've done it." But Luciana leaped up impatiently, opened the cupboard under the washbasin and Erdosain smiled enthusiastically.

In the hand of the blond girl, the copper rose glistened.

In that sad hovel the marvelous metal flower spread its coppery petals. The flickering of the acetylene lamp played red patterns across it, as though the flower had taken on the botanical life that was now burned off by the acids that made up its soul.

The deaf man took his nose out of his plate of stew and in a solemn voice, after an examination of the hieroglyph of the rose, exclaimed:

"No two ways about it, Erdosain, you're a genius. . . ."

"Thoon we'll all be rich—"

"Let's just hope God heard that," muttered the old lady.

"But Mama, don't be such a skeptic!"

"Did you put in a lot of work?"

Elena, with a grave smile and a scientific manner, explained:

"See, Remo, he let the first rose have too many amps and burned it—"

"So there was no problem with the stability of the chemicals in the bath?"

"No, well, yes, we did cool it down a bit."

"To bathe this rose here; we put on the fixer—"

"You know . . . a nice coating of fixer . . . gently. . . ."

Remo examined the copper rose again, admiring its perfection. Each red petal was nearly transparent, and under the metal coating the branching nerves of the natural petal barely showed; the chemicals turned them black. The rose was lightweight, and Erdosain added:

"How delicate! . . . It weighs less than a five centavo piece."

Later, looking at a yellow shadow that covered the pistils of the flower, streaking as it settled against the petals, he added:

"But look, when you take the flowers out of the bath you must rinse them in water. You see these yellow streaks? That's where cyanide from the bath is attacking the copper." They formed a huddle around and listened in religious silence. He went on: "Then what you get is cyanate of copper; you don't want that, because it will damage the nickel coating. How long did it take?"

"An hour."

As he looked up from the rose his eyes met Luciana's. The girl's eyes were velvety with mysterious warmth and her smile half revealed her brilliant teeth. Erdosain looked at her in amazement. The deaf man was examining the rose and they all crowded close in and peered attentively at the yellow cyanide stripes. Luciana did not lower her eyes. Suddenly Erdosain remembered that the next day he would be a party to Barsut's murder, and an immense sadness made him cast his eyes to the floor; then, all at once feeling hostile to these people, who were full of hope and unaware of what sufferings and anguish he had borne for months, he got up and said:

"Well, so long."

Even the deaf man was flabbergasted.

Elena leaped up from her chair and the old lady froze with one arm holding up a plate she had been about to set in front of Eustaquio.

"What's the matter, Remo?"

"Say, hey, Erdosain—"

Elena looked at him seriously:

"Is something wrong, Remo?"

"Nothing, Elena . . . believe me—"

"Are you angry?" Luciana asked with her eyes full of that mysterious sad warmth.

"No, it's nothing . . . I felt I had to see you . . . but now I must go—"

"You really aren't angry?"

"No, señora."

"You've got tho much on your mind . . . I thee—"

"Shut up, you dolt!"

The deaf man managed to tear himself away from his hieroglyphs to reiterate his earlier claim:

"I'm telling you, take this seriously now, because it will make you rich."

"But nothing's the matter?"

Erdosain got his hat. He felt repugnance at having to mouth useless explanations. It was already resolved. So why talk? Nonetheless, he forced himself to say:

"Believe me . . . I love you all a great deal . . . as always. I'm not angry . . . don't be upset . . . I have more ideas—we'll set up a dye shop for dogs and sell dogs dyed green, blue, violet—you see, I'm brimming over with ideas . . . You'll get out of this misery . . . I'll get you out. . . . You see, I'm running over with ideas."

Luciana looked at him with pity and said:

"I'll walk you to the door," and they went together as far as the street.

The fog occupied a great cube in the street inside which the wicks of the streetlamps reverberated sadly.

Suddenly Luciana took Erdosain's arm and said in a soft voice:

"I love you, I truly do love you."

Erdosain looked at her ironically, his pain transformed into cruelty. He looked at her.

"I gathered as much."

She went on.

"I love you so much that so you'd like me I learned about high-temperature processes and Bessemer-ing steel. Shall I tell you what a hydraulic lift does or how refrigeration works?"

Erdosain enclosed her in a cold stare, thinking, "This girl is in questionable shape."

"I always was thinking about you. Shall I tell you how to run an analysis on steel and how to smelt copper, how to extract gold from ore, and about recessed-flame furnaces?"

Erdosain, obstinately pressing his lips together, walked down the street thinking man's existence was absurd, and again unjustified rancor sprang up in him against that sweet girl who, pressing against his arm, was saying:

"Do you remember that time you talked about how your goal was to run a high-temperature furnace? I was mad about you then. I set out to study metallurgy. Shall I explain to you the difference between an irregular carbon configuration and a normally occurring molecule? Why don't you say anything, my love?"

The train rumbled by with a muffled clattering far off; the milky fog turned into darkness a little way from the street lamp, and Erdosain would have liked to say something, to reveal his troubles to her, but that clogged-up, hard malignancy kept him stiffly mute beside the girl, who insisted:

"But, what's wrong? Are you angry with us? But we have you to thank for our fortune!"

Erdosain looked her over from head to toe, gave her arm a squeeze and told her in a flat voice:

"You don't interest me."

Then he wheeled around and before she could manage to look at him, he had stepped away and was lost in the fog.

He knew he had been gratuitously crude to the girl, and that knowledge gave him such cruel joy that he muttered with clenched teeth:

"They can all drop dead and leave me in peace."

Two Souls

At two in the morning, Erdosain was still walking through walls of wind, through downtown streets, in search of a brothel. Waves of muffled noise washed against his ears, but borne along by the frenzy of instinct he walked under the storefronts where the street was darkest. There was a horrible sadness inside him. At that moment he was headed nowhere.

He went along like a sleepwalker with his eyes fixed on the ornaments on top of police helmets, which flashed at each intersection in the cylinders of light flowing from the arc lights. Something extraordinary was impelling his body along with great strides. Thus he reached Plaza Mayo and now, on Cangallo, he left behind the Once Station.

There was a horrible sadness inside him.

His mind, stuck on one thought, repeated:

"It's no use, I'm a murderer," but, suddenly, when some red or yellow cube of light showed the entryway to a brothel, he would stop and hesitate in the wash of reddish or yellowish fog, thinking "No, not this one," and resume his walk.

A silent automobile rolled by him and sped away,

and Erdosain thought of the happiness he would never have and his lost youth, and his shadow went racing ahead on the paving stones, then shrank toward him and, not to be trod underfoot, leapfrogged over him, or flickered across a sewer grating. But his anguish grew heavier with each moment, as if it were a mass of water that sloshed him around until he was weak and nauseated. In spite of it, Erdosain imagined that by special providence, he had entered a singular brothel.

The madam let him into the bedroom, he threw himself onto the bed clothed—water was boiling on a kerosene burner in one corner—suddenly the girl appeared, half-naked, and stopping short in surprise, the reason for which only he and she knew, the whore exclaimed:

"It's you? . . . You! . . . you're here at last! . . ."

Erdosain answered her:

"Yes, it's me. . . . Ah, if you knew how I've looked for you!"

But since that was never to be, his sadness rebounded like a lead ball off a rubber wall. And he could see how his desire to have an unknown whore become seized with pity for him would be, as days went by, as useless as that ball to take a stance against the oppressions of life. Again he repeated to himself:

"Ah! it's you? You . . . Ah! At last you've come, my sad love . . ." but it was no good, he would never find that woman, and a pitiless energy born of desperation swelled his muscles, coursed through the seventy kilos of his weight, as in the cubic space of his chest an enormous sadness made his heart beat heavily.

Tiptoeing down the hall, he went up to his door and sneaked it open. Then, holding out his hands in the dark, he went to the corner where the sofa was and slowly curled up onto it, being careful not to make the springs groan. Later he could not see why that should have mattered to him. He stretched his legs out on the sofa and remained for a few minutes with his hands laced behind his neck. And there was more darkness in him than in that room, which would have been transformed into a wallpapered cube had he switched on the light. He wanted to pin his thoughts onto something objective, but it was no use. So he felt a certain childish fear; for a few minutes he paid close attention, but no sound came and then he closed his eyes. His heart was working in hard thumps, pushing the mass of his blood, and a watery chill made the hair on his back stand on end. With stiff eyelids and body rigid he waited for something to happen. Suddenly he realized that if he kept on like that he would break out in screams of fear, and pulling up his heels, with his legs crossed like Buddha, he waited in the dark. He was utterly annihilated, but he could not call out to anyone, nor could he weep. Yet he could not very well keep on crouching there all night.

He lit a cigarette and a wave of cold immobilized him.

The Lame Whore was standing by the room divider screen, examining him with her cold poison stare. The woman's hair was bound back in halves that covered her ears with their red wings, and her lips were pressed together. Everything about her was overattentive; Erdosain was frightened. Finally he got out:

"You!"

The match burned his fingers, and suddenly, an impulse stronger than his timidity forced him to his feet. He went over to her in the darkness and said:

"You! Weren't you asleep?"

He felt her reach out; the woman held his chin in her fingers. Hipólita said in a deep voice:

"Why aren't you asleep?"

"You are stroking my chin?"

"Why aren't you asleep?"

"You are touching me? . . . But how cold your hand is! Why is your hand so cold?"

"Light the lamp."

As the light poured down, Erdosain stood contemplating her. She sat on the sofa.

Erdosain murmured timidly:

"Shall I sit beside you? I couldn't sleep."

Hipólita made room for him, and next to the stranger, Erdosain could not resist a force that raised his hands, and he brushed her forehead with his fingertips.

"Why are you the way you are?" he asked.

The woman looked at him calmly.

Erdosain contemplated her for an instant with mute desperation and finally took her delicate hand. He would have kissed it, but something went off in the depths of his being and he drooped over into her lap, sobbing.

He wept convulsively in the shadow of the stranger, who sat upright and rested her gaze on his shaking head. He wept blindly, his life twisted with hard fury, holding back screams whose unreleased wrenchings renewed his horrible grief, and suffering poured forth endlessly from him, he was flooded with fresh grief, pain was coming up through his throat in great sobs. Thus he agonized for several minutes, biting his handkerchief to keep from shrieking, while her silence was a softness on which his weary spirit lay down. Then the screaming agony spent itself; the last tears welled up in his eyes, a rough snoring sound came up from his chest and he found it soothing to half lie, wet-cheeked, across the woman's lap. A vast tiredness seized him, the image of his faraway wife vanished off the surface of his pain, and as he lay there, a sunset calm fell, reconciling him to all the disasters laid in store for him.

He raised his flushed face, stamped with the imprint of the folds of her skirt and wet with tears.

She looked at him serenely.

"Are you sad?" she asked.

"Yes."

Then both fell silent and a violet flash lit up the corners of the dark patio. It was raining.

"Shall we drink some maté?"

"Yes."

He heated the water in silence. She looked vaguely at the rain drumming on the panes, while Erdosain readied the leaves. Then, smiling through his tears, he said:

"I have a special way of steeping it. You'll like it."

"Why are you sad?"

"I don't know . . . this anguish . . . I haven't had a tranquil life for some time."

Then they drank the maté in silence, and in that room with the paper peeling off in one corner the woman took on a special perfection, wrapped in her fur coat and with her red hair drawn back in smooth bands that covered the tips of her ears.

With a childish grin, Erdosain added:

"When I'm alone, sometimes I drink."

She smiled in friendly fashion, her legs crossed, a bit bent over, one elbow in the palm of the one hand and the other holding the maté, sipping out of the nickel-plated straw.

"Yes, I was distraught," Erdosain repeated. "But, how cold your hands are! . . . Are they always that cold?"

"Yes."

"Will you give me your hand?"

The stranger straightened up and reached out her hand with great dignity. Erdosain took it carefully in his hands and kissed it, and she looked at him at length, the coldness of her eyes melted into a sudden warmth that flushed her cheeks. Then Erdosain remembered that man in chains, and not letting it blot out the pale happiness now in him, he said:

"Look . . . if you were to ask me to kill myself now, I would do it. That's how happy I am."

The heat that had a moment ago convulsed him with weeping was again dissipated into a cold gaze. The woman looked at him with curiosity.

"But in all seriousness. Look . . . it's better, even . . . ask me to kill myself—tell me, doesn't it seem to you it would be better if certain people just went away?"

"No."

"Even if they do the worst actions?"

"That should be in God's hands."

"Then no point in us trying to discuss it."

Again they drank maté in silence, a silence that came about so he could drink in the sight of the red-haired woman, wrapped in her fur coat, with her transparent hands clasping her knee over the green silk dress.

And all at once, unable to hold back his curiosity, he exclaimed:

"Is it true you were a servant?"

"Yes . . . what's so strange about that?"

"But how odd!"

"Why?"

"It is odd, though. Sometimes I feel as if I'll find in someone else's life what's missing from my own. And then you think how there are these people who have found the secret of happiness . . . and if they would tell us their secret we would be happy, too."

"But, my life is no big secret."

"But you never felt the strangeness of living?"

"Oh, yes, I've felt it."

"Tell me about it."

"It was when I was a little girl. I worked in a beautiful house on Avenida Alvear. There were three girls and four servants. I'd wake up in the morning and it was so hard to believe that I was there living around all this furniture that didn't belong to me and those people who only talked to me so that I'd wait on them. And sometimes it seemed to me that the others all had a niche in life, and fit into their houses, while I felt like I was loose, just barely tied with a cord to life. And their voices would come floating out to me like when you're asleep and can't tell if you're dreaming or you're awake."

"It must be sad."

"Yes, it's very sad to see other people be happy and see how other people can't see how you're unhappy for all your life. I remember how at siesta time I would go to my room and instead of doing my mending I'd think: will I be a servant all my life? And the work wasn't what tired me anymore, it was my thoughts. Haven't you noticed how stubborn sad thoughts are?"

"Yes, they never go away. How old were you then?"

"Sixteen."

"And you'd still never been to bed with a man?"

"No . . . but I was furious—furious at being a servant all my life—besides, one thing happened that really made an impression on me. It was one of the sons. He was engaged and very Catholic. More than once I came on him loving up a cousin who was his fiancée, I remember now, she was a very sensual girl, and I wondered how you could reconcile Catholicism with such nasty stuff. Involuntarily, I got so I was spying on them . . . but even though he was so eager-handed with his fiancée, he was always correct with me. Later I realized I had wanted him . . . but it was too late . . . I was working in a different house. . . ."

"And then . . ."

"I could feel my ideas weighing in on me. What did I want from life? Didn't I know, then? Everywhere they were good to me. Since then I've heard people say harsh things about the rich—but I couldn't see it. Think how they lived. So, why should they have to be bad, right?

They were the girls of the family, I was the servant."

"And?"

"I remember one day I was on a streetcar with one of my employers. Two young men were having a conversation in one row. How you ever noticed how some days certain words go off like bombs in your ears—as if you'd always been deaf and were hearing people speak for the first time? Anyway. One of these two men was saying 'An intelligent woman, even an ugly one, if she set about selling her favors right would get rich, and if she'd just keep out of love she'd be queen of the city. If I had a sister that's what advice I'd give her.' Those words left me frozen where I sat. That was the instant end of my timidity and when we got to the end of the line it seemed like instead of those strangers having said those words, I had, I who had not even known about them up till then. And for days I puzzled over how one sells her favors."

Erdosain smiled:

"Amazing."

"I spent my next month's pay on a lot of books about prostitution. That was dumb, because they were nearly all pornography—stupid—not even about prostitution, but really about prostituting one's soul running after pleasure. And, can you believe it, not one of my friends could give me an explanation in so many words of prostitution."

"Go on . . . I'm not surprised now Ergueta should fall in love with you. You're an admirable woman."

Hipólita smiled, blushing.

"Don't exaggerate . . . all I am is a sensible one."

"So then, you delicious creature?"

"Silly kid! . . . Anyway—" Hipólita pulled her coat together over her chest and went on: "I went on with my work, all day long, but the work got to seem strange—I mean, while I'd be scrubbing or making a bed, my mind would be off far away and yet so much inside me sometimes I thought if it grew any bigger it would split open my skin. But I couldn't get it figured out. I wrote a bookstore asking if they didn't have a manual for women starting to sell themselves and they didn't answer, till one day I decided to see a lawyer and have him set me straight on the matter. So I went down street after street where the lawyers hung out their signs, sign after sign until, making my way down Calle Juncal, I stopped in front of a splendid house, talked to the doorman, and he ushered me in to see a doctor of jurisprudence. I remember as if it were today. He was a thin, serious man with a face like a perverted bandit, but when he smiled his soul was like some young kid's. When I thought it over later I concluded that he must have been a man who suffered a lot."

She sipped the maté, then, handing it back to him, she said:

"How hot it is here! Could you open the window?"

Erdosain opened one side a crack. It was still raining. Hipólita went on:

"So, not making it a big thing I said, 'Professor, I'm here to see you because I want to know how a woman sells her favors.' He just sat there staring at me in amazement. After a few moments' thought, he said, 'What's your purpose in wanting to know?' And I calmly explained to him my plans and he listened to me attentively, frowning, weighing my words. Finally he said, 'A woman is said to be selling her favors when she carries out sexual acts without love and for profit.' So you mean, I said then, that by selling her body, she can get free of it . . . and then she's free."

"You said that to him?"

"Yes."

"How strange!"

"How do you mean?"

"And then?"

"Hardly saying good-bye, I went out. I was happy, I've never been happier than that day. To sell one's body. Erdosain, that was it, to get free of your body, to have your will free to do anything that popped into your head. I felt so happy that as soon as a nice-looking fellow came along and murmured sweet things to me under his breath, I gave myself to him."

"And then?"

"A real surprise! Because when the man—I told you he was nice-looking—well he fell over like an ox when he was satisfied. The first thing I thought was he must be sick—I never imagined that. But when he explained to me that that was natural for any man, I couldn't help but laugh. So that a man who seems as immensely strong as a bull . . . well, have you ever seen a thief in a room full of gold? Just then I, the servant girl, was that thief in a room full of gold. And I saw the world lay in my hand . . . Later, after I got into prostitution, I resolved to study—yes, don't look so astonished, I read all kinds of things—I came to the conclusion from reading novels that men are ready to see an educated woman as having a great capacity for love . . . I don't know if I'm making it clear . . . I mean that a veneer of education could cover over the merchandise and raise the value."

"Did you take pleasure in the moment of possession?"

"No . . . but back to what I was saying: I read all kinds of things."

Erdosain warmed to the woman's cynicism, and, feeling tender toward her, he asked:

"Will you give me your hand?"

She gave it to him gravely.

Erdosain took it carefully; then he kissed it and she looked at him at length; but Remo suddenly remembered that man in chains; now he would be awake in

the stables, and not letting it chill the sweet warmth
lulling his senses, he said:

"Look if you . . . if you asked me to kill myself now,
I'd do it gladly."

She looked at him at length through her red eyelashes.

"I say that seriously. Tomorrow . . . today . . . it's
better . . . ask me to kill myself . . . tell me, doesn't it
seem to you certain people should just disappear from
earth?"

"No, that's no way to do things."

"Even though they might turn out criminals?"

"Who's to judge someone else?"

"Then no point us talking about it."

Again they sipped the maté in silence. Erdosain
understood the sweetness of many things. He looked
at her, then he said:

"What a strange creature you are!"

She smiled, pleased, and rejoicing broke out inside
his soul.

"Shall I put in more leaves?"

"Yes."

Suddenly Hipólita looked at him seriously.

"Where did you get that soul you have?"

Erdosain was about to speak about his sufferings,
but he felt inhibited and said instead:

"I don't know . . . I've often thought about purity—
I would have liked to be a pure man," and, waxing
enthusiastic, he went on, "Often I've felt sad over not
being a pure man. Why? I don't know. But can you
imagine a man with a white soul, in love for the first
time . . . and everyone like that? Can you imagine how
great love would be between a pure woman and a pure
man? Then before they gave themselves to one another,
they'd kill themselves—or wait, no; she'd be the one
to offer herself to him for one day—then they'd kill

themselves, realizing the uselessness of living with no illusions."

"But still, that's not possible."

"But it exists. Haven't you ever noticed how many shopkeepers and dressmakers kill themselves together? They love one another . . . they can't marry . . . they go to a hotel . . . she gives herself to him, and then they kill themselves afterward."

"Yes, but they don't do it with any plan in mind."

"Maybe not."

"Where did you have supper last night?"

Erdosain spoke about the Espilas, explaining to her how those people had fallen into penury.

"And why don't they work?"

"Where do they get work? They look for it and don't find it. That's the terrible part. It even seemed I was seeing how misery had killed off their desire to live. Deaf Eustaquio is good at math—he knows infinitesimal calculus—but it doesn't do him any good. He also knows *Don Quixote* by heart . . . but something's a bit skewed in his reasoning. . . . Here, I'll show how: when he was sixteen they sent him out to buy leaves for maté and he went to a drugstore instead of a grocery. After a lot of explanations, he said that maté leaves were a medicinal product—that that was what botany taught."

"He has no common sense."

"Exactly. Besides, he's a fool for gambles—to solve a riddle he'll miss a meal, and when he has a few centavos he goes to a sweet shop and eats himself silly."

"How odd!"

"But Emilio, he's a good sort. He says—as he's told me, he's sure the psychic state they're in, strange and weak-willed, is a hereditary affliction, and so that's how he runs his life, he's as slow as a tortoise. He can take two hours to get dressed. It's as though he did

everything in an atmosphere of extraordinary indecision."

"And the sisters?"

"The poor girls do what they can . . . they sew . . . one
looks after a friend's hydroencephalitic child with his
head bigger than a pumpkin."

"How dreadful!"

"What I can't understand is how they can get used
to all that. That's why after I visited them, I felt I had
to give them hope—and since I know how to talk to
people, I managed to. And they dedicated themselves
to the copper rose."

"What's that?"

Erdosain explained to her about his life as an inventor. It was at the first, right after he married, that he
dreamed of getting rich through a discovery. His imagination filled up the nights with extraordinary ma-
chines, incomplete pieces of mechanisms that spun
their lubricated gears.

"So then you are an inventor?"

"No . . . now I'm not. That did seem important to
me then. There was a time when I was hungry—terribly hungry for money—perhaps I was infected with
an insanity time has changed. . . . So when I talked to
them about it, it wasn't because I was interested in the
matter economically, but just to see them full of hope,
I had to see with my own eyes those poor girls dreaming
about silk dresses, a nice-looking boyfriend, and a car
in front of a townhouse they would never have, and
now I'm sure they believe in all that."

"Were you always like that?"

"Only some of the time. Has that never happened
to you, to get this urge to do charitable deeds? Now I
remember this other thing. I'll tell it to you because
you were just now asking what kind of soul I had. I
remember. A year ago. It was a Saturday and two in

the morning. I remember I was sad and I went into a brothel. The lobby was full of people waiting their turn. Suddenly the door opened and the woman stood there— imagine—a little round sixteen-year-old's face . . . blue eyes and a schoolgirl smile. She was wearing a green wrap and was quite tall . . . but she had a schoolgirl face . . She looked around her . . . it was too late; a dreadful black with lips like inner tubes had gotten up and then, after having wrapped us all in a promise, went sadly back to the bedroom, under the hard gaze of the madam."

Erdosain stopped for a moment, then, in a purer and slower voice, he went on:

"Believe me . . . it's a shameful thing to wait in a brothel. You never feel sadder than there with all those pale faces around you trying with false, shifty smiles to hide the terrible urgency of the flesh. And there's something humiliating besides . . . I don't know what . . . but time goes rushing through your ears, while your sharpened hearing listens to the bedsprings groan inside, then silence, then the sound of washing up— but before anyone could take the black man's place, I got up and took that seat. I sat waiting with my heart banging in great thumps, and when she appeared in the doorway I got up."

"That's how it always is—one after another."

"I got up and went in, the door closed again; I left the money on the washbasin, and when she was about to open her wrapper, I took her arm and said, 'No, I'm not in here to sleep with you.' "

Now Erdosain's voice had grown fluid and vibrant.

"She looked at me and surely the first thing she thought was that I must be some pervert; but looking at her seriously, believe me, I was moved, and I said to her: 'Look, I came in because I felt sorry for you.' Now we were sitting together on a bureau with a gilded mirror, and she, with her schoolgirl face, was looking

me over gravely. I remember! I can still see it. I said,
'Yes, I felt sorry for you. I know you must earn two or
three thousand pesos a month . . . and there are fami-
lies who would be content to live on what you throw
away on shoes . . . I know . . . but I felt sorry for you,
terrifically sorry, seeing so much beauty so shabbily
insulted.' She looked at me in silence, but I didn't smell
of alcohol. 'Then I thought—right then it occurred to
me as the black man was going in, to leave you with
a sweet memory . . . and the sweetest memory I could
come up with was this—to come in and not touch
you . . . and then forever afterward you'd remember that
gesture.' And see, while I'd been talking the prostitute's
wrapper had come open over her breasts, and while
above her crossed legs you could . . . suddenly she caught
sight of that in the mirror and quickly pulled her robe
down over her knees and covered up her chest. That
gesture made a strange impression on me . . . she looked
at me without saying a word—who knows what she
was thinking—suddenly the madam rapped with her
knuckles on the door and she looked at me with a
pained expression, then her little face turned toward
me . . . she looked at me a moment and got up . . . she
took the five pesos and forced them into my pocket as
she said, 'Don't come back, if you do I'll have the
bouncer kick you out.' We were standing up . . . I was
headed out the other door, but suddenly, not taking
her eyes from mine, she wrapped her arms around my
neck . . . she was still looking into my eyes and kissed
me on the mouth . . . I can't tell you what that kiss
was like . . . she ran her hand across my forehead and
said: 'Good-bye, noble man.' "
  "And you never went back?"
  "No, but I hope we'll meet again someday . . . who
knows where, but she, Lucién, will never forget me.
Time will go by, she'll go through the most miserable
brothels . . . she'll grow horrible, but I'll always remain

in her as what I set out to be, as the most precious memory in her life."

The rain beat on the windows of the room and the mosaics of the tiled patio. Erdosain sipped his maté slowly.

Hipólita got up, went over to the windowpanes and peered for a moment into the blackness of the patio. Then she turned around and said:

"Do you know, you're a strange man?"

Erdosain hesitated for an instant.

"I'll tell you the truth—I don't know what's to become of my life—but believe me, I wasn't given the chance to be a good man. Dark outside forces twisted me, pulled me down."

"And now?"

"Now I'm going to do an experiment. I met an admirable man whose firm conviction it is that lying is the basis of human happiness and I'm going along with him in everything he does."

"And does that make you happy?"

"No . . . some time ago I figured out that I was never going to be happy again."

"But do you believe in love?"

"Why talk about it!" But suddenly he realized why he had been rambling on like that a few minutes ago, and he said: "What would you think of me if tomorrow . . . I mean any day . . . if any day now you found out I had killed a man?"

Hipólita, who had sat down, raised her head slowly and leaning it back against the sofa, studied the ceiling for some time. Then, looking down, she said as she filtered a chilly gaze from between red eyelashes:

"I'd think you were immensely unfortunate."

Erdosain got out of his chair, put away the cooker, the leaves, and gourd for the maté in the cupboard, and then Hipólita said to him:

"Come here . . . at my feet here."

He sat on the carpet with one side leaning against her legs, let his head droop onto her knees, and Hipólita closed her eyes.

It was an easy, peaceful feeling. He rested in the woman's lap, and the warmth of her limbs came through the cloth, warming his cheek. Moreover that scene seemed very natural; life was getting to look like a movie, which is what he always tried for, and it did not enter his head to think about Hipólita, stiffly sitting on the sofa, who thought that he was a weak and sentimental man. The ticktock of the clock dribbled out a drop of sound at each movement of the gears; it plopped like dripping water into the cubical silence of the room. And Hipólita said to herself:

"All he'll do in his life is complain and suffer. What good is a fellow like that to me? I'd have to support him. And the copper rose, that's silly. What woman would wear metal ornaments on her hat, that are heavy and going to tarnish? But still, they're all like that. The weak ones are intelligent and useless; the others are boring brutes. I still haven't come across one of them who'd deserve to cut the others' throats or be a tyrant. They're pitiful."

She often thought those things, whenever reality did something to fade the brightly colored version of life her imagination had painted a moment before. She could sort them like eggs by now. That straight-backed, sweet-smelling, severe-looking one who liked to come across as silent and contained, he was a lecherous wretch, and that other little well-dressed one, eternally polite, discreet and sensible, harbored the most horrendous vices, while that lumberjack sort of brute, strong as an ox, was as inexpert as a schoolboy, and so they filed past her eyes, linked together by that same never-flagging desire, they had all at some point let their heads droop over onto her bared knees, while she, alien to the clumsy hands and fits of frenzy that animated those sad puppets thought, bitterly, that a feeling for life was like being thirsty in the middle of a desert.

"That's how it was. All that ever kept men going was hunger, lust, and money. That's how it was."

In anguish, she told herself the only one she had cared for was the pharmacist, who at moments rose above all this vehement carnality, but in the course of the terrible game his workings had gotten gummed up, and now he was lying more broken than any of the other puppets.

What a life she had had! Before, when she was a penniless girl, she thought she would never have money or a fancy house with fine furniture, or shining silverware and china, and to see riches so far beyond her reach made her as sad then as today it did to know that none of the men who would lie in her bed had the makings of a tyrant or a conquerer of new lands.

HIPÓLITA'S INNER LIFE

What dreams had filled her head!

Some days she fantasized a meeting with a man who would talk about jungles and have a tame lion at home. He would never grow tired of embracing her and she would love him like a slave; then she would find it a joy to shave under her arms and apply makeup to her breasts, all for him. Disguised as a boy, she would traverse with him those ruins where centipedes sleep and villages where blacks build their huts in the forks of trees. But nowhere did she find lions, only flea-bitten dogs, and the most adventurous gentlemen brandished a quick fork and kept their gaze ever upon the gleaming stewpot. She fled these stupid little lives in disgust.

As time went on, it turned out the strange novelistic characters she met were not as interesting as in the novel; in fact, that what seemed best about them in the novel was exactly the odious bits that made them so repulsive in life. But still, she had given herself to them.

Once they were sated they turned away from her as if ashamed to have offered her a look at their weak sides. Now she sank into the sterility of her life like some well-explored sand basin.

Just as it was impossible to transform lead into gold, it was impossible to transform the soul of man.

How often had she fallen naked into the arms of a stranger and said to him: "Wouldn't you like to go to Africa?" The man would react as though he were in bed with a rattlesnake. And then she would feel that those bodies made out of bones with muscles stretched over them were weaker than those of tender infants, more fearful than children in the woods.

She found women odious. She watched them give in to the sensuality of males and then offer the whole world the sight of their bloated bellies. All they knew how to do was suffer, this was a world of tired people, half-waking ghosts that infested the earth with their gravid sleepiness, like the gigantic lazy monsters at the dawn of time. Thus her soul, attempting to soar, was smashed to earth by the overwhelming pointlessness of those who lived around her.

Because Hipólita would have liked to live in a universe of lesser density, a world as light as a soap bubble where matter was not subject to gravity, and she imagined the surge of joy she would have running hither and thither over the planet, metamorphosing at will and imparting to her every day the reality of a game that would compensate for the games she had never played as a child.

Everything had been denied her as a child. She remembered how one of the fantasies of her childhood was to dream she would be the happiest creature on earth if only she could live in a room with wallpaper.

She had seen in shop windows paper printed with patterns that to her limited imagination seemed ready to make a dream of the life of whoever lived surrounded by them, printed papers that were like transplanting the enchanted forest into a house, with arbitrary flowers of various blues twining away across gilded backgrounds, and that seven-year-old's dream was as intense in her as her later idea when she was a maid about the pleasure she would feel if she could have a Rolls-Royce, whose leather upholstery was as precious in her imagination as the impossible patterned papers that really only cost sixty centavos a roll.

She had wandered off into the past. She remembered now, with the man's head on her knees, those Sundays when suddenly at dusk the weather changed and the cold breeze drove her employers out of the garden and back to the parlor. The rain pattered on the panes, and she took refuge in the shiny clean kitchen, and one could hear the voices of guests through the rooms, the women conversed while the girls leafed through magazines, pausing over the photographs of weddings, or played the piano.

And she, sitting at the table, twisting one corner of her apron in her fingers, leaning forward a little, let the sounds wash over her, always melancholy to her ears, even when they spoke of happy things. She felt isolated like a leper, cut off from happiness. The music wafted to her a vision of new places, mountain resorts, and she would never be that new bride who lilted down to the dining room on the arm of her handsome husband, while the silverware and china tinkled softly and the birds fluttered around the windows, and a waterfall sent forth crystal sounds.

She twisted the corner of her apron slowly between her fingers, her head bowed over, her legs crossed.

She would never have a husband like the dashing gallant who sweeps the heroine off her feet in novels, nor would she festoon a mantilla across the velvet railing of her box at the opera, while diamonds glittered in the ears of duchesses and violins poured sweet strains from the orchestra pit.

Nor would she be a young matron, a lady of the house like women she had served, with husbands who tenderly placed solicitous palms to feel the stretching and swelling of their gravid abdomens. And her sorrow swelled up gently like the darkness coming on at the close of day.

Forever, forever and ever to be a servant!

Then anger tinged her grief, her forehead felt heavy and her red-rimmed lids drooped in resignation.

And the parlor piano sent foreign lands streaming through her fantasies, and she thought how the painstaking effort of turning out young *ladies* must make their souls lovelier and sweeter for the suitor's desiring, and her head was heavy as if the cranium had gotten turned into a helmet of lead bones.

Everything around her, pots, stove burners, the clean wood of the kitchen cupboards, and the bathroom mirrors and red lampshades, seemed to have some substance in it so that it was beyond her reach, as if the dishcloth, the carpet, the children's tricycle were all made to bring happiness to beings not even made out of the same stuff she was.

The very clothes the misses wore, the fine light fabrics with which they adorned their pretty bodies, the embroidery and ribbons, all struck her as basically unlike any such she might buy for herself with the same money. This feeling of being set down among people who inhabited a different realm from the one she belonged to upset her, so much so that despair showed on her face plain as a stigma.

How could she ever be anything but a servant, forever a serving-girl!

A half-smothered *no* welled up in her throat, in answer to the invisible presence that gave it no rest. Her life seemed to pit itself against such servitude. She did not know how she might escape from the evil fate that bound her like fetters, but she kept repeating to herself that it was only a temporary state of things, although she had no notion what might materialize to free her. And she was always watching the misses' deportment, how they carried their heads, how they said their goodbyes in the doorway, later reproducing in front of a mirror the phrases and gestures from memory. And these motions she went through alone in her cramped quarters left her with a sensation of high birth and delicacy on her lips and in her soul for several hours, during which her old clumsy ways seemed to her a betrayal of her genuine persona, now recaptured: a *lady*.

For a few hours her life was aglow with a delicacy as soft and penetrating as the fragrance of a scented cream, a waft of vanilla, and it seemed as though it was her throat that pealed forth those mellifluous yesses and noes, and finally she imagined herself in conversation with a beautiful partner who wore a blue fox wrapped about her neck.

Her serving-girl's quarters held a host of nuance-laden figures of fantasy, and sitting in an armchair lined in alligator silk, she received friends who were just dashing off to Paris and chatted about engagements. "Her mother won't let her go to X for the summer because they'd run into S— that fellow who made a play for her before." Or she'd sail the seas, seas as calm as the Palermo Lakes or some other playground of the rich, perched on a wicker basket, just as she'd seen ladies in photographs of luxury liners, or on her way through the streets to the market to shop. She would have a Kodak lying carelessly in her lap while a young man, cap in hand and inclined toward her, spoke to her timidly.

Her housemaid's soul was flooded with happiness. She knew it was all so fine that if she ever came to live her dream, she'd be Lady Bountiful. And she could see herself in the wintry dusk, hurrying down mean streets in a coat of costly weave, seeking out an orphan child, the blind man's girl. She would save her, adopt her as her own child, and one day the orphan girl would make her debut; she would have blossomed into a lovely young woman; bare shoulders from amid clouds of tulle and, above the chiseled forehead, a lock of golden hair would set off the delicacy of her almond eyes.

And all at once a voice would call her:

"Hipólita . . . serve the tea."

A CRIME

Erdosain suddenly looked up, and Hipólita, as though she had been thinking of him, said:

"You, too . . . you've been through a lot, too."

Erdosain took the woman's cold hand and brought it to his lips.

She went on, slowly:

"Sometimes this life seems to me a bad dream. Now that I feel yours, the pain of times gone by comes back to me. Always, everywhere, life was cruel."

Then she said:

"What must you do not to suffer like that?"

"The thing is, we're carriers of suffering. One time I thought it floated airborne . . . it was a silly idea; really we're the carriers of our own sickness."

They fell silent. Hipólita slowly stroked his hair,

then suddenly she took her hand from his head and Erdosain felt her pressing her hand against his lips.

Erdosain, sitting beside her, murmured:

"Tell me, what have I done for you that you should make me so happy? Don't you see you're my heaven on earth? Never had I hit such depths."

"Nobody ever loved you?"

"I don't know; but love was never shown me in all its terrible strength. When I got married I was twenty and I believed in love as something spiritual."

He hesitated an instant, but then he got up quickly and after turning out the light, sat on the sofa next to Hipólita. Then he said:

"Maybe I was just a pathetic dolt. But when I got married I had never kissed my wife. It's true, I'd never felt any need to do it because I took her lack of warmth for great purity and besides . . . because I believed a *lady* was above all that kissing."

She was smiling in the dark. He was sitting on the edge of the sofa, his elbows on his knees and his cheeks buried in the palms of his hands.

The room was flooded with violet lighting.

He continued slowly:

"I had this idea of a *lady*, the utmost expression of purity. Besides—don't laugh—I was bashful . . . and on our wedding night, when she got undressed naturally with the light on, I turned my head not to see . . . and then I went to bed with my pants on."

"You did?" Indignation vibrated in the woman's voice.

Erdosain burst out laughing, now all wound up:

"Why not?" as he watched the Lame Whore sidelong and wrung his hands. "I've done things a lot stranger, too. And some, I haven't yet done. 'The times have come,' as your husband used to say. I believe he's right. But all this happened way back, when I used to live like an idiot. I'm telling you that so you won't think if

I were to go to bed with you now I'd keep my pants on."

Hipólita felt afraid for a moment. Erdosain kept his sidelong gaze trained on her, and wrung his hands, but nothing more. Prudently, she added:

"No doubt it was all a kind of sickness with you. Like what I had when I was a servant. You never touch down to the earth."

"Yes, you never touch down. That's just how I was. Yes, I remember when they'd call me an idiot."

"That, too?"

"Yes, to my face . . . I stood looking at the man who'd insulted me, and my muscle tone went slack, leaving me like a dishrag. I wondered how I'd taken so many humiliations and intimidations. I'd been through a lot— so much—that more than once I felt like hiring myself out as a servant in a wealthy household— How much could I grovel? Then I felt the terror, the blackest fear, of having a life with no noble object, no great dream, and now finally I've got one . . . I've condemned a man to death . . . No, stay where you are, listen, tomorrow, because I let it happen, a man will be murdered."

"No!"

"Yes, it's true. The man with the beautiful lies, the one I was telling you about before, needed money to carry out his plan. So it will be carried out, because I want it to happen. Tomorrow he'll give me a check to cash. When I come back he'll be executed."

"No . . . it can't be like that."

"Yes, and if I don't come back they won't kill him, because without the money there's no point to the crime . . . fifteen thousand pesos—I could run away on that . . . to hell with them and society—each man for himself. You see? It all depends on my being an honorable criminal."

"My God!"

"I want the experiment to be carried out. You see,

there are ways a man can become a god. For a long
time I've been set on killing myself. If when I asked
you, before, you'd said for me to, I'd have killed myself.
If you just could know how great and beautiful I feel!
Don't talk to me about that other business—it's all set
to go; in fact, I like to think about the black hole I'm
throwing myself into. You know? . . . And any day now—
no, it won't be daytime—any night, when I've had
enough of this crazy-quilt excuse for a life, just like
that, I'll be gone."

A wrinkle shot down the middle of Hipólita's forehead. No doubt remained. The man was mad. She was
already, with an adventuress's wisdom, plotting out the
future. "This imbecile calls for some very careful, cautious handling." And so, crossing her arms over her
wrapper, she asked, as if in doubt:

"You'd have the guts to kill yourself?"

"It's not that kind of thing. There's no more courage-
versus-cowardice at suicide point. I intuitively know
that committing suicide is really like extracting a tooth.
And thinking that makes me feel easy about the whole
thing. Sure, I've thought of travels I might go on, other
places, another life. Part of me wants everything delicate and beautiful. I've often thought that—say those
fifteen thousand pesos I'll get tomorrow—I could go to
the Philippines . . . to Ecuador, start a new life, marry
a refined millionaire's daughter . . . we'd spend the siesta hour cuddled together in a hammock, underneath
the coconut palms, while blacks offered us orange sec-
tions. And I'd gaze sadly out to sea—you know? I'm
sure wherever I'd be I'd end up gazing sadly out to sea—
and I'd know I'd still never be happy . . . at first thinking about it drove me wild . . . and now I'm resigned
to it."

"Then why go through with the experiment?"

"You know? I still haven't plumbed my own depths,

but this crime thing is my last hope—and the Astrologer knows, because when I asked him if he wasn't afraid I'd make off with the money, he answered: 'No, not at the moment, no. You're the one who needs the society to get going because you don't know what to do with yourself . . . ' So you see how deeply I'm into it."

"I'd never have imagined anything like it. So they'll kill him out in Temperley?"

"Yes. But still. . . . What's really going on? All this anguish. Do you know what anguish is? To have anguish boring right down into your bones like syphilis? Look, four months before this: I was waiting for a train at a country depot. It was going to be forty-five minutes late—and then I went over to an open square out in front. A few minutes after I'd sat down on a bench, a girl—she must have been about nine, she came and sat by my side. We began to talk—she had a white apron on—she lived in one of the houses across the square— Slowly, unable to stop myself, I started to introduce obscene bits into the conversation—but prudently— watching her reaction carefully. An atrocious curiosity had taken me in its grip. The child, hypnotized by her half-awakened instinct, listened to me, trembling . . . and I, slowly, must have had it written all over my face, because a couple of clerks from the switchman's station kept a watch on me. . . . I revealed to her the mysteries of sex, encouraging her to corrupt her little friends, too—"

Hipólita squeezed her forehead between her fingers. "But you're a monster!"

"Now I've come to the end. My life is horrible. I need to create terrible complications for myself . . . commit sins. Don't look at me. Possibly . . . look . . . people don't know what sin means anymore—sin's not just a failing, an error. I've come to see how sin is an act that lets man break the slender thread that kept him linked to God. I'm going to break that slender thread that tied me to divine charity. I feel it. From tomorrow on I'll be a monster on the face of the earth— imagine a creature . . . a fetus . . . a fetus able to live outside its mother's womb—it never grows . . . hairy . . . small . . . without fingernails or toenails it goes among men without being a man . . . its fragility horrifies everyone around it, but there's no way of returning it to its womb again. That's what will happen to me tomorrow. I'll cut myself off permanently from God. I'll be alone on earth. My soul and me, just the two of us. And infinity in front of us. Always alone. And night and day—and always a yellow sun. You see? The infinite will grow—a yellow sun hanging overhead and the soul cut off from divine love will wander alone and blind under that yellow sun."

Something thumped onto the floor, and all at once something extraordinary happened. Erdosain fell silent in amazement. Hipólita was kneeling at his feet. She took his hand and covered it with kisses. In the darkness the woman exclaimed:

"Let me . . . let me kiss your poor hands. You're the most unfortunate man on earth."

"Get up, Hipólita."

"No, I want to kiss your feet." He felt her arms hugging his legs. "You're the most unfortunate man on earth! What you haven't been through, my God! How great you are. What a great soul you have!"*

Erdosain made her rise with infinite gentleness. He felt the softening effect of an infinite pity, he drew her to him, he smoothed back the hair over her forehead and said:

---

* Commentator's note: Later Hipólita was to tell the Astrologer: "I kneeled to Erdosain exactly when it occurred to me to blackmail you, taking advantage of his having told me all about the murder plan."

"If you knew how easy it will be to die. Like a game."

"What a soul you have!"

"Are you feverish?"

"My poor boy!"

"But why? If we've become like gods. . . . Sit down next to me. Are you fine like that? Look, little sister, everything I've been through is all made up to me now, with what you've just said. We'll live a little longer—"

"Yes, like an engaged couple—"

"On the great day only will you become my wife."

"I love you so much! What a soul you have!"

"And then we'll go away."

They said no more. Hipólita's head had fallen forward onto her chest. It was nearly dawn. Then Erdosain eased that tired body onto the sofa. She smiled exhaustedly; then Remo sat on the carpet, leaned his head on the edge of the sofa, and curled up like that went to sleep.

A Subconscious Sensation

Half sitting up on a sofa, with his arms crossed and his hat down over his forehead, the Astrologer was mulling over his various preoccupations that night in the darkened study. The rain beat against the windowpanes, but he did not hear it, totally engrossed as he was in numerous projects. Besides, something strange was happening to him.

The proximity of the crime to be committed accelerated within the flow of normal time a second, particular time. Thus he got the feeling he was existing in two different frames of time's passage. One, common to all states of normal life, the other fleeting, heavy to his beating heart, running through his meditatively intertwined fingers as water runs out the interstices of a basket.

And the Astrologer, still inside clock time, felt the other kind of time pour through his brain, rapid and endless, like a film running dizzily by, its juxtapositions of images somehow exhausting, injuring, wounding to the mind, since before one idea could be grasped, it was gone and another took its place. So when he lit a match to check the time, he found only a few minutes had gone by, while in his head those mechanical minutes, impelled along by his anxiety, were a totally different length, one no clock could measure.

A feeling kept him waiting expectantly in the dark. He knew that any error committed while in such a state could prove fatal.

The big worry was not Barsut's murder, but just all the care that had to be taken to keep it from becoming a needlessly big problem. Though he tried sketching out his alibi, it was hard to keep at it. He felt the man worrying in the darkness was not him, that he watched his double, a double made out of emotion and looking just like him, with the same rhombus-shaped face, crossed arms, and hat pulled down over the forehead. Nonetheless, he could not really say for sure what thoughts went through the double's mind, so closely linked to him and yet so far beyond his grasp. Because at that moment he felt that his feeling of existing was more important than the existence of his body. Later, puzzling over this phenomenon, he was to say it was his awareness of the different time his emotions ran in, that time inside of the other, mechanical time, like when people say, "That minute seemed like a century."

Unthinkable, yet it could not be taken lightly since it was a question of taking a man's life, paralyzing the circulation of his five liters of blood, turning all his cells cold, rubbing him out of life like a spot from a piece of paper, leaving behind no trace. Since such a grave problem could not be dismissed, the Astrologer felt how he was himself inside mechanical clock time, the physical him, while in the slower pace of the other time that no clock could tick off, there was his double, pensive, enigmatic, truly mysterious, preparing a set of alibis, perhaps, that would later surprise the thinking man.

The certainty he had been transformed by the imminent crime into a double mechanism with two different systems of time and two different rates of speed left him feeling drained there in the darkness.

A terrible weariness seized his whole frame, his sturdy limbs, his joints.

The rain started the frogs up, sounding like a clacking machine, but he, a man of action, but in such anxiety-induced lassitude, as if they had turned his bones to mush and he could not stand up, "I, a man of action," he told himself, "here I remain, here I am inside my clockwork span of time, throbbing to the beat of another time not my own, that leaves me with my guard down. Because the truth of it is that killing a man is just like slitting a lamb's throat, but other people don't see that, and though they're far from me and my conduct is a mystery to them, this abnormal time brings me closer to them, and I can hardly move, as though they were lurking in the shadows watching me. It must be nervous time that has me all off balance, or the subconscious Astrologer who says nothing but squeezes me out like an orange, creating thoughts I'd never come up with. But still, once Barsut is dead, life will just go on as if nothing had ever happened— and really nothing has unless our cover story falls through."

He lit another match. The room was shot through with arrowhead shapes of light. Not even a minute had passed. His thoughts came simultaneously and contained in the nothingness of time facts that, if they were given the time they would have needed under normal circumstances, would have taken months and years. He had been born forty-three years and seven days ago, and his past was continually being annihilated as it hit the present, a present so fleeting that it was always the Astrologer of the minute beyond, inside the time of the next coming minute or second. Now his whole life centered on a fact which was not yet a fact, but which would come to be in a few hours, a fact so full of contained violence that it imparted that extraordinary tension to that other, anxiety time that ran alongside clock time.

And though he had often thought that if it fell to his lot to murder someone he would not let the occasion pass him by, his thoughts returned again to those times of mystery. Then he started up a fantasy about a dictatorship that kept running by means of terror imposed through numerous executions, and the only way to blot out this repugnant momentary impression was to imagine those dead as horizontal men. Indeed, he pictured, lying in the middle of a clearing, the small body of a man, and comparing the dead man's length with the many thousands of kilometers of the earth he tyrannized, he was utterly sure that the life of one man had no value.

He would consign that man to the worms, and having cleared away the human clutter on one tiny part of the earth, he would proceed to conquer more and more land.

Then he thought about Lenin, how he had wrung his hands and repeated to the Soviet commissars:

"What's this garbage? How can we make a revolution if we don't shoot anyone?" And this put joy in the Astrologer's heart. He would set forth such a principle in his own society. The future patriarchs of new races would be brought up to consider murder standard procedure; and again his hopes grew. Then he realized that every innovator has to struggle against the obsolete ideas that have been programmed into him, and that the doubts that plagued him now were the result of a conflict between what society held to be right now and what it would sanction in the future.

Time ran through his fingers, which, in the course of his ponderings, he had interwoven.

Today's murderer would be tomorrow's conquering hero, but for now he would have to withstand the bitter warring of the present all mixed in with yesterdays. He got up, angry now. It was still raining. He went out to the stairs, where he stood peering intently into the darkness and wildness, where trees shook under the water buffeting them thickly and heavily. The darkness there seemed to form part of the existence of a monster who was panting heavily in the darkness. The wet ground had turned ocher. And he was a firm man in the night, the *metteur-en-scène* of grandiose events, and yet no phantom emerged out of the foliage to sanction his attitude. Now he wondered if the men of other ages had suffered such indecision, or if they had marched straight to their goals satisfied that Death would give to their determination the thickness of armor. He told himself that as a philosophical being the only thing that could interest him was the species, not the individual, that it was his feelings that now lay siege to him with scruples, turning the time that must go by into two strange times, all against his will.

A flash of lightning put blue spaces between the blocks of the mountains of clouds.

Sopping and with his hair messed up, the Man Who Saw the Midwife stood to one side of the stairs.

"Ah! It's you!" said the Astrologer.

"Yes; I wanted to ask you what you think of this interpretation of the verse that says: 'The Heaven of

God.' That means clearly that there are other heavens not of God—"

"Then whose are they?"

"I mean there can be heavens where God isn't there. Because the verse adds: 'And the New Jerusalem shall descend.' The New Jerusalem? Is that the New Church?"

The Astrologer meditated an instant. The matter did not interest him, but he knew that to maintain his image with the man he had to answer, and he answered:

"We, the illuminati, know secretly that the New Jerusalem is the New Church. That's why Swedenborg says: 'Since the Lord God cannot show himself in person, and having announced that he will come and establish a New Church, then he must do it by means of a man who will not just receive the doctrine of this church, but will also publish it by means of the press . . .' but, why do you, without any other passage, think there are several heavens in existence?"

Bromberg, sheltering under the porch, looked off into the heavy-breathing darkness, shaking under the pummeling of the rain, then answered:

"Because heavens are something you feel, like love."

The Astrologer looked at the Jew in amazement, and the man went on:

"It's like love. How can you deny love if love is in you and you feel the angels strengthening your love? It's the same with the four heavens. Admittedly, all the words of the Bible are of mystery, since if it weren't that way, the book would be absurd. The other night I was reading the Apocalypse, filled with grief. I was thinking how I'd have to murder Gregorio, and I wondered if it was permitted to shed human blood."

"But when you strangle someone you don't shed any blood," objected the Astrologer.

"And when I got to the part about the 'Heaven of God' I understood the reason for mankind's sadness. God's heaven had been denied to them by the church of darkness—and that's why so many sinned so greatly."

In the darkness, the childish voice of Bromberg sounded as sad as though he were lamenting how they had excluded him from the true heaven. The Astrologer argued:

"The man with wings who speaks to me in dreams said the end of the church of darkness is near—"

"And so it must be—because hell grows every day. So few are saved that heaven compared to hell is smaller than a grain of sand next to the ocean. Year after year hell grows, and the church of darkness, that ought to save man, swells the numbers in hell instead, and hell grows, grows, without any chance existing of making it smaller. And the angels gaze in fear upon the church of darkness and fiery hell all swollen like a belly heavy with dropsy."

The Astrologer replied, assuming a lofty tone of voice:

"That's why the man with wings has told me: 'Go, O holy man, forth to edify men and announce the glad tidings. And exterminate the Antichrists and reveal your secrets and the secrets of the New Jerusalem to Bromberg the Jew.'" Suddenly the Astrologer, taking his companion's arm, said: "Don't you remember when your spirit conversed with the angels and served them white bread at the side of the road, and you bade them sit at the door of your abode and washed their feet?"

"I don't remember that."

"Well, you ought to remember. What will the Lord say if he hears that? How am I to answer for your soul before the Angel of the New Church? He'll say to me: 'What is become of that beloved son, my pious Alfon?' And what will I tell him? That you're an animal. That you've forgotten the days when you lived an angelic life and now you spend the whole day in a corner breaking wind like a mule."

Bromberg objected in a bristly rage:

"I do not break wind."

"Yes you do, and it makes a lot of noise, too—but what's the difference?—the Angel of the Churches knows that your soul is aglow with sincere devotion, and that you are an enemy of the King of Babylon, of the Dark Pope, and so you are chosen to be the friend of him who with the mandate of the Lord shall establish the New Church on earth."

The rain beat quietly on the leaves of the fig trees and all the acrid, soft darkness wafted into the night its humid greenery smell. Bromberg predicted gravely:

"And the Pope, the very Pope, in terror, will dash out into the street barefoot, and they'll all shrink back from him in horror and fear and the walls along the roads will spill over with flowers when the Holy Lamb comes by."

"That will happen," continued the Astrologer. "And up in heaven, the doors will open to the sight of all the repentant sinners, the golden portals of the New Jerusalem. Because so great is the charity of God, beloved Alfon, that no man shall enter directly into contact with it without being smitten to earth with his bones jellied."

"That's why I shall bring to men my interpretation of the Apocalypse and then go off to the mountains to do penitence and to pray for them."

"Indeed, Alfon, but now go to sleep because I have to meditate and it is time for the man with wings to come speak words in my ear. And you also must sleep because otherwise, tomorrow, you will have no strength to strangle this reprobate—"

"And the King of Babylon."

"Indeed."

Slowly the Man Who Saw the Midwife walked away from the stairs. The Astrologer went back inside and climbing a staircase to one side of the entry hall, he went into a very long thin room, with beams running exposed across it at the top to hold up the oblique extension of the roof.

The peeling walls held not a single etching. In one corner were the trunks belonging to Gregorio Barsut and under an oeil-de-boeuf window, a red painted wooden bed. A black bedspread contrasted bizarrely with the white sheets. The Astrologer sat down pensively on the edge of the bed. His smock fell half-open, showing his naked, hairy chest. He arched his fingertips covering his seallike mustache, and, frowning, he sat contemplating a trunk in the corner.

He wanted to force his thought to leap upon some extraneous novelty, which by breaking up the monorhythm of his feelings would restore him to the frame of mind he had been in before he decided to murder Barsut.

"Twenty thousand pesos," he thought. "Twenty million pesos that will let me set up the brothels and the colony . . . the colony . . ."

Still he could not think clearly. Ideas slipped away from him elusive as shadows, his thoughts, gone berserk with shock, made it impossible to concentrate. Suddenly he slapped his forehead and, jubilant, dragged a box with him into the vestibule, a thick dust sifting from the box's loosely tied top.

Not caring that his smock sleeves were getting all full of white dust, he opened the box. There were lead soldiers mixed in with wooden dolls, and really it was a whole population of clowns, generals, jesters, princesses, and strange roly-poly monsters with lopsided noses and mouths like frogs.

He picked up a piece of rope and, turning to one corner, he fastened it to two nails, thus uniting the angle formed by the two walls with an improvised bisecting line. Then he took several puppets from the box, throwing them onto the bed. Then he strung up each of the figures by the neck, and so engrossed was he in this task, that he failed to notice that the wind was driving the rain in through the open window, as it was raining harder.

He worked enthusiastically. As soon as he had wound cords around the neck of each figure and cut them to varying lengths, he dragged all the puppets by their ropes off to the corner. When it was done, he sat looking at his handiwork. The five hanged figures threw moving hooded shadows on the rose-colored wall. The first, a Pierrot figure without the puffed breeches but a black-and-white checked blouson; the second, an idol with chocolate skin and vermilion lips, whose watermelon head was level with the Pierrot's feet; the third, still lower, was a windup Pierrot, with a bronze plaque in its belly and a monkey's face; the fourth was a blue cardboard sailor, and the fifth an open-nosed black man with a plaster sore showing through the white coating on his patrician neck. The Astrologer contemplated his work in satisfaction. He had his back to the lamp, and his black silhouette projected up to the ceiling. He said aloud:

"You, Pierrot, are Erdosain; you, roly-poly, are the Gold Seeker; you, clown, are the Ruffian; and you, black man, are Alfon. So that's settled, now."

His speech finished, he pulled Barsut's trunk out from against the wall, pulled it up in front of the puppets and sat in front of them. And thus there began a silent dialogue whose questions came from inside him and received their answer inside him when he fixed his gaze upon the figure he was interrogating.

His thoughts became surprisingly clear. He needed to express his ideas by telegraphic, clattering staccato, as if all of him had to keep the rhythm of the thoughts in time with a mysterious trepidation of enthusiasm.

He thought:

"We've got to set up factories for poison gas. To hire
a chemist. To think big, not just trucks, cells, great
covered structures. Training camp in the mountains,
nonsense. Or, no. Yes. No. Also beside Paraná River a
factory. Cars armor plating chrome steel nickel. Poison
gas important. Up in the mountains and in Chaco Forest to spark revolution. Find brothels, kill owners. A
killer band in airplane. Everything possible. Each group
radio-equipped. Use a code and keep switching the
wavelength. Electric current falling water. Swedish turbines. Erdosain's right. Life is so great! Who am I? Production of bubonic bacillus and super strains of typhus.
Set up academy comparative studies Russian French
Revolution. Movies an important element. Not to be
neglected. See filmmaker. Have Erdosain look into that.
Filmmaker in the cause of revolutionary propaganda.
That's it."

Now the flood of thoughts eased up. He told himself:

"How are we to instill in every mind the revolutionary enthusiasm I bear in my own? There's our problem. What lie or truth do we use? How time goes by.
And how sad! Because it's true. There's such sadness
within me that if they could only see it they'd be amazed.
I carry it all on my own shoulders."

He curled up on the sofa. He was cold. His veins
throbbed hard in his temples.

"Time slips away. Just like that. And they all fall
down, like so many sacks of potatoes. Nobody tries to
take wing and soar. How can I get these clods to take
wing? And yet, life can be so much more. More than
they've ever imagined. The soul like an ocean surging
inside seventy kilos of flesh. That same flesh yearns
to soar away. Everything in us longs to soar up to the
clouds, to reach hidden lands up there in the clouds—
but, how? There's always that 'how' and I . . . here I
am, suffering over them, loving them as though I'd

given birth to them, because I love those men . . . I love them all. They were just randomly plunked down on earth, and that's not how things ought to be. And yet I love them. I can feel it now. I love Humankind. I love them all as though slender threads bound them to my heart. Through that thread they suck my blood, my life, and yet, in spite of it all, there's so much life in me I'd gladly have millions more of them, to love them even more and give them my life. Yes, give them my life like a cigarette. Now I understand Christ. How much he must have loved Humankind! And yet I'm ugly. My big wide face is ugly. And still I must be beautiful, the way only gods are. But I have a cauli-flower ear and a great bony nose like a punched-up boxer's. But what does that matter? I'm a man and that's enough. And I need to conquer. That's it. And I would not give up a one of my thoughts for the love of the most beautiful woman."

Suddenly some earlier words flashed into his memory, and the Astrologer said:

"Why not? . . . We can make cannons, just as Erdo-sain said. It's an easy procedure. Besides, they don't have to last through a thousand volleys. A revolution that dragged on for that long would be a failure."

The words fall silent inside him. In the darkness a dark pathway opens inside his skull, with exposed beams running across to join the sides, while in a fog of coal dust the blast furnaces, with cooling stations looming like armored men, fill up the space. Clouds of fire flare from the armored slats and the jungle beyond stretches out thick and impenetrable.

The Astrologer feels he has his own personality back, the one that the strange dislocation of time had taken from him.

He thinks, he thinks it is possible to make chrome-plated steel and construct cannons from cast-metal tubes. Why not? His thoughts race on to the possible obstacles with flexibility. Then with the money the brothels bring in land could be bought up in different spots in the country at an insignificant cost. There the members of the society would set up reinforced concrete structures to house the artillery, making them look like storehouses for grain.

He thrilled to the thought of setting up a revolutionary party within the country, one that would rise to arms at a radio-broadcast signal. Why not? Steel, chrome, nickel. The words have taken hold in his head. Steel, chrome, nickel. The head of each cell would be in charge of a battery. So, what will we need? For each cannon to fire four or five hundred rounds. And then machine guns mounted on cars. Why not? For every ten men a machine gun, an auto, a cannon. Why not give it a try?

Slowly, in the depths of the black night, a huge white-hot egg of steel, supported on two columns, slowly moves its point to a great dome. This is the Bessemer steel process driven by hydraulic piston. A shower of sparks and flames pours from the top of the steel egg. Iron is being made into steel, being subjected to a blast of air that makes contact at hundreds of atmospheres of pressure. Steel, chrome, nickel. What is there to lose? He thinks of a hundred details. Not long ago a voice inside him had wondered:

"Why is it the sum total of human happiness would occupy so little space?"

The truth of it saddened his existence. The work should belong to the few. And those few should walk with giant strides.

It is necessary to create the complication. And to see things plain. First to kill Barsut, then to set up the brothel, the training camp in the mountains . . . but, how to dispose of the body? Isn't it idiotic that the man who can easily build a cannon and manufacture steel, chrome, and nickel should have such a hard time figuring out how to get rid of a body? But that's unthinkable . . . it could be burned up . . . five hundred degrees are enough to destroy a body contained in a closed receptacle. Five hundred degrees."

Time and exhaustion go streaming through his mind. He would like not to think, and suddenly his voice, as if independent of his mouth and his will, whispers from inside to distract him a little:

"The revolutionary movement will break out simultaneously in every town in the country. We'll launch an attack on the barracks. We'll start by shooting anybody who gets in our way. A few days beforehand in the capital we'll let loose a few kilograms of a strain of typhus and bubonic plague bacilli. From planes, during the night. Every cell near the capital will cut off railway lines. We'll allow no trains to enter or to leave. Then we'll have the nation's heart paralyzed and black out telegraph communications, too, and with the head men shot, the power is ours. All this is crazy, but quite feasible. And when a person is on the verge of great deeds, he lives in a dreamlike state, like sleepwalking. But still, he makes his way forward with such rapid slowness that once he gets where he's going, it surprises him. To do that, the only indispensable elements are will and money. Besides the cells we can set up a special strike force of murderers and assailants. How many aircraft does the army have? But with the communications all cut off, the barracks under attack, the head honchos shot, who's left to send in the troops after us? This is a country of animals. You have to use a gun. That's indispensable. We'll only get respect with terrorist tactics. That's what a coward mankind is. A machine gun . . . How will they get together troops to send in after us? We've cut off telegraph, telephone, railroads. . . . Ten men can keep a population of ten thousand in fear. To have the machine gun is enough. There are eleven thousand total population. The north country, the great plains, they'll join up when we issue the call. Tucumán, Santiago del Estero, if we play our cards right, are ours for the taking. San Juan's full of crypto-Commies. That just leaves the army. We'll attack the barracks by night. If we get their ammo supply, shoot the guys in charge, and hang the sergeants, with ten men we can take a base with a thousand soldiers, so long as we have machine guns. It's so simple. And hand grenades, what should I do about hand-carried explosive devices? With the element of surprise, simultaneously nationwide, ten men per town and Argentina is ours. The soldiers are young and will come over to our side. We'll make enlisted men into officers and put together a Red Army like nothing anybody's ever seen on this continent. Why not? What's to stop us from striking at the San Martín Bank, assaulting the Rawson Hospital, and taking the Martelli Agency in Montevideo? All we need is three newspaperboys with guts and the city's ours.

His hyperactive anger made the blood pound in his veins. It surged bounding through his sturdy body, tensed up as if ready for an attack. He felt stronger than ever, the strength of a man who can use his gun.

The electric light swung with each thundering boom from the storm, but the Astrologer, sitting with his back to the bed, legs crossed, on top of the trunk, chin in hand and his elbow propped on his knee, kept his eyes fixed on the five dummies whose raggedy shadows played across the pink wall.

Behind him, the rain that was coming in the window made a puddle on the floor, the questions went back and forth in silence, at times a sharp crease shot down the middle of the Astrologer's forehead, then his motionless eyes, in his rhomboid-shaped face, answered his own unspoken questions by blinking according to how he felt, and he remained there like that until day broke, then, getting off the trunk, he turned away ironically from the five puppets, leaving them there in the solitude of the room, bobbling about like five hanged men.

He hesitated an instant, then he swiftly went down the stairs, past the portico, and strode off toward the stables where Barsut was confined.

It had stopped raining. The clouds had broken up, leaving a bit of sky with a yellow piece of moon visible.

THE REVELATION

While all this was going on, in Las Mercedes Hospital, Ergueta reached a state he was later to call "the knowledge of God." It happened like this.

He awakened at dawn in the room. A parallelepiped of moonlight painted a blue rectangle on the whitewashed wall by his bed. Through the window bars the sky showed, boxed by the window frame, a sky the same porous, arid blue as plaster tinged with methylene. Between the bars, a trickle from a star trembled.

Ergueta scratched his nose thoroughly, although he felt no great urgency. He grasped that he was in the madhouse, but that was "no problem of his."

He might have worried if they had shut up his spirit, but the one locked up in the madhouse was really his body, his body that weighed ninety kilos, and now he felt somewhat burned remembering how he had made his rounds of the brothels. And he could not help reviewing, like some opprobrious horror show, the sensual life in which he had wallowed. But then, what did his spirit have to do with the excesses of his flesh?

It was such an evident distinction to his mind that it astonished him that the doctors still could not see the difference.

Ergueta marveled at his discovery. He was no longer
a man, but rather a spirit, "a sensation purely of soul,"
with its borders clearly delineated within the fleshly
framework of his body, like clouds in the endless spaces.

He was light as a feather. Other nights he had felt
able to go outside his body, slough it off like a suit.
Knowing he could, suddenly grasping the fact made
him a little bit afraid. At moments his epidermis seemed
only to touch the outermost edges of his soul, so that
the equilibrium between his body, about to drop off
behind, and his skin, made him nauseous. It was like
being in an elevator falling.

Besides, he was afraid of willing his soul to leave his
body, because if it got destroyed, how would he get
back inside? The orderly had a scoundrel's face, and
though Ergueta would have explained to him how body
and soul must reunite, he did not feel it was quite safe
to. But, as the first impression wore off, he began to
relish the thought he was a mere weak child, which
did not prevent him from also laughing in his bed there
at what a farce it was to restrain his ninety kilos when
the whole time he could roam anywhere he felt
like . . . but no . . . this was no game. His goodness could
not allow that. And how fine it felt to be so full of
brotherly love! His mercy spread to cover the world,
like a cloud over the roofs of the city. His body lay ever
farther below.

Now he could see it as if at the bottom of a box, the
sanatorium nestled among the white cubes of houses
like one more cube, the streets tinged blue among great
overhanging shadows, the green of neon signs glowing
feebly, and space flooded his interior as the ocean would
a sponge, while time ceased to exist.

Great lengths of space swooped through his delight.
Ergueta felt quiescence, a reservoir of brotherly love,
willed by something outside him. Thus would he enjoy
the dry pool along with the rain that heaven sent him.

Of the earth onto which he beamed his love, he saw the very edges, round, greenish, with the blue ether lapping up against them. And as it was not natural to remain silent, he only managed to say:

"Thank you . . . thank you, my Lord."

He felt no curiosity. His humility grew stronger in reverence.

Up in the blue expanse he caught sight of a sudden upcropping of rocks. A golden light bathed the rocks in spite of the night, and the blue in the distance fell away into great gullies from the golden heights. Ergueta, with his body restored, advanced with cautious step, his eyes fixed and wary in his hawklike profile.

Naturally he could not feel tranquil because his body had sinned innumerable times, and because he understood that his face, despite the grave expression it now bore, had the energetic lines and the fierceness of a hardened sinner, the sort he had modeled himself on when he was young, out in the slums, and in roving gangs.

But his spirit was contrite and perhaps that was enough, though he still said:

"What will the Lord say when he gets a good look at me? How am I to show myself before Him?" And looking automatically at his shoes he saw they were in need of a shine, which made him feel worse. "What will the Lord say when he gets a good look at me and sees what a pimp and hustler I look like? He'll ask about my sins . . . he'll remember all the hustles I pulled off . . . and what will I say in answer?—that I didn't know? But how can I claim that, if he left proof of his existence in all the prophets?"

He went back to looking at his rundown, dirty shoes.

"And he'll tell me, 'You're a pathetic slob . . . a shameless low-life sort and to think that you went to the university. You were out hustling when you could have used your gambling money to console the orphan, to ease life's sufferings. And you sullied your soul in orgies after I gave it to you, and you dragged your guardian angel with you through brothels and he wept behind you, while your fleshy mouth was full of abominations . . .' And the worst of it is I can't deny anything. How can I deny my sin? What a life of hustling, my God!''

The sky over his head was a blue plaster dome. Remote planets like oranges swung in ellipses, and Ergueta looked humbly at the golden stones.

Suddenly a great upheaval shattered his modest state of mind. He looked up and to his left, standing ten steps away from him, he saw the Son of Man.

The Nazarene, cloaked in a sky blue tunic, turned his bony profile to him with one glowing, almond-shaped eye visible.

Ergueta's soul was cast down, but his body could not kneel, because "if you want people to think you're cool, you have to watch your image," not go on your knees to a Jewish carpenter, but still he felt a sob wrack his soul and in the silence he held out his arms, hands clasped, to the silent god.

He felt his tough hide becoming soaked through and through with devotion to Him.

Silent, he looked at Jesus standing there among the rocks. Ergueta's eyes filled. He could only wish there were someone around he could beat up to show the Lord how much he loved Him, and the silence was so unbearable that, though nearly overcome with feeling, he managed to blurt out this humble entreaty:

"I'd like to change my ways, but I can't."

Jesus stood looking at him.

"Believe me . . . you don't know what it means to me to tell you I love you."

Ergueta turned away, took three paces in the opposite direction, then, facing Jesus again, stopped.

"I've committed every sin. I've gotten myself into
some pretty messy business . . . I'd like to repent and
I can't . . . I want to kneel . . . truly, to kiss your feet,
you who were crucified for us. Ah! if you knew all I've
wanted to say to you but it's slipped away from
me . . . and yet I love you. Is it because we're here man
to man?"

Jesus looked at him.

A new smile graced the face of Jesus.

Ergueta was silent an instant, then blushing he murmured timidly:

"Oh! How good you are." He was another man, half-
crazed in ecstasy. "How good! You have bestowed your
smile upon me, a sinner. Do you see? You gave me
your smile. By your side, believe me, I'm like a child,
a kid. I'd spend my whole life adoring you, I'd be your
constant defender. Now I will sin no more, all my life
I will think of you, and God help anyone who questions
your sovereignty—I'll make him take it back and stuff
it down him—"

Jesus looked at him.

Then Ergueta, wanting to offer his best, said:

"I kneel before you." He went forward a few steps
and coming up in front of Jesus bent his head, put one
knee to the golden stone, and was about to prostrate
himself when Jesus reached out his finely chiseled hand,
placed it on his shoulder and said:

"Come. Follow me and sin no more, because your
soul is as beautiful as that of the angels that sing the
Lord's praises."

He tried to speak, but empty space and silence en-
folded him dizzyingly. Ergueta grasped that he had entered into the knowledge of God. It was clearly so,
because when he turned in the direction of some voices

resounding in the darkened hall, a madman who had been mute from birth exclaimed, looking at him in amazement:

"You look like a man from heaven."

Ergueta looked at him in astonishment.

"Yes, because just like the saints, you have a glowing disk around your head."

Ergueta, gently seized with fear, leaned against the wall.

A one-eyed madman, who had so far kept silent, exclaimed:

"Miracles . . . you do miracles. You made the mute speak."

The conversation woke up a third lunatic, who spent his days killing imaginary lice between his calloused, work-beaten fingers, and the bearded fellow, turning his pale face, said:

"You came to raise the dead."

"And make the blind see," interrupted the mute.

"And one-eyed people, too," asserted the madman with one eye, "because now I can see out of this side."

The mute, propping himself up with both elbows dug into the mattress, went on:

"But you're not yourself, it's God inside your body."

Ergueta, overcome, affirmed:

"True, brothers, I'm no longer myself . . . it's God who's inside me— How could I, a miserable whoremaster, do miracles?"

Then the louse killer, sitting on the edge of the bed and swinging his bare feet, suggested:

"Why don't you do another miracle?"

"I came not for that, but to preach the word of the Living God."

The louse killer hiked one foot up on his knee and malevolently insisted:

"You ought to work a miracle."

The mute put his pillow on the floor of the hall and, sitting on it, said:

"I won't speak anymore."

Ergueta squeezed his temples, stunned by what he was seeing. The one-eyed man reflected amicably:

"Yes, you should revive a dead person."

"But there's no dead person here!"

The one-eyed man limped up to Ergueta, took his arm and nearly dragged him over to one of the beds, where a little man with a round head and enormous nose lay unmoving.

The mute came up, compressing his lips.

"Don't you see he's dead?"

"He died this afternoon," muttered the one-eyed man.

"I tell you the man's not dead," exclaimed Ergueta in irritation, convinced the others were making sport of him; but the louse killer leaped from his bed, came over to the other bed, bent over the little man with the round head and pushed the unmoving body so it would fall off, right onto the floor, where it thumped dully and lay between the two beds with its legs pointed up like the Y-shape of a freshly pruned tree.

"Now you see he's dead?"

The four madmen remained in consternation around the Y-shape, inside the rectangle of pale blue moonlight, with the wind billowing out their shirts.

"You see he's dead?" repeated the bearded man.

"Work a miracle," the one-eyed man begged. "How are we to believe in Him if you don't work a miracle? Go on, it's no big thing for you."

The mute, bending his head down repeatedly, made signs of acquiescence to Ergueta.

Soberly he leaned over the body; he was about to pronounce the words of Life, but suddenly the walls of the room spun the planes of the cube before his eyes, a dark wind howled in his ears and again he caught sight of the three madmen standing inside the blue rectangle of moonlight, their nightshirts flaring out with the wind, while he slipped down a tangent that cut through the giant whirlwind of darkness, into unconsciousness.

THE SUICIDE

Erdosain remained there at the Lame Woman's feet perhaps for an hour. The emotions he had passed through were dissolved into sluggishness now. He felt a stranger to everything that had happened that day. Anguish and malevolence grew hard inside him like mud in the sun. He remained, nonetheless, immobile, in the utter grip of the sleepiness that came raveling forth, dark and heavy, from his tiredness. But his forehead wrinkled. And through the mist and darkness grew his other despair, the hopeless fear of becoming lost like a ghost at the edge of a granite dike. The gray waters formed bands of different heights that ran counter to one another. Iron launches carried half-glimpsed people to remote emporiums. Also there was a woman decked out like a *cocotte*, with diamonds flashing at her throat and her elbows propped on the table of a tavern, pressing her jeweled fingers into her cheeks. And while she was speaking, Erdosain scratched the end of his nose. But since this was an inexplicable attitude, Erdosain remembered that four girls had appeared with dresses down to their knees and yellow hair in wild disorder around their horsy faces. And the four girls, as they passed by him, held out a plate. It was then that Erdosain wondered: "Can they eat on the money they make doing that?" Then the star, the *cocotte*, who wore under her chin a great droopy mass of diamonds, told him yes, that the four girls lived on panhandling, and began talking about a Russian prince, in her most feminine voice, whose way of living, although she tried to arrange things, would not fit in with the way the girls lived. At that point Erdosain was able to understand satisfactorily why he was scratching the end of his nose while the lovely creature was talking.

But his sadness grew when he saw the silent people, turning away, climb into the cars of a long train with all the window blinds pulled down. Nobody asked about itineraries or stations. Twenty paces away, a desert of dust stretched out darkly. He could not make out the locomotive, but he heard the painful clanking of the chains as the brakes were released. He could run, the train started up slowly, catch up with it, climb up the steps, and stand for a minute on the platform of the last car, watching the train pick up speed. Erdosain still had time to get away from this gray solitude without dark cities, but immobilized by his enormous anguish, he stood there looking, a sob trapped in his throat, at the last car with the windows closed tight.

When he saw it go into the curve of rail that the wall of fog covered, he realized he was left forever behind in the ashen desert, that the train would never come back, that it would go always silently onward, with all the windows of its cars closed tight shut.

Slowly he took his face out of Hipólita's knees. It had stopped raining. His legs were frozen and his joints ached. He looked for a moment into the face of the sleeping woman, blurred by the blue-tinged light coming in through the panes, and with extraordinary caution got up. The four girls with horse faces and kinky yellow hair were still with him. He thought:

"I should kill myself." But looking at the red hair of the sleeping woman, his ideas took a more sinister turn.

"It would be cruel, I know. But, I could kill her." He squeezed the butt of his revolver in his pocket. "One shot into the skull would be enough. The bullet is steel and would only make a tiny hole. Well, yes, her eyes would pop out and maybe her nose would bleed. Poor thing! And she must have suffered a lot. But it would be cruel."

A cautious malevolence made him bend over her. As he watched her sleep his eyes assumed a mad fixedness, while with the hand in his pocket he raised the gun, fingering the trigger. Thunder boomed in the distance, and that strange incoherence that shrouded his brain like a veil was gone; then with great care he took up his coat, closed the door with great care to keep it from creaking, and went out.

At the foot of the stairs he realized happily that he was hungry.

He went to one of the grills near Spineto Market, rushing the blocks at a near run.

The moon rode the violet crest of a cloud, the sidewalks stretched out in the moonlight as though zinc-plated, dead silver gleamed in every puddle, and with a whirling purr the water ran up against and lapped the granite curbs. The walkway was so wet that the cobbling seemed freshly soldered to the streetbed.

Erdosain went in and out of the blue shadows that sliced obliquely across the façades. The smell of something wet gave the morning solitude a certain seaborne desolation.

Without a doubt, he was not in his right mind. He was still worrying about the four horse-faced girls, and the sinister sea with iron waves. The heavy odor of burned oil vomiting steadily out the yellow door of a dairy turned his stomach, and then, changing his mind, he headed for a brothel he remembered was on Calle Paso, but when he got there the door was already shut and, disconcerted, shivering with the cold, with a taste like copper sulfate in his mouth, he went into a café where they had just rolled up the iron grating. After a long wait, they served him the tea he had ordered.

He thought about the sleeping woman. He half closed his eyes, and leaning his head against the wall, he let himself sink further into his desolation.

He did not suffer for him, the man whose name appeared on registration lists, but rather now his awareness, at some remove from his body, looked at him as if at a stranger, and wondered:

"Who will have mercy on man?"

And these words, which were the summing-up of his thought, made him churn inwardly, filled with pained tenderness toward his unseen fellowmen.

"To fall . . . to drop ever lower. And yet, other men are happy. They find love, but all suffer. It's just that some figure it out and others never do. Some think it's just because they don't have something. But that's a stupid illusion. But still, she had a beautiful face. What made the most sense was the part she told me about the adventurer prince. Ah! To be free to sleep on the bottom of the sea, in a lead chamber with thick windows. To sleep for years and years while the sand piled up, just sleep. That was why the Astrologer was right. The day will come when people will make a revolution, because they have no God. Men will go on strike until God appears."

A bitter cyanide smell came to him; and sensing through closed eyelids the morning light, he felt watery, as though he were on the bottom of the sea and the sand was piling up endlessly on his lead chamber. Someone touched his shoulder.

He opened up his eyes just as the café waiter said:

"No sleeping in here."

He was going to reply, but the waiter had gone to wake up another sleeper. It was a fat man, who had let his bald head fall onto his arms, crossed on top of the table.

But the sleeper did not respond to the waiter's words, and then, amazed, the owner came up, a man with a mustache as big as bicycle handles, and shook the man in his café until he was doubled over in his chair, still not falling because the table kept him up.

Erdosain got up, astonished, while the owner and the waiter, looking at one another, looked sidelong at the singular customer.

The sleeper remained in an absurd position. His head lolled onto one shoulder, his flat-featured face showed, pockmarked and wearing dark, round glasses. A thread of reddish slaver was staining his green tie, slipping out from bluish lips. The stranger's elbow pressed a sheet of paper with writing down on the table. They realized he was dead. They called the police, but Erdosain did not leave, curious to see the whole spectacle of the suicide in dark glasses, whose skin was slowly becoming covered with blue blotches. And the odor of bitter almonds that hung in the air seemed to come from between his slack jaws.

First a police aide came, then a sergeant, then two patrolmen and an inspector, and they all ringed around the dead man, as though he were a steer. Suddenly the aide, turning to the inspector, said:

"Don't you know who he is?"

The sergeant took out of the dead man's pocket a hotel receipt, several coins, a revolver, and three worn letters.

"So this is the guy who killed the girl in Calle Talcahuano?"

They took the dead man's glasses off, and now his eyes showed, crossed, the cornea turned upward, the eyelids red-tinged as though he had wept tears of blood.

"Didn't I tell you?" went on the aide. "Here's his identification."

"He was going to go to Ushuaia forever."

Then Erdosain, when he heard that, remembered it as if he had read about it a long time ago. (And yet, it was not long ago. He had found out about it the morn-

ing before in the paper.) The dead man was an embezzler. He abandoned his wife and five children to go live
with another woman by whom he had three children,
but two nights ago, maybe having grown tired of the
hag, he showed up in a hotel on Calle Talcahuano with
a seventeen-year-old girl, his new mistress. And at three
that morning he covered her head with a pillow, shooting a bullet into her ear. Nobody in the hotel heard
anything. At eight that morning the murderer got
dressed, left the door half-open, and calling the em-
ployee told him not to wake his wife until ten, because
she was very tired. Then he left, and only at twelve did
they find the dead girl.

But what most impressed Erdosain was to think that
the murderer had spent five hours in the presence of
the dead woman, five hours next to the body of the girl
in the solitude of night . . . and that he must have loved
her greatly.

But had he not harbored the same thought a few
hours ago in front of the redheaded woman? Was that
an unconscious memory or the suicide doubled over
next to him?

The ambulance came up and the dead man was loaded
into it.

Then they interrogated him. Erdosain told what little he knew as witness, and went out into the street,
still pondering. An undefined and painful question lay
at the bottom of his awareness.

He remembered then that the dead man's pants bot-
toms had been muddy, his shirt dirty and damp, so in
spite of everything, how had he made the girl he killed
love him? Did love exist then? Despite his two wives
and eight children here and there and his life of hustling
and embezzling, the murderer felt love. And he imagined him in the harsh night, there, in that hotel fre-
quented by prostitutes and persons whose profession
could only be imagined, in a room with the wallpaper

peeling off, looking down to see on the blood-soaked pillow the waxen face of the now cold girl. Five sobering hours looking at the dead girl, who had taken him in her naked arms. Thinking these things, he came to the Plaza Once, stunned and in pain.

It was five in the morning. He went inside the railway station, looked around, and since he was sleepy huddled up in a corner of the waiting room.

At eight he was awakened from deep sleep by a passenger bumping his suitcase into things. He rubbed his fists into his sore eyelids. The sun was shining in a cloudless sky.

He went out and took the bus out to Constitution Station.

The Astrologer was waiting for him at the Temperley station.

His sturdy form enveloped in a smock, with the hat pulled down over his eyes and his drooping mustache ends, was spotted right away by Erdosain.

"You're really pale," said the Astrologer.

"I'm pale?"

"Yellow."

"I didn't get a good sleep . . . and worse, this morning I saw a guy kill himself."

"Okay, then, here's the check."

Erdosain looked at it. It was for fifteen thousand three hundred and three pesos, made out to "Cash," but the date was for two days ago.

"Why did he date it for two days ago?"

"It'll look better. See, the teller knows that if the check were lost, then by the time that you showed up to cash it there'd be a stop payment on it."

"Did he protest?"

"No—he smiled. That man plans to send us all to jail . . . ah! . . . before you go to the bank, go to a barbershop and get a shave—"

"And does he know already?"

"No, we'll wake him when it's time."

The train would not arrive for a few minutes. Erdosain looked at the Astrologer, smiling, and said:

"What would you do if I ran away?"

The other man, arching his fingers, sucked on his mustache, and then:

"That's as impossible as for the train that's coming not to stop here."

"But just supposing, then."

"I can't. If I supposed that for a moment, you wouldn't be the one to cash the check . . . Ah! Who was that suicide this morning?"

"A murderer. Funny thing. He killed a girl who wouldn't go live with him."

"Energy lost down the drain."

"Do you think you could kill yourself?"

"No. You see I'm cut out for a higher destiny."

Erdosain asked a strange question:

"Do you think redheads are cruel?"

"Not so much that, but rather asexual; that gives them that coldness toward things that makes such a disagreeable impression. The Melancholy Ruffian told me that in his long career as a pimp he'd known very few redheaded prostitutes. Well, then. Don't forget to get a shave. Go to the bank at eleven, no, before. You're having lunch with me today, right?"

"Yes, see you then."

After Erdosain, the Major got on, waving good-bye to the Astrologer in a friendly fashion. Erdosain did not see him.

Sunken into his seat, Erdosain thought:

"He's an extraordinary man. How is it he can be so sure I won't run out on him? If he's as right the rest of the time as now, he'll win out," and lulled by the rocking of the train he fell asleep again.

The Major was behind him. And in the bank itself,

with his heart hammering, he went up to the window
when the teller called him:

"Big bills or little?"

"Big."

"Sign here."

Erdosain signed the back of the check. He thought
they would ask for identification, but the teller, blank-
faced, wearing a jacket with fake alpaca sleeves, counted
out ten thousand-peso bills, five five-hundreds, and the
rest in small bills. Erdosain would have liked to flee
in fear, but he scrupulously counted the money, put it
in his wallet, put the wallet back in his pants, keeping
hold of it firmly, and went out to the street.

Between forests of white clouds there showed, like
clean metal, a curlicue of sky. Erdosain felt happy. He
thought that in a different climate, under a perpetually
blue sky like the curlicue he could see now there must
be astounding women, their hair luxuriant and their
faces smooth, their eyes huge and almond-shaped, long
lashes casting shadows. And the softly scented air would
waft out of the morning countryside into the city in-
tersections, the green lawns terraced to fit the rolling
hills, spherical towers rising from the highest eleva-
tions of parks and terraces.

And the Astrologer's rhombus face, with his walrus
mustache drooping down over the corners of his mouth,
and his chauffeur hat, made him enthusiastic; then he
thought how being part of the conspiracy would let
him continue his experiments with electrotechnology,
and now he crossed streets like some emperor fallen
upon bad days, not realizing his presence was seducing
the washerwomen who went by with hampers under
their arms and exciting the seamstresses coming back
from their shops with heavy bundles.

He would invent the Death Ray, a sinister violet zap
flash of millions of amps that would make the steel of

a battleship melt like a bit of wax in an oven and blow whole concrete cities to smithereens, as if volcanos of dynamite had been detonated there. He saw himself, now made Head of the Universe. The Ambassadors of the World Superpowers were at his beck and call. He sat in a vast hall with glass paneling, and in the center a round table stood. All around it, crouching low in their plushy seats, sat the old diplomats, bald, leaden-faced, with hard, shifty eyes. Some drummed with their pencils on the glass tabletop, others smoked silently, and a huge black man in green livery stood motionless beside the red velvet draperies at the entrance.

And there he was! Erdosain, Augusto Remo Erdo-sain, ex-thief, ex-accountant, got up. The top half of his body in its fine black jacket was reflected in the glass tabletop and his four right-hand fingers were thrust into his pocket, while in his left hand he held some papers. Standing, he looked with icy eyes into the impassive faces of the Ambassadors. A terrible pallor held him in its grip, deliciously cold feeling. Heroes from every age lived on within him. Ulysses, Demetrius, Hannibal, Loyola, Napoleon, Lenin, Mussolini all flashed before his eyes like great wheels of fire, and were gone to the place where the solitary earth curved away, lost in a dusk not belonging to this world.

His words fell in quick chunks, solid as steel. And, seized by the splendor of the moment, he regarded his own image in an imaginary mirror, haughty and swelled with lofty emotions.

He set the conditions.

He had them hand over entire national navies, thousands of cannons, and great quantities of rifles. Then hundreds of men would be handpicked from each people, set on an island and the rest of humanity wiped out. The Ray would blow up cities, make soil barren, turn peoples and woodlands to dust. Forever gone and lost would be all trace of science, art, and beauty. An elite of cynics, bandits who had grown jaded about civilization, total skeptics, would seize power, with him at the helm. And since man can only be happy with some metaphysical lie to give him hope, they would support the clergy, and a new Inquisition would go after any heresy that might imperil the official dogma or the uniformity of belief that would be the absolute basis of human happiness, and man, restored to an earlier stage of society, would devote himself, as in the days of the pharaohs, to farming work. Grand metaphysical lies would bring man back to the joy that too much knowledge had withered away to nothing within his heart. His words came out in brief, dry chunks, like steel cubes falling together. And he said to the Ambassadors:

"Our city, the City of the Kings, will be wrought of white marble and set beside the sea. It will be seven leagues across, with rosy copper domes, lakes and woodlands. There we'll lodge false saints, swindlers, godfathers, fake magic men, apocryphal goddesses. Science will be nothing but magic. Doctors will make their rounds dressed like angels, and when the population goes up too fast, they'll be punished for their misdeeds with flying dragons, all lit up, that will seed the city from the air with Asian cholera.

"Man will live in the age of miracles, and will be a millionaire in faith. At night we'll beam up onto the clouds, with powerful projectors, the 'Entry of the Good Man Into Heaven.' Get the picture? Suddenly, from above the mountains there's a green and purple flare, and the clouds show a garden where the white airs drift like snowflakes. An angel with rosy wings approaches through heavenly fields, comes to the gate of Paradise, and with open arms welcomes in 'The Good Man,' a country fellow with a battered hat, a long beard, and a walking stick. Do you see it, my hustlers, pros, cynics, the best in your fields? See? The angel with rose-colored wings welcomes in the man who has suffered and sweated on earth. You see what a terrific idea, what an easy but stunning miracle? And the multitudes will fall on their knees and worship God, and only for us will heaven not exist, we sad bandits who hold the power, the science, and the useless truth."

He trembled as he spoke.

"We shall be as gods. We will give to men stupendous miracles, fine beauties, and divine lies, we will bestow upon them the certainty of a future so extraordinary that all the promises of priests will pale beside the reality of our apocryphal prodigies. And then, they will be happy. Do you see, imbeciles?"

Someone shoved him into the wall. Erdosain stopped short, startled, convulsively gripped the money in his pocket, and in excitement and as fiercely happy as a little tiger set loose in a brick forest, spit on the façade of a dress shop, saying,

"City, you will be ours."

The Major was following him.

THE WINK

In Temperley the Astrologer was waiting for him. A kindly smile lit up his face. Erdosain nearly ran over to him, but the other man, taking hold of his arms, stopped him short and looked a minute into his eyes, then, speaking to him for the first time in familiar form, said:

"Are you happy?"

Erdosain blushed. At that instant a double mystery was revealed to his consciousness. The man was not lying, and he felt so much his friend that now he would have liked to converse indefinitely, tell him everything there was to tell of his unhappy life, and he only managed to say:

"Yes, I'm very happy."

The Astrologer stood still a moment in the train station. Now he had gone back to addressing him in the formal form.

"You know? Many of us bear a superman within us. The superman is the will exerted to its utmost, beyond all moral norms, and carrying out the most terrible acts, a sort of ingenuous joy, almost—what you might call the innocent sport of cruelty."

"Yes, the point where you stop feeling fear or anguish, it's as if you were walking on clouds."

"Sure, the ideal would be to awaken in many men this cheerful, naive ferocity. It's our task to launch the era of the Innocent Monster. Everything will be done, no doubt of that. You just need to have enough time and guts, when they catch on to how spirituality has them bogged down in the cesspool of this civilization, they'll change before they go under for the last time. It's just that man hasn't seen how diseased he is with cowardice and Christianity."

"But weren't you going to Christianize humanity?"

"Oh, no, just the dregs . . . but if that plan doesn't work we'll try just the opposite approach. We haven't set up any principles so far, and the best thing would be just to use all sorts of different ones. Like a pharmacy, we'll have perfect lies for all purposes—set to dispense for the most amazing diseases of heart and soul."

"You know, you really are crazy, I have to agree with what Barsut told you yesterday."

"What we call madness is just new thoughts people aren't used to. Look, if that guy over there were to tell you everything he had on his mind, you'd have him put away. Of course, there should only be a few like us . . . the big thing is for our actions to bring us vitality and energy. Yonder lies salvation."

"And Barsut?"

"He doesn't even have an inkling what he's in for."

"And how will we eliminate him?"

"Bromberg will strangle him . . . I don't know, it's not my affair."

Under the sun, avoiding the puddles, they walked back to the house. And Erdosain was thinking:

"And the City of the Kings, us, will be of white marble and placed along the sea . . . and we shall be as gods."

And looking at him with his eyes aglow, he said to his companion: "Did you know one day we shall be as gods."

"That's what these idiots can't grasp. They've killed the gods. But a day shall come when they'll be running down the roads in the sun shouting 'We love God, we need God!' What pathetic slobs! I can't see how they ever managed to kill God. But we'll bring them back to life. We'll invent some fine gods—supercivilized—and then life will be something to see!"

"And if it all falls through?"

"It doesn't matter . . . there'll be another . . . there'll be another to fill my shoes. It must happen that way. The only thing we should want is for the idea to take root in people's imaginations—the day when it's in many souls is the day fine things will happen."

Erdosain was astonished at his serenity.

He was no longer afraid, and again he remembered the hall with the Ambassadors, and his malevolent eyes looked around, unsettling the elderly diplomats with their bald heads and leaden faces and hard, shifty eyes, and then, unable to contain himself, he exclaimed:

"So we wring one guy's neck, what the fuck, big deal."

The other looked at him with surprise.

"Are you jumpy or do you get mad for no reason, like an elephant?"

"No, it bothers me to be stuck with all these obsolete scruples."

"That's you young people all right," replied the Astrologer. "Like a cat that can't decide whether to come in the door."

"Should I be there at the execution?"

"Do you want to be?"

"I really want to."

But as they left the villa, his stomach gave a sick lurch and he felt in his throat a spasm as if he were about to vomit. He could hardly keep his footing. He saw shapes through a blur of milky fog. His arms hung from the joints like bronze limbs. He walked with no perception of distance; the air seemed vitreous, the ground rippled beneath him, at moments the trees seemed to zigzag before his eyes. He felt tired breathing, his tongue was dry, he could not wet his dry lips and burning throat, and only embarrassment kept him from falling. When he got his eyes half-open, he was going down the stable steps with Bromberg.

The Man Who Saw the Midwife walked along in a trance, his hair a wild mess. His belt was not threaded through the beltloops and a bit of white shirt like a handkerchief stuck out of his zipper. He covered his mouth with a fist and kept yawning cavernously. But his sleepy, faraway gaze did not fit with his tough-guy stance. He had fine eyes, grave and incoherent as those of huge animals, gazing out from between thick lashes that threw shadows on the circles under his eyes in a rounded, dainty face. Erdosain looked at him, but the man seemed unaware, lost to the world inside his magnificent incoherence. Then he gazed toward the Astrologer with his fine fool's eyes, got a nod from him, and opened the lock, then all three went into the stables.

Barsut leaped to his feet; he was about to say something. Bromberg took a flying leap and there was the cracking of skull against wood in the stables. The sunlight painted a yellow lozenge in the dust. Muffled grunts came out of the shapeless huddle. Erdosain watched the fight with cruel curiosity, and suddenly Bromberg's pants came undone, as he was bent over Barsut with his huge arms straining, squeezing the man's throat against the floor, and came half off leaving his white rump sticking out bare and his shirt all hiked up. And the muffled grunting stopped. There was a moment of silence, while the murderer, half-naked, motionless, squeezed the dead man's neck harder.

Erdosain just stood there looking.

The Astrologer stood by holding a watch in his hand. They stayed standing like that for two minutes, endless to Erdosain.

Erdosain just stood there looking.

"Okay, that ought to do it."

Awkwardly, his hair plastered across his forehead, Bromberg turned around, and not looking at anyone with his incoherent gaze, he grabbed his pants, red in the face, and did them up hastily.

The murderer had left the stables. Erdosain followed him, and the Astrologer, who came last, turned around to look at the strangled man.

He was flat out on the floor, his face to the ceiling, his jaws distended, and his twisted mouth showing some teeth at one corner and his tongue protruding.

Just then something extraordinary happened, but Erdosain did not see. The Astrologer, pausing at the stables door, turned to the dead man, and then Barsut

heaved his shoulders up, stretched his neck and, look-
ing at the Astrologer, winked.* The Astrologer touched
one finger to his hat brim and went out to join Erdosain
who, unable to hold it in, exclaimed:
"That's all?"
The Astrologer looked at him mockingly.
"You were expecting something more theatrical?"
"And how will you dispose of him?"
"Dissolve him in nitric acid. I have three jugs full.
But, off the subject, anything new on the copper rose?"
"Yes, it came out just fine. The Espilas are overjoyed.
Just tonight I saw one of them that was fine."
"All right, let's have lunch—we deserve it by now."
But when they were just entering the dining room,
the Astrologer said:
"What—aren't we going to wash our hands?"
Erdosain looked at him in surprise and instinctively
raised his hands up to get a good look at them. Then,
hurriedly, in silence, they went to the bathroom, and,
removing their jackets, ran the water. Erdosain took
some soap and, with his sleeves rolled up to the elbows,
he scrubbed up. Then he let the water run over his
arms and dried them vigorously on the towel. But, before leaving, the Astrologer did a curious thing.
He grabbed the towel and threw it into the bathtub,
took a bottle of alcohol, poured it over the towel, then
lit a match, and for a minute both their faces were lit
up in the dark room by blue flames from the fuel ig-
niting the cloth. Then only a blackish heap of ash was
left; the Astrologer turned on the water and it ran down,
washing away the ashy residue, and then they both
went back to the dining room.

---

* Commentator's note: Faking Barsut's murder was decided on
by the Astrologer at the last minute, after a long talk with
that individual.

An ironic smile played across Erdosain's face.
"Pontius Pilate, eh?"
"You're right. And unconsciously."
In the shadowy dining room the garden was visible through half-shut blinds. Tall honeysuckle shoots reached the windowsill. Transparent insects buzzed through the air by the lime tree and the white walls made a reflection in the waxed, mellow blond wood of the floor. The tablecloth fringe fell around square table legs. In an Etruscan vase, a bouquet of carnations emitted its spicy fragrance, and the silverware shone against the linen and up into the china; the shadows made curlicue arabesques in the glassy convexity of the wineglasses, or stretched out in triangular bands across the plates. In an oval dish was some lobster spread.

The Astrologer poured wine. They ate in silence. The Astrologer brought in egg drop soup, asparagus swimming in oil, artichoke salad, and then fish. For dessert there was cottage cheese sprinkled with cinnamon, and fruit.

Then they had coffee, and Erdosain gave him the money. The Astrologer counted it out:

"For you, three thousand five hundred. Have some suits made. You're a good-looking fellow and should dress well."

"Thank you . . . but listen . . . I'm dying for some sleep. I'm going to take a nap. Could you wake me at five?"

"Why not, come on." And the Astrologer accompanied him to his bedroom. Erdosain took off his shoes, exhausted by now, and threw his jacket over the bedstead. His eyes burned fiercely, his chest was bedewed with sweat and he thought nothing more.

He awoke when it was dark, to the sound of the Astrologer opening a blind. He turned around surprised, as the other man said to him:

"Finally! You've been sleeping for twenty-eight

hours." As he expressed doubt, the Astrologer handed him that day's paper, and, surely enough, two days had passed.

Erdosain leaped out of bed thinking of Hipólita.

"I've got to be going."

"You slept like a dead man. I've never seen anyone sleep like that, with such exhaustion, even neglecting the natural needs of the body . . . but, by the way, where did you get that story about the suicide in the café? I've seen last night's papers and this morning's. None of them has the story. You dreamed it."

"But I could show you the café."

"Well, you dreamed in the café, then."

"Maybe so . . . it doesn't matter. So?"

"It's all done with."

"All of it?"

"All."

"And the acid?"

"We'll pour it down the cesspool."

"So then?"

"It's as if he'd never existed."

Taking his leave of the Astrologer, he was told:

"Come Wednesday at five. We meet that night. Don't forget to get an off-the-rack suit to wear while the tailor does the others. So be there, and don't miss it, since the Gold Seeker, the Ruffian, and others will be, too. We'll exchange ideas, and remember, I'm very interested in the poison gas thing. Draw up a plan for a small factory to make chlorine and phosgene. Ah, and you can figure out what in hell mustard gas is. It destroys anything not protected by waterproofing soaked in oil."

"Phosgene is produced by the reaction of carbon monoxide and chlorine."

"Don't lose any time, Erdosain. A small factory. One that can double as a school for revolutionary chemistry.

Remember our activities can be divided into three sets. The Gold Seeker will run everything related to the colony, you run the industries, Haffner runs the brothels. Now we need money, so there's no time to lose. You have to get to work. What do you say to setting up an industrial complex that's the Argentine equivalent of what Krupp was in Germany? You must have confidence. Many surprises can come out of what we're doing. We're discoverers who have only a vague notion what we're heading for.* And who even has a vague notion!"

Erdosain fastened his gaze on the man's rhomboid face for a second, then, with a mocking smile, said:

"Do you know you're like Lenin?"

And before the Astrologer could reply, he was gone.

---

* *The story of the characters in this novel will continue in another volume entitled* The Flamethrowers.

Roberto Godofredo Christopherson Arlt was born in Buenos Aires in 1900. He was thrown out of school at the age of eight, reportedly for writing the following note to his teacher: "*Señorita, let us run away to the sea. Dressed in black velvet I shall carry you off to my pirate ship. I swear by the corpse of my hanged father that I love you. Yours till death. Roberto Godofredo, Knight of Ventimiglia, Lord of Rocabruna, Captain of the Whaler* Taciturn." Despite this lack of formal education, he wrote stories, publishing his first in a neighborhood newspaper when he was fourteen. Arlt left home at sixteen, and for the next six years worked at various jobs in Buenos Aires and Córdoba. His first novel, *El jugete rabioso* (*The Rabid Plaything*), took him five years to write and was published in 1925. *Los siete locos* (*The Seven Madmen*), his second book, was published in 1929, and, although it was awarded a municipal prize, it met with the universal dislike of the critics. The same year, Arlt began writing a column for *El Mundo*, and continued to do so until his death in 1942. 1931 saw the publication of *Los lanzallamas* (*The Flamethrowers*), the sequel to *Los siete locos;* the next year, Arlt's final novel appeared, *El amor brujo* (*Love the Sorcerer*). In spite of their popularity with the public, none of these novels received any critical support for some twenty-five years, and, on the advice of a friend, Arlt decided to write a play, "Los 300 Millones" ("The 300 Million"). He produced six more over the course of the next ten years, as well as two volumes of short stories, a collection of his *El Mundo* columns, and a book of commentaries on Spain, *Aguafuertes españolas* (*Spanish Etchings*).

In 1942, Arlt died of a heart attack, leaving behind him a play, "El desierto entra en la ciudad" ("The Desert Comes into the City"), which was finally published in 1953. Six years later, Editorial Hachette released a new selection of his columns, and in 1968 his complete plays were published by Schapire. In 1972, the first English translation of his work appeared—a story, "Esther Primavera," was included in an anthology of Latin American fiction and poetry. The next two years brought two more anthologies containing English translations of stories by Arlt. In 1981, a new edition of Arlt's collected works was published in Argentina, with an introductory essay by Julio Cortázar. *The Seven Madmen* is his first novel to appear in English.

ABOUT THE TRANSLATOR

Naomi Lindstrom teaches Latin American literature at the University of Texas. She is the author of *Literary Expressionism in Argentina* (1977), *Macedonio Fernandez* (1981), and the forthcoming *Woman's Voice in Latin American Literature: Four Fiction Works.*

THE SEVEN MADMEN

has been set in a film version of Trump Mediæval,
a typeface designed by Professor Georg Trump
in the mid-1950s and cast by the C. E. Weber
Typefoundry of Stuttgart, West Germany. The
roman letter forms of Trump Mediæval are based
on classical prototypes, but have been interpreted
by Professor Trump in a distinctly modern style.
The italic letter forms are more of a sloped roman
than a true italic in design, a characteristic shared
by many contemporary typefaces. The result is
a modern and distinguished type, notable both
for its legibility and versatility.

The book was designed by Janis Capone and
composed by NK Graphics, Keene, New Hamp-
shire. The paper is Warren's #66 Antique,
an entirely acid-free sheet. Haddon Craftsmen,
Scranton, Pennsylvania, was the printer and the
binder for this book.